HOSTAGE

Sheldon D. Engelmayer
and Robert J. Wagman

Caroline House Publishers, Inc.
Ottawa, Illinois & Ossining, New York

DEDICATION:
To the United States of America, its people and its freedoms . . . and to 52 very special Americans and their families.

ACKNOWLEDGEMENTS:
The authors have spent a year writing this volume and, in the process, received much valuable assistance on the condition that none of the information be published until the U.S. nationals held hostage were safely back in the United States. For their cooperation, we wish to thank various members of the U.S. Departments of State and Defense, the Carter White House, the intelligence community and, of course, the hostage families who gave so much of themselves to us. We especially thank our researcher, Jill Habermann, whose tireless efforts helped make this book possible. And very special thanks to Donna McCrohan for putting all the pieces together.

All inquiries and catalog requests should be addressed to Caroline House Publishers, Inc., Box 738, Ottawa, Illinois 61350—(815)-434-7905.

ISBN: 0-89803-084-6

Wendy Stone, Art Direction

Contents

The End Of An Ordeal

"We observe today . . . a celebration of freedom, symbolizing an end as well as a beginning, signifying renewal as well as change."

So began the Inaugural Address of John F. Kennedy on January 20, 1961.

Twenty years later, Ronald Wilson Reagan, the 39th man to take the oath of office as President of the United States*, must have wondered as he delivered his Inaugural Address whether his administration would begin with "a celebration of freedom, symbolizing an end as well as a beginning," or whether it would begin with a crisis that, at that very moment, was getting so out of hand that war could now be the only possible solution.

For as Reagan stood on the steps of the U.S. Capitol, his right hand raised high, his choking voice sounding the solemn words prescribed 191 years earlier, his thoughts—as indeed, the thoughts of an entire world—were focused on a runway thousands of miles away in Iran, and on two buses filled with 52 Americans for whom the world had been a living hell for 444 days.

On that runway, too, was an Air Algeria plane. *If* the 52 Americans boarded that plane, *if* it took off, and *if* it cleared Iranian airspace, it would be a "celebration of freedom" unlike any John Kennedy could have imagined. But if none of those things happened, if the two buses left the runway to return to Tehran with its passengers still on board, if hell was to have a 445th day, if all the negotiations, the agreements, the hopes were shattered, the outrage and indignation of the United States would have

been so great that only war could be the balm that would relieve the wounds. No one said it; no one even dared think it. It was just something you knew.

Reagan took the oath of office at 11:58 a.m. EST. Thirty-three minutes later, at 12:31 p.m. EST, the long, agonizing wait ended. The Air Algeria plane was airborne—and the 52 U.S. nationals were on board.

It was to be "a celebration of freedom" after all.

This is the story of those 444 days and the 52 Americans who had to endure them. Elsewhere in this volume, we report on the events and the personalities of the first 354 days of this unconscionable ordeal. On this and the next few pages, however, we focus only on the last 90 days. We do so because a happy ending is a perfect beginning for a "celebration of freedom."

Former Secretary of State Edmund Muskie said of the hostage negotiations, "We really have been on a straight line since about September. Actually, all the elements that went into the final solution were in place, the basic equation of money for the 52, but there were many hurdles to overcome, many false starts, many blind alleys and a great deal of bad faith on the part of the Iranians. But, basically, the final deal is the result of a straight line negotiation that had its beginnings in September."

Actually, those closest to the talks trace the start of the final phase of the negotiations to a series of events which began on October 22, 1980, and ended 11 days later, on November 2.

Despite frantic attempts by religious hardliners to

block any resolve of the hostage question, attempts that would continue virtually up to the time the hostages boarded the Air Algeria aircraft at Tehran airport on January 20, Ayatollah Ruhollah Khomeini, President Abolhassan Bani-Sadr, and the Iranian parliament finally took up the hostage issue in a serious effort to resolve it.

U.S. intelligence agencies believe that by late October a majority of the higher-ups in the Iranian government, including the ayatollah, had decided that the hostages were simply more trouble than they were worth. For the Iranians, the problem became getting the most they could while, at the same time, placating the clerics who in great measure felt the continued holding of the hostages was the glue still binding the revolution together.

The realization that the time was right to begin the process of meaningful negotiations was underscored by the election of Ronald Reagan and by the fact that the war with Iraq had been reduced to a stalemate, with neither side having the will or the ability to end it. With the prospects of a long, drawn-out conflict facing them, the Iranians clearly needed the money and supplies tied up by the freeze imposed by President Jimmy Carter and they feared that, despite all the rhetoric about Carter as Satan, they would have a much more difficult time dealing with Reagan.

On November 1, after a delay of several days, the Majlis, Iran's parliament, finally took up the hostage issue and, the next day, November 2, formally set the conditions for the hostages' release. These conditions were really embellishments of the four conditions first set down by the ayatollah on September 12: return of the shah's wealth; cancellation of claims against Iran; non-intervention in the internal affairs of Iran; and the unfreezing and return of all Iranian assets.

Blindfolded, with hands bound, one of the hostages is paraded before the crowds by a group of Iranian students. (WIDE WORLD PHOTOS)

There is considerable evidence that the Majlis, which turned Khomeini's four broad conditions into concrete demands, believed that Carter would instantly accept them in an effort to win the hostages' release before November 4, and thus turn the election to his favor. They, therefore, were surprised by the almost instant rejection of the demands by Carter.

The United States, however, did indicate its willingness to negotiate on the basis of these four conditions while, at the same time, making it clear that it was legally impossible for it to comply absolutely with any of the demands except the non-interference condition.

The Iranian parliament for the first time appeared to approach the problem on a more or less mature and reasonable basis and agreed to accept Algeria as an intermediary in negotating a release. U.S. officials point to the Algerians entering the picture as a significant event at the start of the final process.

On November 10, Deputy Secretary of State Warren Christopher arrived in Algiers, on the first of many flights there, to begin the process. He carried with him a formal response to the demands of the Majlis. From documents obtained from the State Department, it is clear that initial response, delivered to the Algerians in early November, is basically the same as the actual agreement signed on January 19.

In the November 10 response, the United States agreed to the immediate and unconditional transfer to Iran of $2.5 billion in frozen Iranian assets; binding international arbitration of all legal claims against Iran; the freezing of all identifiable assets of the late Shah Mohammed Reza Pahlavi and his family in this country to allow the Iranians to proceed against those assets in U.S. courts; the withdrawal of the U.S. case against Iran in the World Court, and an agreement to prevent any further claims being filed against Iran for its actions in seizing the embassy and the hostages.

The next day, the Algerians took the five-page U.S. response to Tehran where Iranian officials, with the advice of lawyers working for them in Paris and London, formulated a series of nine "questions." These were brought by the Algerians to Washington on November 25.

At the same time, both U.S. and Iranian officials in separate announcements revealed that the United States had agreed "in principle" to the four Iranian conditions, but that a large number of "technical points" remained to be worked out by the parties. Evidence now indicates that neither side really expected the final agreement to take as long as it did to work out and, when U.S. negotiators reviewed the nine Iranian questions, they thought the hostages would be home by Christmas.

On December 2, Christopher returned to Algeria. He took with him a new set of documents which were described as answers to the Iranian questions.

Actually, one document was a re-working of the original proposal of November 12, not changing in a material way what the United States was willing to do but, rather, redrafting the November 12 proposal to bring it more in line with the form of the four conditions set forth by the Iranian government.

The second document Christopher carried on this trip is described as a series of comments on the U.S. proposal that attempted, at some legnth, to set forth for the Iranians the extent to which the president could legally comply with the Iranian conditions.

U.S. negotiators believed that the information contained in these two documents was sufficient to win the quick approval of the Iranians.

The Iranians then threw a major monkey wrench into the negotiations, one which apparently stunned both the Algerian intermediaries: On December 19, after studying the U.S. reply, Iran's chief negotiator, Executive Affairs Minister Behzad Nabavi, demanded that a total of **$24 billion** be deposited with Algeria before the hostages could be freed!

Once again, the Iranians had miscalculated how much Jimmy Carter wanted the hostages home before Christmas. The Iranians apparently believed the United States was willing to pay any price to get its nationals back and that, once Iran put a "firm" figure on the table, the United States would fall all over itself to make the deal.

The Iranians tried to cloak this new demand, to make it easier for Carter to sell it to the American people. It was simply a "reasonable statement" of the value of Iranian property and assets held by the United States. They said that $14 billion of the "deposit" would guarantee the return of Iranian assets and that $10 billion would be held until the late shah's wealth was returned.

But the United States rejected the proposal out-of-hand. President Carter called it a ransom demand and said no such demand ever would be met, despite the Iranians' claim that it was their final word on the matter. The $24 billion, they insisted, was not open to any negotiation.

The Christmas "deadline" came and went and U.S. television viewers were once again treated to the media event of a Christmas visit by clergymen to the hostages. An Algerian negotiating team also was allowed to see the hostages and, according to those close to the negotiations, it was at this time that the Algerians quietly dropped their role as message-passers and became more active in the process.

The Algerians stayed in Iran for four days, meeting with Nabavi and other Iranian officials. They then went to Washington and held similar talks at the State Department.

Based on these talks, the United States formally rejected the Iranian $24 billion demand and proposed

All over the nation, yellow ribbons tied around trees, posts, and buildings become the symbol of America's vigil. (WIDE WORLD PHOTOS)

a counter-offer which for the first time upped the initial amount the United States was willing to place in escrow pending the release of its citizens. The new U.S. offer was to place $4.5 billion of Iran's estimated $8 billion in frozen assets in escrow with the Algerians, plus another 1.6 million ounces of gold belonging to the Iranians but on deposit with the Federal Reserve Bank of New York.

On January 2, the Algerians took this new proposal to Tehran along with a warning from the White House. The Carter administration told the Iranians that, as far as it was concerned, if no agreement was reached by January 16 the Iranians would have to deal with the new Reagan administration.

This date, Carter spokesmen made clear, was not an ultimatum, but simply an operative fact. After January 16, there simply would not be time to implement an agremeent before Inauguration Day. If no deal were reached by the 16th, therefore, all bets were off.

At the same time, President-elect Reagan was making statements which indicated that he would be a lot harder to deal with than was Carter, that he would not be bound by what was being discussed with the then U.S. administration and that, above all, he had no intention of "signing a blank check" in order to gain the hostages' release. The Iranians, he said, were "barbarians" and he would not deal with barbarians.

Obviously, none of this was lost on the Iranians. When the Algerians arrived in Tehran, they were met by statements from Iranian officials that they were not willing to make any concessions whatsoever and that they would not be intimidated by this new "Wild-West cowboy" president. At the same time, they transferred the three U.S. diplomats who had been held at the Foreign Ministry to another location.

But while making all this noise publicly, the Iranians privately sat down with the Algerians and reviewed the newest U.S. offer. Three days later, they came up with a series of "questions" about this offer which the Algerians immediately transmitted to Washington.

A number of the questions were of a highly technical nature indicating that, despite its public rhetoric, the Iranians were seriously looking at the latest U.S. proposal. On January 7, therefore, Warren Christopher assembled a group of experts and flew off to Algeria with answers.

Christopher went to Algers with the idea of returning almost at once to Washington, but it quickly became apparent that the Iranians really wanted to find a solution to the problem before the Reagan presidency became a fact. Negotiations began to intensify and Christopher remained in Algiers.

Christopher and his team, along with Algerian Foreign Minister Mohammed Benyahian (who, with West German Chancellor Helmut Schmidt, emerged as a hero in the negotiation process for the forceful roles they played in bringing the parties together) began a series of meetings that lasted through the weekend of January 10-11. Throughout those two days, Benyahian and other Algerian officials were in constant contact with Tehran.

By the end of the weekend, both sides were in virtual agreement on all major issues and discussions now centered on the procedural matters of exactly how the funds were to be transferred.

The last major roadblock to the eventual agreement was the passage by the Majlis on January 14 of a resolution allowing U.S. claims against Iran to be settled by binding arbitration. Iranian officials had indicated they could not agree to this key provision without the approval of the parliament; the passage

of the resolution, over the objection of the hardliners, cleared the final hurdle.

On January 15, the Iranians passed to the Algerians a set of proposals for the procedural process to transfer the funds. Some of these procedures were not totally acceptable to Christopher, however, and a new series of progressively more frantic talks were held at the Algerian Foreign Ministry.

Enter now several Englishmen whose work became key to the eventual agreement. On Friday, January 16, a U.S. military jet carried a group of bankers and lawyers from London to Algiers for the final set of talks. Included in the party were Roger Brown, a lawyer representing the National Bank of Iran; Christopher McMahon, the deputy governor of the Bank of England; and David Somerset, the bank's chief cashier. The three, working with officials of the Algerian National Bank and the U.S. Federal Reserve System, came up with a set of proposals on which both the Iranians and the United States could agree. By Sunday, January 18, the agreement was made and, as far as the United States and Algeria were concerned, it was time to break out the champagne.

On the morning of January 19, Christopher, having been given special authority by President Carter, sat next to Benyahian in the Treaty Room of the Algerian Foreign Ministry and signed the final agreements on the part of the United States. At the same time, the agreements were signed in Tehran. Both the U.S. and Algerian officials thought it would be only a matter of hours before the hostages would be put on planes then waiting at Tehran airport to fly the hostages to Algeria, where they would be turned over to U.S. control.

But there was one more hitch to overcome, one which in hindsight was built up more for progaganda effect than real substance, but which in the late evening hours of January 19 was very real indeed:

Before funds could be transferred from the Federal Reserve Bank in New York to the Bank of England, Iran had to file certain documents with the British bank setting up the necessary escrow account. But Iran did not do so. Chief Iranian negotiator Nobavi said this was because U.S. banks had tried to pull a fast one on Iran by including in the last-minute documents a new 12-page addendum which the Iranians had never before seen.

The U.S. and Algerian negotiators in Algiers were dumbfounded. They did not have the slightest idea of what Nabavi was talking about. The only addendum they were aware of long ago had been approved by the Iranians.

Privately, Nabavi told the Algerians a different story. He said he was holding up the signing of the escrow documents because of the deletion of a single word in a clause. In one document, which had thrice

Only two of the 52 hostages were women—Kathryn Koob and Elizabeth Ann Swift—shown here with Msgr. Annibale Bugnini and the Rev. Jack Bremer during a 1980 Easter mass. (WIDE WORLD PHOTOS)

been translated, the word "minimum" had been deleted in a sentence which had originally read that the United States would deposit a "minimum" of $8 billion in the Bank of England. Nabavi said that, by dropping the word in the final text, the United States was saying it would deposit only $8 billion and this would cheat the Iranians out of at least $900 million.

The U.S. negotiators considered this nonsense and said so. But the Iranians remained firm. So British lawyer Brown redrafted the clause to the mutual satisfaction of both parties. The Bank of Iran then went ahead with the filing of the escrow documents and the asset transfer process began.

The Iranians, however, were not yet finished. They had dealt with "Satan" and, in truth, they had been bested by "Satan." There was to be no ransom; at least some of its debts—debts incurred by the hated shah's regime—would have to be paid; and they would have to agree to binding arbitration on other debts. For this further humiliation, "Satan" must pay.

In Washington, in Algiers, in Frankfurt, and in homes the world over, the long wait began. Day 443 ended and day 444 was underway. The clock ticked away. Soon, in Tehran, it would be day 445.

The Iranians knew that "Satan," in the person of *President* Jimmy Carter, was waiting to give the message of freedom before the end of his watch. They were determined that his watch would end without that message. Only when "Satan" was *Citizen* Jimmy Carter would the hostages be freed.

But to Carter, it did not matter when the hostages were freed, only that they had been freed, as witness his remarks upon arriving home in Plains, Ga.:

"There is no way for me to describe how I feel now. I would like to say, although I haven't had a chance to see my bed either Sunday night or Monday night, in the last few hours, I've had a lot of very emotional experiences. I won't mention them all, but I will say that one of them was this morning—I won't say exactly what time yet—I got word from sure sources that both planes in Iran were lined up on the runway waiting to take off. That was a thrilling experience for me.

"The next time was when I came out to Andrew Air Force Base having had a chance to serve as president of the greatest nation on Earth and stood there with my wife and the vice president and his wife, Joan, and heard "The Star Spangled Banner" played and they fired the 21-gun salute for a president.

"And my heart was filled with the realization of what it means to be free and what it means to be a citizen of the greatest and the strongest and the most decent nation on Earth and I had to fight back the tears.

"And for the last 14 months Rosalynn and I and the secretaries of state and others have stayed in close touch with the hostage families. And as . . . I came toward . . . Air Force One, Mrs. Schaefer, who is the wife of the senior military man held hostage, said to me, 'Mr. President, I hope someday you'll have a chance to meet my husband.' And I put my arms around her . . . and I said, 'I'll be with him tomorrow and I'll tell him you love him.' That was another experience that I'll never forget—all emotional.

"And . . . I'd like to say that when those planes were lined up, when they played 'The Star Spangled Banner,' when I put my arms around Mrs. Schaefer and when I saw this crowd of friends and neighbors—all three (sic) were emotional, but they weren't sad. Every single one of them, including coming back to Georgia, is a happy experience for me and I thank God for it.

"There are still restraints on me—some self-imposed, some agreements with foreign nations—about mentioning the American hostages who have been held so long in Iran. But I have not had a chance yet to make a statement about them and I felt that, because of the intense interest in these 52 people around the world, that I would say a few words to you about them.

"Just a few moments ago on Air Force One before we landed at Warner Robins (Air Force Base), I had received word officially for the first time that the aircraft carrying the 52 American hostages had cleared Iranian airspace on the first leg of the journey home and that every one of the 52 hostages was alive, was well—**and free**."

*Reagan is officially the 40th President because Grover Cleveland was both the 22nd and 24th President, having lost his first bid for re-election.

The Rise And The Fall Of The Shah

October 1971. Tehran. The most expensive party in all history is about to begin. Shah Mohammed Reza Pahlavi sitting on his Peacock Throne is spending an estimated $60 million to celebrate "the 2,500th anniversary of the founding of the Persian empire by Cyrus the Great." Ten million dollars alone is being spent to construct a series of massive "royal tents" of ancient design, only these will be equipped with electric lighting, sound equipment, toilets and bathrooms for the greater comfort of his guests.

After all, these guests are the kind of people who are accustomed to being comfortable.

The list is impressive. Heads of state and the world's jet set will come together for a week of pomp and ceremony unmatched in the modern world. Among those who will attend: Prince Philip of Britain; King Olav of Norway; Emperor Haile Selassie of Ethiopia; Soviet President Nikolai Podgorny; Romania's Nicolae Ceausescu; King Frederik IX and Queen Ingrid of Denmark; Spain's Juan Carlos and Princess Sofia; King Hussein of Jordan; King Constantine II and Queen Anne-Marie of Greece; and Philippine President Ferdinand E. Marcos.

A march-past of the armies of 10 main Persian dynasties, including the shah's own, required the construction of exact replicas of the ancient chariots, armor and weapons, besides uniforms and dresses. It will be a glorious spectacle all by itself.

The celebration has been carefully designed to be a tribute to Iran's tradition of monarchy and to the shah. Among highlights of the celebration will be a wreath-laying at the tomb of Cyrus, where the shah will address "the spirit of the founder of the Persian empire" and bid his long-dead predecessor, "Rest in peace, for we are awake."

Perhaps Cyrus will hear these words. Certainly, he will not respond. If he could answer the shah's felicitations, however, the great emperor of all Persia might warn Mohammed Reza Pahlavi that peace for him will be short-lived, that others also are awake and they will move stealthily in the shadows until their day arrives. And the "2,500-year-long dynasty" will come to a bloody end.

(The shah's plans for the anniversary celebration were meant to instill in those attending and the millions around the world who would watch the extravaganza on television the thought that the Pahlavi family traced its right to the Peacock Throne back through those 2,500 years. The shah himself often seemed to forget that, in fact, his dynasty traced its roots back only to 1921, when, to end foreign influence, Col. Reza Pahlavi of the Persian Cossack Brigade, a self-educated officer of rising influence, led a coup against the then ruling but very weak Qajar dynasty.)

Iran is a huge non-Arab Islamic country that, as Persia, traces its history back to almost 600 years before the birth of Christ. References to it even can be found in several books of the Old Testament. Cyrus, Alexander the Great and Ataxerxes were among its famed monarchs.

The Greeks eventually conquered Persia, followed next by the Turks and finally by Mongol invaders. It was conquered again in 1501 and the present day Iran slowly began to emerge. The Qajar Dynasty began its lengthy reign in 1795. Until 1906, however, there was no legislative body to share power with the shahs on the Peacock Throne. That was rectified by the signing of a new constitution which for the first time established a parliament (majlis).

The downfall of the Qajar dynasty actually began in 1908, when oil was discovered, leading to a decision by Britain and Imperial Russia to divide Iran into two commercial zones. This foreign influence was increased during and after World War I and eventually led to the Reza Pahlavi coup in 1921.

Four years later, the majlis offered the throne to the victorious colonel, who at his coronation as Reza Shah on April 25, 1926, named his 7-year-old son Mohammed crown prince.

Mohammed Reza was born on October 26, 1919, and with his parents and twin sister lived the next few years in a modest house in one of the older residential districts of Tehran. With his father on the throne, this quickly changed. Soon, he had private tutors and then was sent to Switzerland where he went to school at the very exclusive Le Rosey.

Meanwhile in Iran, the storm clouds of World War II were gathering and Reza Shah was starting to get himself and his country in deep trouble. An autocratic ruler who governed with an iron hand, Reza Shah had begun taking advantage of the oil income to begin modernizing Iranian society. But the monarch made no secret of his admiration for Nazi Germany and, given the strategic location of Iran, this made the allies very nervous indeed. To prevent Iran falling into Hitler's hands, British and Soviet troops occupied Iran in August 1941. It virtually was a bloodless invasion that resulted in Iran surrendering after two days.

The shah spared no expense when it came to celebrating the 2500th anniversary of ''the founding of the Persian empire by Cyrus the Great.'' One of the highlights of the festivities were the cavalrymen, dressed in the historically accurate and incredibly expensive gold and silver armor of ancient Persian horsemen. (WIDE WORLD PHOTOS)

The first action of the occupiers was to remove Reza Shah from the throne. He was allowed to abdicate and to flee into exile to South Africa, where he died three years later at age 66. In his place, the British placed on the throne Reza Shah's 21-year-old son, called back from school to lead his country in what the allies were certain would be a much more anti-German line.

Despite his young age, Mohammed Reza Pahlavi was ready to rule. While in school in Switzerland, he had dreamed of the day he would accede to his father's throne and rule Iran in a less autocratic and more considerate way.

The shah was to recall those early days of his reign in an interview given late in his monarchy, but well before his troubles really began to mount.

''When I took the throne at the age of 21, I found myself plunged into a sea of trouble,'' he said. ''The allied commands were treating Iran like a conquered nation. Their continual interference in political life and affairs disgusted me and my people.''

He took advantage of the almost accident that in 1943 brought U.S. President Franklin D. Roosevelt, Soviet Premier Josef Stalin and British Prime Minister Winston Churchill to Tehran for what was to become the historic meeting in which they agreed to cooperate in the defeat of Nazi Germany.

Their host, the young shah, took advantage of the Tehran Conference and the good-will that existed between the participants to extract from them a firm agreement that all foreign troops would leave Iran within six months of the war's end.

For their part, Britain and the United States honored the deadline in 1946, but the Soviets refused to remove their troops. Also, the Moscow-oriented Tudeh Party rose in revolt and Soviet agents convinced a number of tribal leaders to join the growing rebellion by separating their territories and joining the USSR. But the shah's troops, helped by U.S. supplies and advisers, and a very sharply worded warning by President Harry S. Truman, smashed the uprising. The separatist movement conceded defeat on December 12, 1946.

After his victory, the shah—in what was to be the keynote of his regime—told cheering crowds: ''There is no honor to be the king of a poor people.''

This led to a period of growing Iranian nationalism as the young shah solidified in power. He was not without his enemies within the country, however. In 1949, the shah survived the first of two public assassination attempts. On February 4, 1949, a gunman attacked him outside Tehran University. Three bullets hit his military cap; a fourth entered his right cheek and upper lip, emerging under his nose. The gunman's revolver then jammed and bodyguards killed him on the spot.

Then, in 1950, it was disclosed that the Anglo-Iranian Oil Company, which produced virtually all of Iran's oil, paid $142 million in taxes to Britain, but only $45 million in royalties to Iran. On April 29, 1951, the shah nationalized the company.

The situation led to the rise of the emotional, charismatic, 70-year-old Mohammed Mossadegh, whom the shah named prime minister to replace Rezmara who was assassinated in 1951.

Mossadegh broke diplomatic relations with Britain on October 22, 1952, accusing London of attempted economic strangulation in support of the oil company.

Mossadegh, at the time his country's most powerful politician, became the focal point for the anti-shah (or, more accurately, a combination of anti-monarchy and anti-Pahlavi) forces. Given this backing, Mossadegh made a raw bid for control. He proclaimed martial law, threatened the shah with civil war and began to arrest those loyal to the monarch.

With their capital in turmoil, the shah and wife Soraya fled to Bagdad on August 16, 1953, and then went to Rome. In a scene that would be repeated 27 years later, mobs in Tehran tore down statues erected to the "King of Kings."

At this point, the Central Intelligence Agency stepped in. CIA station chief Kermit Roosevelt moved quickly to convince the army to stand behind the shah. CIA operations personnel began sowing seeds of discontent throughout the ranks of the rebel forces. They also began compromising leaders of the anti-shah crowds, eventually getting them to turn from yelling "Death to the shah, long live Mossadegh," to "Death to Mossadegh, long live the shah."

After a few days of fighting, troops loyal to the shah beat back Mossadegh's forces. The shah returned home in triumph August 22, less than a week after his hasty departure.

When he resumed his throne, the shah made a vow that such a revolt would never again take place. His remedy was to rule more autocratically than he had first planned. Rule by force was the order of the day, now, but the shah nevertheless continued his program to modernize his country.

Then, in 1960, the shah decided it was time to relax somewhat the tightness of his rule. A year later, he announced details of what he called his "White Revolution"; land reform to abolish the serf-master relationship, profit-sharing for workers, equal rights for women, elimination of illiteracy, a national health program and a reformed political structure.

This reform program for the first time brought the shah into sharp conflict with his country's conservative religious leaders. On religious grounds, they were opposed to equal rights for women. On economic grounds, they especially disapproved of the land reform measures. After all, much of the land that was to be handed out to the people was owned by them. As a class, the Iranian religious community of ayatollahs, mullahs and mujtahids was richer even than the Pahlavi family itself. And it intended to stay

The 1971 celebration was in fact the most expensive party in history, costing some $60 million. The "Tent City" of Persepolis, seen here, and equipped with electricity, sound equipment, and all the comforts of home, housed foreign dignitaries. Price tag: about $10 million. (WIDE WORLD PHOTOS)

that way.

Instead of attempting to reach some sort of accommodation with the clerics, however, the shah chose to crush their opposition. Religious leaders who spoke out against reform were harassed, jailed and even executed.

When the White Revolution was formalized by a national referendum in 1963, the mujtahids called their followers out into the streets and, during a period of rioting, many were killed when the shah's troops opened fire on the crowds. (See the article on Ayatollah Khomeini on page 94 for explanation of the power religious leaders wield in Iran and why.)

Finally, after Prime Minister Mansur was assassinated, the shah ordered the mullahs and mujtahids back to their mosques and arrested and ordered exiled their principal leaders, including Ayatollah Ruhollah Khomeini.

The key to the reform program was the redistribution of the land. It was going well, resulting in the head of the program, Agriculture Minister Hassan Arsanjani, becoming so popular among the peasants that the shah began to fear that he was creating another Mossadegh. He, therefore, packed Arsanjani off to Rome as ambassador to Italy. Almost immediately, things began to go badly in the land reform program.

The opposition attempted a second public assassi-

nation attempt on April 10, 1965, when a guard in the Marble Palace suddenly turned his machinegun on the shah. Luckily, the man apparently was a very poor shot. The burst of fire resulted in two guardsmen being killed, but others were able to fatally wound the assassin. The shah was unharmed.

Finally, after waiting 25 years, Mohammed Reza Pahlavi decided it was time to be formally proclaimed "King of Kings." On his 46th birthday, October 26, 1967, a massive coronation was held in the Hall of Mirrors in Golistan Palace. There, the shah placed the jeweled crown on his own head, an ancient custom. Here, again, the shah made a dangerous judgmental error: Many traditionalists were angered when the shah named his wife Farah the country's first empress in all of its 2,500 years.

Farah was his third wife. He had married Queen Fawzia, sister of King Farouk of Egypt, and a daughter Shahnaz was born. Fawzia could not conceive again, raising a constitutional problem since the crown is inherited by the direct male line only. The marriage was dissolved in 1950.

In 1951, he married Soraya Esfandiari, daughter of a Bakhtiari tribesman who had a German wife. Later, it was discovered that Soraya was sterile and that marriage, too, was dissolved.

The shah met Farah, daughter of an Iranian army

officer, in 1959 when she was a student of architecture in Paris. Popular legend said he shouted his proposal during a noisy helicopter ride on Air Force Day in 1959.

The shah had four children by Farah, two sons and two daughters. Prince Reza, the eldest, became heir apparent.

The coronation marked another period of autocratic rule and further modernization. Because the shah recognized that Iran's future rested in its oil production, in 1967 he demanded major concessions from the multinational consortium that had replaced the Anglo-Iranian oil company, including the return of a sizeable area for Iran's own exploration.

Opposition to the shah continued. Many in the population believed the shah was trying to Westernize them against their wills (a thought implanted in their minds by the religious leaders who stood to lose their fortunes and their power); others in the new emerging middle class opposed the shah because they felt they were not getting their fair share from the modernization program, which was marked by widespread corruption, waste and mismanagement.

With the shah in control of most of the segments of society and public expression, the opposition centered itself in the country's mosques. Almost by default, the country's 200,000 mullahs found themselves spearheading the opposition, a role they quickly came to like.

The shah countered by wooing the military. Anything the military wanted, it got. Lavish salaries and perquisites went to the officer corps. The shah himself appointed all officers above the rank of major and the main test of appointment was loyalty to the person of the shah.

In the period between 1971 and 1976, the shah once again cracked down on his opposition, this time with SAVAK, the secret police organization, doing the dirty work. Street violence became commonplace in Tehran and other major cities, and all demonstrations against the shah were dealt with very strongly by police and SAVAK.

At the same time, it was a boom time for Iran economically. The shah led the oil-producing nations in quadrupling oil prices in December 1973 and the money just kept rolling in after that.

Politically, however, repression continued. Mohammed Reza Pahlavi was determined to leave this world a richer, more powerful Iran than had existed when he was born. His Iran would be better educated, poverty would be on its way out if not already eliminated, women would have equal roles with men in Persian life and the people would own their own land. He could not allow the selfish opposition to threaten his noble vision.

In March 1975, a year after he launched a $68 billion development program, the shah banned all political parties and created a new one dedicated to "the great civilization." In the process, he throttled even the feeblest voices of dissent.

Insulated in his palaces, the Shah went ahead with plans to speed industrialization. With vast infusions of oil money, inflation soared and corruption caused a near collapse of the nation's power generation network.

Then, in early 1977, partially as a result of efforts from the new Carter administration in Washington, the shah announced a new policy of liberalization. There was a general release of political prisioners, a relaxation of censorship and an attempt to introduce legal reforms. It was the beginning of the end for the shah and the 2,500-year-old monarchy, but it made Washington happy.

The shah appointed a new premier, Jamshid Amouzegar, to fight the problems posed by the opposition. But it was too little, too late.

In the new relaxed atmosphere, there were calls for a complete change of system. Lawyers demanded restoration of all liberties and students rioted at Tehran University.

And, once again, the clerics led the opposition.

On New Year's Eve 1977, in the midst of growing turmoil, Jimmy Carter chose to accept the shah's invitation for a visit. Saying that "Iran under the great leadership of your shah is an island of stability in a troubled area of the world," Carter complimented Mohammed Reza Pahlavi on the "respect, admiration and love which your people give you." Needless to say, from this day on anti-Americanism became synonymous with anti-shah sentiment in Iran.

Perhaps buoyed by the lavish praise from Carter, the shah quickly made three fatal errors. In his 12th year of exile, 78-year-old Ayatollah Khomeini had become the focal point of opposition to the shah. In an attempt to silence Khomeini, the government published an article bitterly attacking him.

This led to a January 8, 1978, demonstration by some 4,000 religious students in the holy city of Qom and the second fatal error, a massive confrontation with the shah's troops. When the day was done, dozens of the students lay dead and hundreds more were wounded.

As a result, all during 1978, street rioting was the norm in Iran and the estimated death toll from the almost constant confrontations with police and soldiers is said to have totaled over 3,000.

Advisers to the shah begged him to form a new government, giving a large role in it to the clergy in the hopes that they would calm the rioters. He refused, however, thinking instead that he could somehow bring the situation under control. It was his last wrong decision.

When clashes between anti- and pro-shah forces continued unabated, martial law was declared in September.

It had little effect. In a final attempt to restore

The shah, even to his last days, never really comprehended the hatred of his people whom he had led for 38 years. They did not share his vision of making Iran the fifth most powerful country in the world, and bitterly denounced him for the means he employed to reach his ends. (WIDE WORLD PHOTOS)

calm, the shah named one of his top political opponents, Shahpour Bakhtiar, as prime minister. This only spurred on the opposition.

By November, the only segment of Iranian society that remained loyal to the shah was the army. On November 5, a massive riot had left much of downtown Tehran gutted and many dead. It was now only a matter of time.

The monarch's friends insisted he was unaware until very late of the threat to his survival. In the last days, those close to him found the shah deeply dispirited and bewildered. He could not understand how this people whom he had led for 38 years did not appreciate his master plan for making Iran the Middle East's dominant power. He believed that Iran would become the fifth most powerful country in the world, with solar and atomic energy supplementing its oil and gas, with education going to the remotest villages by satellite and (with continued U.S. cooperation) the most powerful military machine in the Middle East.

But the people clearly did not share this vision. So on January 16, 1979, the imperial family flew into exile. First, the shah went to Egypt, at the invitation of President Anwar Sadat. A few days later, he and Empress Farah went on to Morocco at the invitation of King Hassan. Then, on March 30, they flew to Paradise Island, the Bahamas. From there, they went to Mexico and, following deterioration of his health, to New York for surgery.

Mexico, however, refused to allow the shah to return after he had recovered sufficiently to travel. Working behind the scenes, therefore, the Carter administration found the Pahlavis a new home in Panama. This, too, was not to last, though. The Iranians were putting intense pressures on the regime of Gen. Omar Torrijos Herrera to extradite the shah. In a fit of paranoia, the ousted monarch, realizing that he was dying, decided to live out his days in relative peace. He accepted an invitation tendered by President Sadat to live out his days in Egypt.

On July 27, 1980, Mohammed Reza Pahlavi, Shah of Shahs, Keeper of the Peacock Throne, died in exile a broken, embittered man. But not a poor one. The shah and his family had not left Iran empty handed. No one, least of all Iran's new Islamic regime, has any idea how much the shah exported abroad for personal use. His accounts with Swiss, U.S. and other banks never may be fully disclosed. The main channel through which he and his family exported wealth was the Pahlavi Foundation, a so-called charity whose holdings in Iran and abroad were estimated at $20 billion.

"Rest in peace, for we are awake," the shah had told Cyrus the Great of Persia in 1971. But for the King of Kings, life no longer held any peace as his days drew to a close. For others, too, were awake and they did not share his dreams of a greater Iran.

The Hostage Rescue That Worked

It was in the final days of Shah Mohammed Reza Pahlavi's regime.

In Tehran, the situation had deteriorated to such an extent that moment-to-moment survival depended upon who was the better shot.

The situation was so out of control, in fact, that Texas-based Electronic Data Systems, known commonly as EDS and owned by multimillionaire H. Ross Perot, ordered all of its company's personnel out of Iran.

EDS held several multimillion-dollar contracts with the shah's government to install and maintain major computer systems. Perot says the country was $5 million behind in its payments to EDS by December 1978 and, with things getting worse and the shah clearly getting ready to escape, he decided EDS should, too.

Within hours of EDS's December 28 announcement that it was "temporarily" ceasing operations in Iran, two of its Tehran-based engineers, William Gaylord and Paul Chiapparone, found themselves in jail. The charge: offering Iranian officials bribes in order to win EDS a major new contract.

On the face of it, the charges were absurd. Perot said the two men were being held as "hostages" to insure that EDS would not leave Iran and would continue to service and maintain the computer systems it had installed.

This was born out when the public prosecutor offered to drop the charges in exchange for EDS guaranteeing that it would remain in Iran and renegotiating its contracts so that the Iranians would have to pay less money.

Perot, however, refused to give in to the blackmail. He immediately decided to rescue his two employees. To accomplish this, he did not turn to Washington and official government channels. Rather, he turned to Col. Arthur Simons, USA-Ret.

Simons had become famous during the Vietnam war for leading a 1970 raid against a North Vietnamese prison in an attempt to free U.S. POWs. The

raid succeeded, even though the attackers discovered that the POWs had been moved the night before. Simons was considered an expert in such missions and Perot knew he was the right man to get the two EDS employees out.

Simons agreed to take on the job on one condition: He would be paid only for his expenses.

At first, Simons considered a flat-out military raid against the Ghasr prison, where the two men were being held. But he decided that such a raid, which would have been much like one President Carter ordered, would surely fail.

Instead, he decided to do what many people have suggested the United States should have done against the embassy: accomplish the rescue using native Iranians to do the work by letting them believe they were doing a political act beneficial to the revolution.

A hand-picked team of EDS employees was put together. All were volunteers with military service who previously had been in Iran with the company. Over a short period of time, the rescue team infiltrated Iran and was put into place.

The plan was a simple one. The prison held thousands of men who were regarded as political prisoners. So the EDS agents simply would incite a mob of Iranian revolutionaries to commit a political act which it wanted to do in the first place: storm the jail.

On Feb. 11, 1979, the plan was put into effect. The mob was gathered and whipped into a frenzy. It attacked and, within minutes, the prison's fences were down and some 7,000 inmates poured out, including the EDS employees who had been tipped off in advance. The two linked up with the EDS raid team at a preplanned location outside the jail.

Using a carefully laid-out escape route, the men traveled overland to Turkey and freedom.

Within 48 hours, both EDS employees and their volunteer rescuers were back with their families in Texas.

Chronology Of The Hostage Crisis:

Sunday, November 4, 1979
DAY 1: 500 Moslem ''students'' seize the U.S. embassy in Tehran. Revolutionary guards do nothing to intervene. Approximately 90 people are taken hostage, 61 of them U.S. nationals. The ''students'' demand that ousted Shah Mohammed Reza Pahlavi, receiving cancer treatment in a New York hospital, be returned for trial. Ayatollah Ruhollah Khomeini supports the takeover, calling it ''a natural reaction to the U.S. government's indifference to the hurt feelings of the people of Iran.''

Monday
DAY 2: Militants release all Iranians who had been seized in the attack and announce that their hostages include U.S., Pakistani and South Korean nationals. The State Department refuses to turn over the shah and demands the immediate release of all the hostages. President Carter sends former Attorney Ramsey Clark and William Miller, staff director of the Senate Intelligence Committee, to Iran with a personal letter for the ayatollah. He also asks the Pentagon and intelligence agencies for contingency plans for a rescue mission. The militants seize and occupy the British embassy for several hours.

Tuesday
DAY 3: Prime Minister Mehdi Bazargan and his government resign in protest, leaving the Revolutionary Council as the ruling power. The militants at the U.S. embassy say they will ''destroy'' all hostages if the United Nations attempts to free them. Reports begin to circulate that the leader of the militants are Palestinian-

speaking and possibly Palestinian-trained. The Palestine Liberation Organization announces that its leader, Yasser Arafat, will seek release of the hostages. Presumably, ''Charlie's Angels,'' under the command of Vietnam escape-and-evasion veteran Col. Charles Beckwith, are placed on alert this day.

Wednesday
DAY 4: Two more U.S. nationals, identified as ''spies working for Bell Helicopter,'' are seized at their hotel and taken to the embassy. The PLO sends a delegation to Tehran and the State Department says, ''We would welcome help from anyone.'' The Revolutionary Council agrees to

An Iranian artist puts the finishing touches on his portrait of the Ayatollah Khomeini—on the wall of U.S. Embassy. (WIDE WORLD PHOTOS)

The three hostages released in November, 1979—from top to bottom, Marine Sgt. William Quarles, Katherine Gross, Marine Sgt. Ladell Maples. (WIDE WORLD PHOTOS)

allow in the Clark-Miller mission. Later in the day, however, Khomeini reverses the decision, calling the embassy a "den of corruption" and a "place of spying." Anti-Iranian demonstrations break out in several U.S. cities.

Thursday

DAY 5: Militants reject PLO mediation efforts and parade a bound and blindfolded hostage through the embassy compound. New anti-Iranian demonstrations break out in the United Nations. Carter suspends shipments of military spare parts to Iran. Iran orders oil deliveries to the United States reduced.

Friday

DAY 6: Whipped up by new Khomeini speeches, thousands of Iranians gather at the embassy to show support for the militants and to denounce the shah and the United States. "Death to the shah, death to Carter, death to the United States" reverberates through the streets surrounding the embassy compound. The U.N. Security Council urges Iran "in strongest terms" to free the hostages. President Anwar Sadat of Egypt offers asylum to the shah and denounces events in Iran as "a crime against Islam." Khomeini appoints a new foreign minister, Abolhassan Bani-Sadr, who was finance minister in the Bazargan government. Bani-Sadr will now hold both posts. Reaction in the United States to the appointment is guarded. Privately, however, officials say Bani-Sadr is considered a moderate and his appointment could lead to a swift end to the hostage crisis.

Saturday

DAY 7: Carter orders all Iranian students in the United States to report to immigration authorities. He says "illegals" will be deported. The American Civil Liberties Union denounces the move and says it will challenge the order in court.

Sunday, November 11, 1979

DAY 8: Iranian students occupy

the courtyard of U.S. embassy in Beirut, but are evicted by Syrian troops. Khomeini rejects Pope John Paul II's plea to free the captives.

Monday

DAY 9: Carter orders a suspension of oil imports from Iran; at the same time, Iran, anticipating the move, announces it will not sell "another drop" of its oil to the United States. The PLO announces it has failed in its mediation efforts.

Tuesday

DAY 10: Iran requests an urgent Security Council meeting to air its charges against the shah. The United States responds negatively, saying release of the hostages must come first. For the first time, the exact demands of the Iranians are made known in a statement from Iran's broadcasting chief, Sadegh Ghotbzadeh: The United States must condemn the shah as a criminal, he must be returned for trial, his wealth must be returned to Iran, and an international commission must investigate the charges against him and the United States.

Wednesday

DAY 11: In the early hours of the morning (Washington time), Carter freezes all Iranian assets in U.S. banks, estimated at as much as $11 billion. The action comes within minutes of an Iran announcement saying it will withdraw those funds. Ramsey Clark is called home from his futile diplomatic effort.

Friday

DAY 13: Militants detain an NBC television crew for several hours on the embassy grounds. They then threaten "harsher" measures against the hostages if the shah is moved to any other country but Iran. More than 100,000 Iranians march on the embassy in support of the militants. Carter asks the nation to refrain from abusing innocent Iranians living in the United States.

Saturday

DAY 14: In what appears to be the first break in the crisis, Khomeini goes on television to tell the militants that, in the name of Islam, they should free black and women hostages not involved in spying. At the same time, he says the hostages who are spies will be put on trial unless the United States returns the shah.

Monday, November 19, 1979

DAY 16: Three hostages, two black marines and a woman, are taken to Tehran airport and put aboard a plane for West Germany.

Tuesday

DAY 17: Ten more hostages—four women and six black men—are also released after facing reporters and making some anti-shah statements. They are also flown to West Germany. For the first time, Carter says the United States may have to use force if the remaining U.S. nationals are not freed. He orders the Indian Ocean fleet to station itself off the coast of Iran and orders the carrier Kitty Hawk from the Pacific to join the growing task force. "Charlie's Angels" begin training for a rescue mission at about this time. The grand mosque in Mecca, Saudi Arabia, Islam's holiest city, is seized by terrorists.

Wednesday, The Day Before Thanksgiving

DAY 18: Khomeini goes on radio all through the Islamic world and announces that the seizure of the grand mosque is the work of "American agents." Within hours, an Islamic mob seizes the U.S. embassy in Islamabad, Pakistan, killing two U.S. marines. The embassy staff is terrorized, especially several women who are subjected to vile indignities, according to secret State Department reports. After a delay of many hours, Pakistani troops rescue the embassy staff and the building is then sacked and burned. Meanwhile, in Tehran, the militants say all hostages will be killed and the embassy blown up

if the United States attempts to rescue them. Hundreds of thousands of Iranians demonstrate in what is so far the biggest anti-U.S. demonstration.

Friday

DAY 20: Khomeini expresses "great joy" at the sacking of the U.S. embassy in Pakistan; he repeats the threats of the militants to "destroy" the hostages if the shah is not returned. The 13 freed hostages arrive in Washington. Rep. George Hansen, R-Idaho, leaves for Tehran on what he says is a "peace mission." The trip is denounced by the White House and politicans from both parties.

Saturday, November 25, 1979

DAY 22: U.N. Secretary General Kurt Waldheim, with White House approval, calls an urgent meeting of the Security Council. Hansen visits the U.S. embassy where he is allowed to see some of the hostages. Later, he says they are generally in good health. He proposes a congressional investigation into Iran's charges against the shah.

Tuesday

DAY 24: Iran asks a week's delay in the Security Council meeting so that Foreign Minister Bani-Sadr can get to New York. The shah is operated on in New York for removal of gallstones and his doctors say he should be well enough to return to Mexico within a week.

Wednesday

DAY 25: In his first news conference since the embassy takeover, President Carter warns that Iran faces what he calls "grave consequences" if any hostage is harmed. In a move interpreted as showing his opposition to the Security Council meeting, Khomeini fires Bani-Sadr and names Sadegh Ghotbzadeh to replace him. Ghotbzadeh immediately announces that Iran will boycott the Security Council meeting.

Thursday

DAY 26: A Mexican airliner is sitting on a Kennedy Airport runway awaiting the shah when, in a surprising move, Mexico announces it will not take him back. The White House says the Mexican government is going back on a specific promise. Meanwhile, the State Department takes the U.S. case to the International Court and asks that it orders the hostages released. For the first time, the United States says the exact number of hostages is 50.

Saturday, December 1, 1979
DAY 28: Embassy militants announce that the hostages will be tried as spies unless the shah and his "stolen billions" are returned. The U.S. Security Council approves a U.S. sponsored resolution and demands that Iran releases hostages.

Sunday, December 2, 1979
DAY 29: The shah leaves New York for Lackland Air Force Base in Texas. The White House says the move is temporary while efforts continue to find him what is called a "permanent place of residence" in another country.

Monday
DAY 30: Iranian workers overwhelmingly approve a new Islamic constitution, making Khomeini ruler for life.

Tuesday
DAY 31: The Security Council in a new and tougher stance unanimously demand release of the hostages.

Wednesday
DAY 32: The Soviet Union, in its first word on the subject, condemns the holding of the hostages, but attacks Washington for protecting the shah and for the build-up of the U.S. fleet in the Arabian Sea south of Iran. The task force now numbers 21 ships, including the carriers Midway and Kitty Hawk. In Iran, in the "holy city" of Qom, Khomeini loyalists storm the home of rival Ayatollah Shariat-Mandari and three men are killed.

Thursday
DAY 33: Rioting breaks out in Iran's Azerbaijan and Kurdistan provinces in opposition to Khomeini, the Revolutionary Council and the new constitution. In Qom, hundreds march on Khomeini's headquarters to protest the previous night's attack.

Friday
DAY 34: In Paris, in the first assassination of a member of the shah's family, a son of his twin sister Princess Ashraf is gunned down by a Khomeini assassination team.

Saturday
DAY 35: Foreign Minister Ghotbzadeh says that Khomeini has agreed to the formation of an international panel of "anti-imperialists" to investigate charges of U.S. espionage and crimes against the people of Iran. He says that the hostages will be required to appear before the group to give testimony. At the same time, he assures U.N. Secretary General Kurt Waldheim that all the hostages are safe and can be visited by neutral observers.

Monday, December 10, 1979
DAY 37: In the first appearance of any of the hostages, Marine Col. William Gallegos, in a filmed interview, says the hostages are well. The United States warns against any "parading" of the hostages before an Iran-appointed international tribunal.

Tuesday
DAY 38: Lawyers for Iranian students in the United States win a ruling from a federal judge in Washington ordering a halt to immigration checks on Iranian students.

Thursday
DAY 40: Ghotbzadeh up's his demand from an "international

November 22, 1979. U.S. Congressman George Hansen was the highest ranking U.S. official to arrive in Iran since the hostages were taken. (WIDE WORLD PHOTOS)

tribunal'' to an ''international grand jury'' to try ''hostage spies.''

Saturday

DAY 42: The shah flies from Texas to Panama, and establishes his residence on the exclusive Contadora Island. On landing, he says he hopes his departure from the United States will ease the crisis. This results in the militants saying that hostage trials ''will definitely begin.'' The International Court at the Hague orders Iran to free hostages.

Sunday, December 16, 1979

DAY 43: Ghotbzadeh calls the shah's arrival in Panama a ''victory'' for Iran.

Friday

DAY 48: In a news conference, Carter for the first time announces that the United States will ask the United Nations to impose sanctions against Iran in order to force that country to halt its ''arrogant defiance'' of the world organization.

Monday, December 24, 1979

DAY 51 (Christmas Eve): The militants allow Christmas services to be conducted at the embassy by three specially invited U.S. clergymen: the Rev. William Sloane Coffin of New York; the Rev. William Howard, president of the National Council of Churches; and Bishop Thomas Gumbleton of Detroit; French Cardinal Leon Duval of Algiers joins them.

Tuesday

DAY 52: The clergymen report seeing only 43 embassy hostages —41 men, 2 women—all generally in good condition.

Thursday

DAY 54: The clergymen hold a meeting with Ghotbzadeh to receive a promised list of all 50 hostages. Ghotbzadeh says the militants will not supply such a list. The clergymen say they gave Ghotbzadeh a letter from the ayatollah in which they ''tried to clear up the Iranian misconception that President Carter is not

December 1979. Iranians ''vote'' on a new Islam constitution. But there are no secret ballots, and the mullahs are in full control. (WIDE WORLD PHOTOS)

''It is a strange faith, indeed, which allows the holding of innocent hostages during their holy days while captors celebrate . . .''

— *Letter from hostage William Keough*

Meanwhile, Americans flood the hostages with mail. Here U.S. radio newsman Alex Paen sorts about a quarter-million such greetings. (WIDE WORLD PHOTOS)

supported by the American people in his actions.'' At this meeting, Ghotbzadeh repeats that all the hostages will be tried as spies if the U.N. imposes economic sanctions.

Sunday, December 30, 1979

DAY 57: Secretary General Waldheim leaves New York for Tehran in hopes of meeting with Khomeini and seeing the hostages.

Monday, New Year's Eve

DAY 58: The Security Council votes 11-0 (with the Soviet Union, Czechoslovakia, Kuwait and Bangladesh abstaining) to give Iran until January 7 to release the hostages; otherwise, the council will impose sanctions.

Tuesday, January 1, 1980
New Year's Day

DAY 59: Waldheim arrives in Tehran. Newspapers there feature front-page photographs of Waldheim with the shah and the royal family, including on in which he is embracing the outsted monarch. Demonstrators, including many Afghan studens and clergymen, attack the Soviet embassy to protest Soviet moves in neighboring Afghanistan.

Wednesday

DAY 60: Anticipating that the U.N. may impose sanctions, Iran moves $13 billion from European banks to others in the Middle East.

Thursday

DAY 61: After two meetings with Ghotbzadeh and one with the Revolutionary Council, at which Iran's grievances with the shah are stated, Waldheim is told that Khomeini refuses to meet with him and that he will not be allowed to visit the embassy.

Friday

DAY 62: Waldheim returns to the U.N. and tells a news conference that the hostage crisis is much worse than he expected, and that ''the situation is more grave and serious than people believe.'' Militants demand that the goverment turn over to them Charge d'Affaires Bruce Laingen, who is being held at the foreign ministry. At the same time, they charge one of the hostages, Air Attache Lt. Col. David M. Roeder, with war crimes for flying bombing missions in Vietnam. They invite Vietnam to send representatives

to testify against Roeder ''when he is put on trial.''

Monday, January 7, 1980

DAY 65: Iran ignores the Security Council deadline for release of the hostages. Waldheim, in a closed-door meeting, tells the Security Council that Iran's Revolutionary Council simply does not have enough power to respond to the international community's call to release the hostages.

Tuesday

DAY 66: Battles between forces loyal to Ayatollah Shariat Madari and those loyal to Khomeini leave at least six killed and 80 wounded. A nationwide dusk-to-dawn curfew is enforced. Foreign Minister Ghotbzadeh announces that Laingen will remain at the foreign ministry. In Washington, President Carter and Secretary of State Cyrus Vance tell a group of congressmen that a solution to the hostage crisis may be months away. Full-dress rehearsals of an Iranian rescue mission begin at about this time. Col. Beckwith will be in charge and the force will be made up of volunteers from all the services.

Thursday

DAY 68: The Iranian government says it prevented the terrorists from assassinating Waldheim while he was in Tehran.

Friday

DAY 69: Ghotbzadeh says Iran is ready to release the hostages if the U.N. recognizes the ''legitimacy'' of Iran's demands for return of the shah and his assets. This delays for 24 hours a Security Council vote on a U.S.-sponsored sanctions resolution. At the same time, Iranian Oil Minister Ali Moinfar says any country imposing sanctions or abiding by the U.N. sanctions would be cut off from Iranian oil.

Saturday

DAY 70: Washington and Waldheim both seek clarification of Iranian proposals regarding hostage release.

Sunday, January 14, 1980

DAY 71: When no clarifications

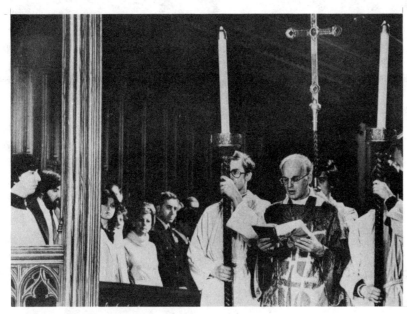

Christmas 1979. Family members of about a dozen of the hostages attend services in Washington National Cathedral. (WIDE WORLD PHOTOS)

are forthcoming, the Security Council votes to impose an embargo on all shipments to Iran except food and medicine. The Soviet Union vetoes the proposal.

Monday

DAY 72: The Revolutionary Council orders all Journalists working for U.S. media, about 100 reporters and technicians in all, expelled from Iran because of "biased reporting." In an interview, Ghotbzadeh says sanctions will make it more difficult to win release of the hostages and that Iran is prepared to hold them "more or less forever" unless the shah is returned.

Wednesday

DAY 74: A French court refuses to allow the Paris branch of Citibank to seize an Iranian account with $51 million in it. In Tehran, a massive search celebrates the first anniversary of the shah's ouster.

Saturday

DAY 77: American Indian John Thomas is allowed into the embassy to see some of the hostages. He brings out with him 151 letters for families.

Sunday, January 21, 1980

DAY 78: Waldheim announces that he is continuing negotiations with Iranian officials in New York, trying to find some "mechanism" that might win the release of hostages.

Monday

DAY 79: In his State of the Union message, Carter takes a generally conciliatory tone to Iran and offers to help it counter the Soviet threat in Afghanistan; the United States has "no basic quarrel with Iran" once the hostages are freed, he says. In Tehran, Ghotbzadeh says Soviet troops within 19 miles of Iran's border pose a "real danger."

Tuesday

DAY 80: The militants accuse embassy press attache Barry Rosen of "being a famous spy and plotter" because he tried to get moderate Iranian newspapers to

January 1980. Finance Minister Bani-Sadr and Ayatollah Khomeini are pictured in campaign posters for the Iranian presidential election. (WIDE WORLD PHOTOS)

write favorable stories about the United States. This, the militants say, was "an attempt to subvert the Iranian pess."

Wednesday

DAY 81: Khomeini is rushed to a Tehran hospital with a heart problem. Ghotbzadeh announces in Iran that Panama has told him the shah is "under arrest." Panama strongman Gen. Omar Torrijos Herrera immediately denies this, but does say that Iran will be given 60 days to formalize an extradition request.

Thursday

DAY 82: Waldheim meets with the Security Council and says Iran and the United States are "near agreement" on a hostage release in exchange for an international commission to hear Iranian complaints against the shah.

Friday

DAY 83: Finance Minister Bani-Sadr, ousted as foreign minister by Khomeini only weeks before, wins an overwhelming victory in Iran's first-ever presidential contest, getting some 75 percent of the votes cast. Khomeini's apparent choice, Foreign Minister Ghotbzadeh, runs way behind the field. Unofficial U.S. reaction is that Bani-Sadr's election will help moderate the situation in Iran.

Saturday
DAY 84: In his first public speech, President-elect Bani-Sadr announces he will not share power with the militants. Further, he says he considers the hostages "a minor matter" and that Iran's biggest problem is Soviet expansionism. This speech, considered hopeful by the State Department, causes the United States to delay plans to impose economic sanctions on Iran.

Monday, January 29, 1980
DAY 86: In another speech, Bani-Sadr takes a somewhat harder line, saying that it was "up to the United States" to end the hostage crisis.

Tuesday
DAY 87: Canada helps six U.S. diplomats, four men and two women, escape from Iran. The Canadian embassy had hid the six for three months and provided them with false passports. The six fly to West Germany with the last of the Canadian diplomats in Iran. Canada closes its embassy.

Wednesday
DAY 88: Ghotbzadeh warns that "sooner or later, somewhere in the world, Canada will pay" for its efforts in getting the six U.S. diplomats out of Iran.

Friday, February 1, 1980
DAY 90: Militant spokesmen go on Tehran television to complain that no one in the government is paying attention to the documents they have collected showing "U.S. spying in Iran." Carter officially thanks Canada for its help in the escape of the six U.S. embassy employees.

Monday
DAY 93: From his hospital bed, Khomeini swears in Bani-Sadr as the first president of the new Islamic republic; he also pledges unconditional support for Moslem insurgents fighting the Soviets in Afghanistan. U.S. immigration officials admit that, of 226 Iranians in this country on diplomatic passports in December, when President Carter announced he was sending many home, only 49 have left; 125 cannot be found at all.

Wednesday
DAY 95: Bani-Sadr, having called the militants holding the U.S. embassy "self-centered children who don't know what they are doing" and saying they were "a government within a government," bars them from unrestricted use of Iran's broadcasting facilities.

Thursday
DAY 96: Khomeini announces Bani-Sadr's appointment as head of the Revolutionary Council. The United States announces a further postponement of any sanctions to give the new Bani-Sadr government time to consolidate its power and possibly start real negotiations for the hostages' release. A group of 49 U.S. nationals sympathetic to the Iranian revolution arrive in Tehran where they have been invited by the militants. Government authorities hold the 49 at the airport for six hours before admitting them into the country. This is viewed as part of the growing struggle between Bani-Sadr and the militants.

Friday
DAY 97: Melkite Archbishop Hilarion Capudji, a long-time friend of the Palestinians who had served a jail term in Israel for gun-running, visits the hostages and pronounces them in "good condition."

February 1980. Holding Canadian flags, Kathleen and Joseph Stafford stand by Tennessee Governor Lamar Alexander during welcoming ceremonies. (WIDE WORLD PHOTOS)

Saturday

DAY 98: Militants respond to Bani-Sadr's criticism by saying they have a direct mandate from Khomeini to continue holding the hostages. The visiting U.S. delegation meets with the militants, but is not allowed to see any of the hostages.

Monday, February 11, 1980

DAY 100: Bani-Sadr says the hostages might be freed "even within the coming days." Washington rejects his condition that the United States admit guilt for past policies.

Tuesday

DAY 101: A militant spokesman says compromise on the hostages will be accepted if Khomeini orders it. Carter orders 1,800 U.S. Marines and four ships to join the U.S. naval forces off Iran.

Wedneday

DAY 102: Bani-Sadr says the hostages could be free in 48 hours if Carter accepts a "secret" plan already approved by Khomeini. The plan centers on the United States "admitting" its past crimes against Iran, promising not to interfere with Iran's internal affairs, and recognizing Iran's right to try to get back the shah and his wealth. The demands fall short of actually insisting that the shah be returned. The White House says it will support a U.N. plan to send an international commission to Iran to hear grievances, but cautions that it could be several weeks before release, indicating no terms have been worked out.

Friday

DAY 104: Ghotbzadeh, in Paris, says the hostages will be free only if both Iran and the United States accept the findings of an international inquiry into alleged crimes of the shah.

Sunday, February 17, 1980

DAY 106: Waldheim assembles a five-man commisison of international jurists and diplomats to investigate Iran's grievances.

Monday

DAY 107: Iran accepts the membership of the commission. Vance

Five of the six who escaped, shown at Canadian Embassy in Washington—R. Anders, C. Lijek, T. Boehm, J. Stafford, M. Lijek, K. Stafford. (WIDE WORLD PHOTOS)

confers with Waldheim in New York.

Tuesday

DAY 108: Khomeini announces he is making Bani-Sadr "supreme commander" of Iran's armed forces, a post Khomeini himself has held since the revolution.

Wednesday

DAY 109: Khomeini, in a major address on Iranian television, makes strong statements against the shah and the United States, and exhorts "our young people (meaning the militants) to not stop until you achieve your victory." In Washington, Carter demands the "prompt return" of the hostages, saying the United States "has no desire to interfere in the internal affairs of Iran."

Thursday

DAY 110: As a U.N. commission begins its work with meetings in Geneva, Iranian officials and militants deny any link between the work of the commission and release of the hostages. Buoyed by Khomeini's television address, the militants say there is no hope of the hostages being released until the shah is returned.

Saturday

DAY 112: The U.N. commission arrives in Tehran for an expected two-week visit which, Washington hopes, will speed the hostages' release. As they arrive, Khomeini, in a prepared text read on Iranian television, says that the fate of the hostages will have to be decided by the new Islamic parliament, to be elected in April.

Sunday, February 24, 1980

DAY 113: Iran's U.N. representative says an end to the hostage crisis is now "in sight for the first time"; Washington is cautious, but Carter says, "I think progress is being made." The commission meets with Bani-Sadr, who promises his full cooperation.

Tuesday

DAY 115: The Revolutionary council says some U.S. journalists will be readmitted to Iran.

Wednesday

DAY 116: The Revolutionary Council's secretary and Supreme Court head, Ayatollah Behesti, a major rival to Bani-Sadr, says the new parliament, as yet unelected, cannot consider the hostage release before May.

Iran's President Bani-Sadr, at left of photo, listens as one of the militants holding the U.S. Embassy and hostages speaks in Tehran. (WIDE WORLD PHOTOS)

Thursday

DAY 117: Meeting with U.N. commission members, Foreign Minister Ghotbzadeh promises that a meeting with the hostages will be arranged. Bani-Sadr said the visit would take place "only with the permission of the militants." This statement was viewed as a conciliatory gesture toward them.

Sunday, March 2, 1980

DAY 120: Khomeini ends a five-week hospital stay for a heart condition.

Monday

DAY 121: Iran's public prosecu-tor asks Ghotbzadeh to turn over Victor L. Tomseth, one of three diplomats held at the foreign ministry since the start of the crisis. The prosecutor charges Tomseth is connected with an anti-cleric extremist group, Forghan.

Wednesday

DAY 123: The militants say they will not allow the U.N. commission members to visit the hostages without a direct order from Khomeini. No such directive is forthcoming. As the seige at the embassy enters its fifth month, President Carter warns that if the U.N. commission is not successful in winning the hostages' release, the United States again will be forced to seek international sanctions against Iran.

Thursday

DAY 124: As the disgusted U.N. commission is about to announce that it is giving up and heading back to New York, the militants, in what appears to be a dramatic breakthrough, announce they will hand over control of the hostages to the Revolutionary Council to "deal with them in any way it deems appropriate. We regard our responsibility for the hostages at an end." Asked what it will mean when the transfer takes place, Ghotbzadeh says, "They are hostages and they will remain hostages." But the developments are enough for the commission, which announces it will remain in Iran for the time being. The militants say they will continue occupation of the U.S. embassy after the hostages are transferred.

Friday

DAY 125: Ghotbzadeh says the hostages may be taken from the militants and moved to a secret location for questioning by the U.N. commission. Thousands of Iranians outside the U.S. embassy compound, apparently led by agents of the militants, implore them not to surrender the hostages. The militants respond by taking a harder line, demanding television time to state their case before turning over the hostages to the Revolutionary Council. U.S. reporters are allowed into Tehran for the first time since Jan. 14.

Saturday

DAY 126: The militants ignore their own deadline for transfer of the hostages in open defiance of Ghotbzadeh and the Revolutionary Council. They demand a meeting with the council to discuss transfer terms and say they will effect the transfer "only if it is the clear will of the Iranian people" and on a direct order from Khomeini. An emergency meeting of the council breaks up with substantial disagreement between those allied with Bani-Sadr and those allied with religious hard-liners.

Monday, March 10, 1980
DAY 128: Khomeini strongly backs the militants' refusal to transfer the hostages and sets up stringent guidelines of what the commission must do before it will be allowed merely to visit the hostages. This ends any immediate hopes the U.N. panel had of succeeding in ending the crisis.

Tuesday
DAY 129: Denied access to the hostages during its 17-day visit, the U.N. commission leaves Tehran for New York. Bani-Sadr accuses the Revolutionary Council of "weakness and indecision."

Wednesday
DAY 130: Iranian television shows films of the hostages taken by the militants. Many of the U.S. nationals clearly show the strain of their ordeal.

Thursday
DAY 131: The State Department officially announces that it has evidence all 50 hostages are alive, ending rumors that one had died.

Friday
DAY 132: Bani-Sadr announces that he will ask the new Iranian parliament when it convenes in May to order the hostages' release. In New York, the U.N. commission ends consultations with Waldheim and suspends its work to await a "more favorable climate" in Iran.

Thursday, March 20, 1980
DAY 138: Meetings are held in Panama between White House adviser Hamilton Jordan, the shah, medical experts and Panamanian officials about facilities for the shah's needed spleen operation and his continued stay in Panama. The shah is given assurances by both the United States and Panama that under no circumstances will he be extradited and that hospital facilities are adequate for the needed operation.

The United States returns to the International Court and says that new information from Iran indicates "detention of the hostages may continue indefinitely and no one in this courtroom has any way of knowing" whether they will be held "for a month, a year, or for a decade." It asks for a stronger court order.

Friday
DAY 139: Despite assurances that he can safely remain in Panama, the shah prepares to fly to Egypt, thus thwarting Iranian attempts to win his return from Panama and complicating efforts for release of the hostages. White House Chief of Staff Hamilton Jordan flies to Panama.

Saturday
DAY 140: Foreign Minister Ghotbzadeh accuses former Secretary of State Henry Kissinger and Chase Manhattan Bank President David Rockefeller of trying to block extradition efforts by Iran to get the shah back from Panama.

Sunday, March 23, 1980
DAY 141: The shah leaves Panama for Egypt. Upon landing, he is greeted by President Sadat who says "the shah will stay here permanently." The shah is then taken to Egypt's finest military hospital.

Tuesday
DAY 143: The State Department sees no "foreseeable solution" to the hostage situation. Carter says the United States will continue trying to isolate Iran diplomatically. In Tehran, a fist-waving Iranian mob of some 30,000 besiege the occupied U.S. embassy to protest the shah's move to Egypt and demand that the hostages be tried. The mob was led by clerical groups opposed to the government of President Bani-Sadr who claimed that his actions are opposed to those of the ayatollah. Bani-Sadr's power, if he had any, seems to be at an end.

Wednesday
DAY 144: In a major setback to solution of the crisis, the Revolutionary Council votes to postpone the second round of parliamentary elections because of evidence of widespread fraud in the first round. Because Iran is on record as saying the hostages will not be released until the parliament rules

Front gates of the U.S. Embassy, scene of many anti-American demonstrations, now deserted except for militant guards. (WIDE WORLD PHOTOS)

on their fate, this puts the earliest possible return date sometime in early summer. After the council meeting, religious hardliner Ayatollah Mohammed Beheshti, secretary of the council and leader of the faction opposing Bani-Sadr, says he believes the Iranian president's actions are ''weak'' and that he favors trials for at least some of the hostages.

Friday
DAY 146: The shah's spleen is removed by Dr. Michael DeBakey. The famed physician called the operation a success.

Saturday
DAY 147: The shah's doctors say there is new evidence that his cancer has spread.

Sunday, March 30, 1980
DAY 148: After receiving a note from President Carter delivered through the Swiss, President Bani-Sadr said the Revolutionary Council will take custody of the hostages if the United States refrains from any ''provocation.'' He admits, though, that the conserva-

tive clergy on the council are opposed.

Tuesday, April 1, 1980
DAY 150: After meeting with Ayatollah Khomeini, Bani-Sadr again says the Revolutionary Council will take custody of the hostages until the new parliament meets and decides their fate, provided that the United States refrains from provocations against Iran. Bani-Sadr says Khomeini did not directly oppose the custody transfer. Carter calls the decision ''a positive step.'' He defers further sanctions against Iran. Khomeini calls Carter ''a great Satan'' on the first anniversary of Iran's Islamic Republic.

Wednesday
DAY 151: Bani-Sadr says Carter has agreed to ''terms.'' The White House says it does not know what Bani-Sadr means, but that it is a positive sign.

Thursday
DAY 152: An angry meeting of the Revolutionary Council breaks up without any resolve of the hos-

tage transfer question. Debate is over whether Carter has actually met terms.

Sunday, April 6, 1980
DAY 155: After another long and angry meeting, the Revolutionary Council decides it cannot resolve the exchange question and leaves the decision up to Khomeini.

Monday
DAY 156: Khomeini overrules Bani-Sadr and says the hostages should remain in control of the militants. The decision is a major setback for the Bani-Sadr government and a victory for the conservative clerical forces in the Islamic Republican Party. It is said Khomeini opposed the transfer simply because it was something the United States would have wanted. Col. Beckwith's volunteer rescue force apparently is placed on full alert this day.

Tuesday
DAY 157: The United States breaks diplomatic relations with Iran and formally embargoes all trade except for food and medicine. Iranian diplomats are given 24 hours to leave the United States.

Wednesday
DAY 158: U.S. intelligence source report evidence that anti-Khomeini Iranian groups are active in Iran. Many of these groups are said to be supporters of former Iranian Prime Minister Shapur Bakhtiar, the shah's last prime minister. New pressure is brought on U.S. allies to join in sanctions.

Thursday
DAY 159: The militants once again renew their pledge to ''destroy all hostages immediately'' if the U.S. undertakes ''even the smallest military action against Iran.'' Two unidentified hostages are shown on Iranian television confessing to ''shocking revelations'' that the embassy was used for spying. Secretary of State Vance calls on U.S. allies to impose economic sanctions and to recall their ambassadors from Iran.

Easter 1980. Hilarion Capudji, the exiled Greek Catholic archbishop of Jerusalem, prays with one of the hostages. (WIDE WORLD PHOTOS)

Friday

DAY 160: President Carter once again refuses to rule out the use of force in Iran. The Common Market foreign ministers, meeting in Lisbon, refuse to impose sanctions instead put off the decision until a future meeting. Militants say they have filmed the "confessions" of 12 of the "spies."

Saturday

DAY 161: A major Tehran rally to "celebrate" the breaking of diplomatic relations with the U.S. brings out the largest crowd since the early days of the revolution. Bani-Sadr uses the occasion to vow, "We will overthrow the Iraqui regime."

Tuesday, April 15, 1980

DAY 164: Three Red Cross workers, two Iranian and one Swiss, are allowed to visit the hostages. They emerge to say, "The general condition of the people is OK." They say they saw all 50 being held at the embassy and that they brought out messages for the families. The hostages are reported sleeping on mattresses on the floors of offices and are not tied up as they often were during the early days of their captivity.

Friday

DAY 167: In a news conference, Carter says military force will be the only option left to the U.S. if negotiations fail. He announces a ban on all exports to Iran except medicine and a ban on all travel to and from Iran.

Saturday

DAY 168: Iranian government officials call the new sanctions "a test of our national will" and accuse the U.S. of spiriting the shah out of Panama to keep him from being extradited.

Sunday, April 20, 1980

DAY 169: Kenneth and Barbara Timm, mother and stepfather of hostage Marine Sgt. Kevin Hermening, fly to Iran, defying the Iranian travel ban in an effort to see the young hostage.

The shah's cars, mostly Rolls Royces, to be put on auction in Europe with the proceeds to be turned over to the Mostazafine Foundation for the poor. (WIDE WORLD PHOTOS)

Monday

DAY 170: Mrs. Timm spends 45 minutes with her son in the embassy. The visit is filmed and shown on Iranian television. An administration official asks other hostage families not to follow the Timms' lead. Several were said to be making plans to go to Iran.

Wednesday

DAY 172: Common Market foreign ministers meeting in Luxembourg announce that, if the hostages are not returned by May 15, they will impose sanctions. Japanese and British oil companies announce they will stop buying Iranian oil because of a $2.50 per barrel price increase. Iran counters by saying it will stop selling to the Japanese and British. At the same time, Iran, for the second time, announces the expulsion of all U.S. newsmen for publishing stories "in opposition to the will of the people." For the second time, the Iranian government orders the explusion of all U.S. newsmen. At the same time, the government indicates the same fate might befall other journalists who publish stories "in opposition to the will of the people."

Thursday

DAY 173: "Charlie's Angels" are ordered into Iran in a bid to free the hostages. On orders of the President, the attempt is aborted in the Iranian desert. According to the official version, three of the eight helicopters that were to have carried the rescuers to Tehran were forced out of the mission. After the abort order is given, one of the remaining helicopters collides with a C-130 tanker aircraft and eight men are killed. The remaining four helicopters and the eight bodies are left in the desert while the would-be rescuers and their support personnel make their escape on other C-130s.

Friday

DAY 174: At approximately 1 A.M., the White House tells the world of the aborted raid. In Tehran, a massive rally is held in front of the U.S. embassy to celebrate the "victory." In a radio broadcast, Ayatollah Khomeini warns that any new attempt to rescue the hostages would result in their deaths.

Saturday

DAY 175: In a news conference, President Bani-Sadr announces that "most" of the hostages have been removed from the U.S. embassy compound and spread around Iran "for their own protection." The hostages remain under the control of the militants. At the same news conference, Mrs. Barbara Timm, still in Iran after

April 1980. An Iranian airman inspects ammunition belt for machine gun in one of the U.S. helicopters that survived the aborted raid. (WIDE WORLD PHOTOS)

visiting her son, appears to apologize for the U.S. action. ''We deeply regret the action of our president and apologize to the Iranian people,'' she says.

Sunday, April 27, 1980
DAY 176: The bodies of the eight dead U.S. servicemen are put on display at the U.S. embassy by Ayatollah Sadegh Khalkhali, head of the Revolutionary Court. Khalkhali insists there are nine dead.

Monday
DAY 177: President Carter announces that he has accepted the resignation of Secretary of State Cyrus Vance. Vance says he is quitting because he cannot support the president's decision to use military force in the rescue attempt. In Iran, the Revolutionary Council announces it will not turn over the bodies of the dead servicemen to the United States, but rather only to a representative of the pope.

Tuesday
DAY 178: The Defense Department admits that a sizeable number of U.S. agents had been in place on the ground in Tehran to aid in the rescue attempt. These agents had been infiltrated into Iran some months before in the guise of European businessmen. The DOD spokesman says that all have now left the country.

Wednesday
DAY 179: President Carter appoints Sen. Edmund Muskie, D-Maine, as the new secretary of state.

Thursday, May 1, 1980
DAY 180: Raid leader Col. Charles Beckwith meets with reporters to answer questions about the raid and to deny stories that he had asked to go on with the remaining helicopters. In London, five armed Iranians from Khuzistan province seize the Iranian embassy, saying they will kill their hostages and blow up the embassy unless the Khomeini government releases 91 political prisoners and agrees to a measure of autonomy for the region.

Friday
DAY 181: Iranian Foreign Minister Ghotbzadeh flatly rejects any deals with the five terrorists in London, saying that if any of the embassy hostages are harmed, the political prisoners being held in Iran would be executed immediately. Ghotbzadeh says the matter is entirely in British hands and that Britain can do whatever it wants. He also rejects out of hand the suggestion that there was any similarity between the taking of the Iranian embassy in London and the U.S. embassy in Tehran.

Saturday
DAY 182: In an effort to show it means what it says, the Iranian government orders a firing squad to execute two of the political prisoners whom the London terrorists seek to free.

Sunday, May 4, 1980
DAY 184: Minutes after the Lon-

don terrorists killed their second hostage, British SAS commandos storm the embassy and, in the ensuing battle, kill three of the terrorists and capture the remaining two. All 19 remaining hostages are rescued, although several are wounded. In Iran, a freelance U.S. journalists, Cynthia B. Dwyer, is taken into custody and accused of being a CIA agent. This is immediately denied by U.S. authorities.

Monday
DAY 185: Foreign Minister Ghotbzadeh thanks the British government for its actions, but flatly rejects the idea that the London incident will have any effect on the U.S. hostages in Iran. ''The circumstances are completely different,'' he insists. The bodies of the eight U.S. servicemen killed in the ill-fated raid arrive from Switzerland at Dover Air Force Base, Delaware. President Carter declares three days of national mourning. In Tehran, an official government spokesman says the dispersal of the hostages to 12 different Iranian cities has been completed.

Wednesday
DAY 187: An Iranian firing squad executes the first female member of the Iranian parliament and the former education minister under the shah.

Thursday
DAY 188: President Bani-Sadr seems to have won a major victory in his continuing struggle with clerical militants. He demands three concessions from Ayatollah Khomenini: the ability to name a prime minister, placing the military under the control of the president (himself), and control of the state radio and television. In a radio address, Khomeini announces ''I accept.'' Meanwhile, Iranians go to the polls in the second round of voting for a parliament, the first under the new constitution.

Friday
DAY 189: The Iranian Republi-

can Party, Bani-Sadr's main opposition, has won a clear majority in the new Parliament. With results in 26 districts still to be counted, they already have won 136 seats to 41 for supporters of Bani-Sadr.

Saturday
DAY 190: Bani-Sadr's attempt to convince Adm. Ahmad Madani, former governor of Khuzistan Province, to become prime minister fails after Madani meets with Khomeini but was unable to get the assurances he feels he needs to accept office. This, coupled with the election results, are major blows to Bani-Sadr.

Sunday, May 11, 1980
DAY 191: With the refusal of Madani to accept the prime ministership, the Revolutionary Council declines to give Bani-Sadr authority to seek anyone else for the time being despite his authorization from Khomeini. The decision is seen as a further chipping away of Bani-Sadr's strength.

Monday
DAY 192: Ayatollah Ali Ghodussi, chief government prosecutor, refuses a request from Swiss Ambassador Erik Lang for information about U.S. journalist Cynthia Dwyer. Ghodussi acknowledges she was being held, but declines further information ''so her accomplices will not escape.''

Wednesday
DAY 194: Iran signs a draft trade agreement with the Soviet Union that includes a provision for Iran to ship its goods across land routes

Ayatollah Sadegh Khalkhali, head of the Revolutionary Court, who put the remains of the dead U.S. servicemen on public display. (WIDE WORLD PHOTOS)

if the United States should attempt a naval blockade.

Saturday

DAY 197: Common Market foreign ministers meeting in Naples issue a much watered down set of sanctions against Iran. Instead of forbidding all trade except in food and medicine, as the United States has requested, the ministers decide only to void all contracts with Iran entered into since November 4 and to enter into no new ones. This decision leaves intact almost all major trade agreements.

Sunday

DAY 198: Britain announces that it will not go along with even the watered down sanctions voted against Iran by the Common Market ministers. Instead of canceling all contracts going back to November 4, the British will only agree not to enter into any new contracts. Current British trade with Iran is estimated at about $100 million a month, or about what it was before the revolution.

Monday, May 19, 1980

DAY 199: In a published interview, Iranian U.N. representative Mansour Farhang says it was no longer in the best interests of Iran to continue holding the hostages.

He says all the political and propaganda gains have been won. The militants, however, perhaps in response to this interview, announce from the city of Zenjan, where a number of the hostages are now being held, that they still demand trials for the hostages. They left open the possibility that they might defy any order from the new parliament regarding the hostages if no trials are held.

Wednesday

DAY 201: The watered-down sanctions against Iran voted by the Common Market ministers go into effect.

Thursday

DAY 202: U.N. Secretary General Kurt Waldheim announces that the U.N. Commission to study Iran's grievances against the shah and the United States was being reactivated and that one of its members, Adib Daoudy, was being sent back to Tehran "to prepare for the return of the whole commission."

Friday

DAY 203: The International Court of Justice at the Hague hands down a six-count judgment against Iran, ordering an immediate return of the hostages and warning that, if they are not

returned, Iran might be held liable for sanctions and reparations.

Sunday, May 25, 1980

DAY 205: Adib Daoudy arrives in Tehran. Foreign Minister Ghotbzadeh says that any meeting with Daoudy will be limited to discussing "the shah's and America's crimes" and no discussion of the hostages will be allowed.

Tuesday

DAY 207: Iran's new parliament convenes in Tehran. Of the 241 seats of the 270-seat body that have been decided, 130 are controlled by members of the fundamentalist Islamic Republican Party. The first day's business is limited to a speech from President Bani-Sadr and messages from the ayatollah and from the militants holding the hostages. The militants repeat their demand for trials of the hostages and state, "The hostage question is the biggest question facing this body."

Sunday, June 1, 1980

DAY 212: In violation of a government travel ban, a delegation of 10 U.S. citizens headed by former U.S. Attorney General Ramsey Clark arrives in Tehran for an international conference on "U.S. intervention in Iran."

DAY 214: Clark confers with Bani-Sadr and announces that he has agreed to head a commission to investigate the role of the United States in Iran during the reign of the shah.

Thursday

DAY 216: On the final day of the conference, Ghotbzadeh announces that it was Iran's view that "there are many other issues outstanding that we consider much more important than the hostages." He repeats the Iranian demand for the return of the shah and his wealth and says that Iran would seek compensation "for the policies of the U.S. over the last 27 years" before the hostages are returned.

Sunday, June 8, 1980

DAY 219: In what was considered another slap at the militants,

"Crimes of America" meeting. Delegates from some 50 countries attend the conference in Iran, including former U.S. Attorney General Ramsey Clark. (WIDE WORLD PHOTOS)

President Bani-Sadr cautions against thinking about trying the hostages. Says Bani-Sadr, "What happens if they are tried and found not guilty. What then would have been the validity to have held them for seven months."

Monday

DAY 220: In a major address, the ayatollah warns that Iran is facing "chaos" because of the differences between political forces in the country. Khomeini calls on Bani-Sadr and the fundamentalists to patch up their differences and "not to struggle with people who are with us."

Wednesday

DAY 222: Members of the left-wing Iranian political party, the "People's Mujahedeen," meeting in a Tehran sports stadium with government approval, are attacked by a large group of pro-Khomeini supporters. The resulting riot, called the largest in Tehran since before the shah fled, leaves one dead and over 400 injured.

Sunday, June 15, 1980

DAY 226: Adib Daoudy, a member of the U.N. Commission of Inquiry, leaves Tehran for New York after a 27-day stay. He says the commission's renewed effort to end the stalemate is a failure. Foreign Minister Ghotbzadeh says he sees no reason for Daoudy or any other commission member to return to Iran.

Wednesday

DAY 229: A newspaper owned by President Bani-Sadr publishes details of what it says is a "plot" by the fundamentalist Islamic Republican Party to force Bani-Sadr out of office. Leader of the so-called plot is said to be Ayatollah Behesti, head of the IRP.

Thursday, June 26, 1980

DAY 237: Khomeini, in a television address, attacks the Bani-Sadr government for retaining "vestiges of the government of the shah." He threatens to call out the people to "overthrow" Bani-Sadr if all references to the shah are not "purged" from the

The ayatollah's Iran takes a dim view of scenes such as this one, photographed several years ago at a beach outside Tehran. (WIDE WORLD PHOTOS)

country. It is the first time Khomeini directly attacks Bani-Sadr.

Saturday

DAY 239: In an answer to Khomeini's attack, Bani-Sadr says the fault in the government rests with many of the ministers and "I am not responsible for them . . . I didn't appoint them." He adds, "I can't rule unless I am given the tools to rule." Then, switching to the hostage issue, Bani-Sadr calls the problem "insoluble."

Friday, July 4, 1980

DAY 245: About 5,000 women, angered over newly issued dress codes, protest in front of Bani-Sadr's office. They are especially angered over a threat to fire any women working for the government who did not wear a veil or chador to work. Bani-Sadr speaks to the women and promises no one would be fired because of the clothing she wears.

Saturday

DAY 246: Militants announce in Tehran that an undisclosed number of hostages had been sent to the cities of Nejafabad, Mahallat and Arak. If true, this would bring to 17 the number of cities in Iran now said to be holding the 53 hostages.

Monday, July 7, 1980

DAY 248: In an obvious show of no support for Bani-Sadr and his 3-day-old promise, the military fires 131 civilian women working for it for reporting to work not wearing veils.

Wednesday

DAY 250: Iran announces that it had smashed a plot by Iranian army and air force elements to overthrow the Khomeini regime. An official news release says the plot was centered at an air base near Hamadan and that at least 300 military men were involved. The plotters are said to have planned to return former Premier Shahpur Bakhtiar to power . . . In Washington, Federal Judge George Hart, ruling in a suit filed by three insurance companies, says Iran must pay damages to U.S. companies whose assets have been seized since the revolution. This is the first of over 200 such suits that have been filed to come to trial. The 200 suits ask for some $5 billion in damages. Iranian assets frozen currently are said to be worth in excess of $8 billion. Lawyers for Iran announce they will appeal the verdict.

Thursday

DAY 251: Hostage Richard

Ayatollah Khalkhali ordered the destruction of graves of nobilities and ex-ministers of the deposed Shah Mohammed Reza Pahlavi. (WIDE WORLD PHOTOS)

Queen is ordered released by Khomeini for "health reasons." Khomeini says Queen should go to a country "which enjoys better health facilities." In the same statement, Khomeini, referring to the plot to oust him, says the United States, the Soviet Union, Israel and Iraq are behind it.

Friday

DAY 252: Queen is flown via Zurich to a military hospital in Wiesbaden, West Germany. . . . In an interview with several European journalists, Carter says "military measures are no logner under consideration," for freeing the hostages. Carter says the U.S. now intends to use private and diplomatic means only to get the hostages released.

Monday, July 14, 1980

DAY 255: U.S. doctors say Queen is suffering from a mild case of Multiple Sclerosis, which caused double vision, numbness on his left side and extreme nausea. He reportedly had been experiencing these symptoms since shortly before the embassy takeover.

Tuesday

DAY 256: Iran seals off the country and forbids all travel in or out in what it calls an attempt to catch more of the anti-Khomeini plotters.

Thursday

DAY 258: Queen flies to Washington, where he is met by Secretary of State Muskie.

Friday

DAY 259: Queen meets with President Carter.

Saturday

DAY 260: In his first meeting with reporters, Queen gives details of his imprisonment. He indicates that he was generally well treated, not interrogated, or pressured to sign anything. He describes his former captors as "very dedicated to Khomeini and very anti-communist."

Sunday, July 20, 1980

DAY 261: In Paris, an Iranian death squad attempts to kill former Prime Minister Bakhtiar. In a sharp exchange of gunfire with French security police, one policeman and a woman neighbor are killed. Five members of the professional assassination team are captured. They are identified as two Lebanese, two Palestinians and an Iranian.

Monday

DAY 262: In a Washington suburb, Ali Akbar Tabatabai, a former press attache at the Iranian embassy and now the head of an anti-Khomeini organization, the Iranian Freedom Foundation, is slain at his front door by someone dressed as a mailman. The FBI immediately is called into the case, which is called a "political assassination."

Tuesday

DAY 263: The FBI announces the arrest of two men in the Tabatabai slaying. One is identified as the postman who the day before claimed his mail truck had been stolen at gunpoint. At the same time, the FBI identified the actual killer as David Belfield, who goes by the name of Daoud Salahuddin. The killer is identified as working for the Iranian interest section of the Algerian embassy in Washington and as being a member of a small black Muslim sect which fervently follows Khomeini. Sect members were employed as guards at the Iranian embassy before it was closed. The FBI said it believed Belfield, using a passport supplied by a "third country," had fled to Iran via Switzerland. In Iran, Bani-Sadr is formally sworn in as president by the newly organized Parliament.

Wednesday

DAY 264: Richard Queen is quoted as telling State Department officials that his captors staged a "mock execution" of a number of the hostages. According to the report, Queen and a dozen or so of the hostages were lined up against a wall and their captors pulled the triggers of their unloaded guns. In one version of the story, which the State Department will not confirm, deny, or comment on, the incident is said to have taken place shortly after the abortive rescue attempt. Another version has it taking place before the rescue bid.

Thursday

DAY 265: The last two U.S. journalists in Iran, Jay Ross of the Washington Post and Doyle McManus of The Los Angeles

Times, flee Iran just ahead of possible arrest.

Friday

DAY 266: In a concession to the fundamentalists, Bani-Sadr nominates Deputy Interior Minister Mustafa Mir-Salim as prime minister. Mir-Salim is considered much more militant than Bani-Sadr's original choice of Hassan Habibi, who had been rejected by the majority Islamic Republican Party.

Saturday

DAY 267: Mohammed Reza Pahlavi, the deposed shah, dies of complications from lymphatic cancer at the Maadi Military Hospital outside Cairo. Immediately after the death is announced in Iran (''the bloodsucker of the century is dead at last''), a government spokesman says the shah's death will have no effect whatever on the hostages. In Paris, Bakhtiar says the shah's death would not change his plans ''to bring liberty and independence to Iran.'' In Washington, some 1,500 Iranians gather for demonstrations both for and against Khomeini. By far the larger group, about 1,100, represented the pro-Khomeini Iranian Students Association. Police move in and arrest 172 men and 20 women on charges of disorderly conduct when the group refuses to leave after fighting breaks out with anti-Khomeini groups. Iran's Parliament adjourns without taking any action on Bani-Sadr's nomination of Mustafa Mir-Salim as prime minister, thus effectively killing the nomination. In its action, Parliament criticizes Bani-Sadr for the ''tone'' of his nominating letter, in which he was critical of parliamentary infighting which had led to the prime minister's office going unfilled.

Sunday, July 27, 1980

DAY 268: The arrested Iranian students are arraigned in federal court. The students refuse to give their names and announce they will go on a hunger strike to protest their innocence.

Monday

DAY 269: The shah is buried in Egypt in a state funeral. Egyptian President Sadat is the only head of state present. Most Western countries are represented by their ambassadors to Egypt. The highest ranking dignitary besides Sadat is former President Richard Nixon, who says the Carter administration's treatment of the shah was ''shameful.'' In Iran, Ayatollah Hasheimi Rafsanjani is elected speaker of the new parliament. He long has been an outspoken proponent of putting the hostages on trial.

Tuesday

DAY 270: A letter signed by 187 members of the U.S. House of Representatives is read to the Iranian Parliament. The letter urges immediate discussion be-

Banner headlines in Iranian newspapers proclaim the death of the shah. Iranians poured into the streets of Tehran, flashing their auto lights. (WIDE WORLD PHOTOS)

tween the U.S. and Iran leading to the release of the hostages. In reading the letter, Speaker Rafsanjani blames the U.S. for the hostage crisis and says it is up to the U.S. to end it.

Friday, August 1, 1980
DAY 273: A very large crowd, estimated at more than 50,000, marches on the U.S. embassy to protest the continued holding of the Iranian students in Washington. The Iranian government sends an "urgent plea" to the U.N. to investigate the conditions under which the Iranians are being held.

Saturday
DAY 274: The Iranians, still refusing to give their names, are brought back into court in Washington and the disorderly conduct charges against them are dropped. But they are ordered held while immigration officials determine whether any of them are in violation of their visas. The male detainees are transferred to a new federal prison facility in Otisville, N.Y., and the women to a federal detention center in New York City pending resolution of the immigration question.

Sunday, August 3, 1980
DAY 275: British arrest 67 Iranian demonstrators in London. The Iranians immediately vow to go on a hunger strike until they are released. A number of Iranians who have been weakened by their hunger strike are force-fed nutritional supplements. In Iran, Rafsanjani announces that, because the Iranian students are being held, Parliament's debate of the hostage issue will be postponed indefinitely. In a message to the detained students, Bani-Sadr urges them to resist deportation "until they have to drag you to the plane."

Monday
DAY 276: Immigration and Naturalization officials announce that a check has shown that all but one of the detainees is in this country legally and therefore all but the one is released. The Iranians go by car to Washington where they announce they will take part in another anti-U.S. demonstration.

Tuesday
DAY 277: An INS officer, saying he did not want to be identified, says the Iranians had been released from custody on orders from Washington before any thorough background checks could be completed. According to this unidentified officer, INS did not have a chance to contact schools the students said they were attending to verify that they were registered for classes, or even to veritfy with local INS offices that the students were registered with them as they as required by law. Khomeini calls for worldwide demonstrations against the U.S. for its continued "intervention into the internal affairs of the people of Iran."

Wednesday
DAY 278: A Justice Department official says the department will begin presenting evidence to a federal grand jury that Iran is providing money and other assistance to the pro-Khomeini groups in the U.S. and that these groups have hired criminals and others to attack anti-Khomeini Iranians here.

Thursday
DAY 279: In answer to Khomeini's call, demonstrations are held in a number of world capitals by Iranian students, including 800 students in Washington. In Rome, Iranian demonstrators chain themselves to the main gate of the Vatican to "protest" the "failure" of Pope John Paul II to protest the arrest of Iranian demonstrators in Washington and London.

Friday
DAY 280: Bani-Sadr, bowing to the will of parliamentary fundamentalists, submits the name of Education Minister Mohammed Ali-Rajai to be prime minister. Ali-Rajai is a hardliner who is much more conservative than Bani-Sadr's previous nominees. In the past, Ali-Rajai has favored spy trials for the hostages.

Saturday
DAY 281: Charges by U.S. officials that Iran is covertly funding Iranian demonstrations in the U.S. are denied by Abas Esfa-

July 29. A large audience listens in Tehran as the Iranian Islamic Parliament meets to select a prime minister for the country. (WIDE WORLD PHOTOS)

hani, a spokesman for the Moslem Student Association. Calling the charges "lies," Esfahani, a student in St. Louis, says the demonstrations were spontaneous protests of U.S. intervention in Iran such as "the terrorist attack said to be an attempt to free the hostages."

Sunday, August 10, 1980

DAY 282: In another rebuke of Bani-Sadr, Parliament quickly approves the nomination of Ali-Rajai as prime minister.

Friday

DAY 287: Syndicated columnist Jack Anderson charges in a series of columns that President Carter plans a limited invasion of Iran in mid-October in order to bolster his re-election chances. The White House immediately denies the story, calling it "absolutely false," and says the idea that any president would take a military action for political gain was "grotesque and totally irresponsible." A number of U.S. newspapers, including The Washington Post, New York Daily News, and Long Island's Newsday refuse to publish the columns. Others do print it because, as one newspaper puts it, if the charges are true, Carter should be impeached; if they are false, Anderson should be run out of journalism forever.

Saturday

DAY 288: Ambassadors from a number of European nations meet with Speaker Rafsanjani to urge immediate parliamentary consideration of the hostage question and to allow an international commission to visit them. Rafsanjani immediately rejects both proposals, saying that Parliament would get to the hostage question after it "finishes its current important business" and that a visitation was impossible "because the spies leaked vital information which was used in the rescue attempt."

Sunday, August 17, 1980

DAY 289: The Majlis expels its only Jewish member on charges that he collaborated with Israel

Acting Interior Minister Ali Akbar Hashimi Rafsanjani has confessed, "We never had the intention to move against the Embassy. But the ex-dictator's arrival in the United States pushed the people over the deep end. . . . Even if we had tried to stop them, we would have failed." (WIDE WORLD PHOTOS)

and opposed the taking of the U.S. hostages. Under the new Iranian constitution, one seat in Parliament is guaranteed to the country's Jewish minority.

Sunday, August 24, 1980
DAY 296: The militants announce that the hostages have been moved once again to such distant and secret locations as Gorgan and Gazvin. At the same time, they once again restate that if the U.S. tries any kind of military force, "the attackers and the spies would be sent off to hell together."

Wednesday, August 27, 1980
DAY 299: Amnesty International, the international human rights organization, announces that it believes that over 1,200 persons have been executed in Iran since the Islamic revolution took power. As if to underscore this, 11 more military officers are executed in Tehran, bringing to 92 the number executed in the aftermath of the ayatollah's takeover.

Saturday, August 30, 1980
DAY 302: Prime Minister Rajai announces receipt of a new letter from Secretary of State Muskie urging new talks leading to the hostages' release. This is the first direct contact between the U.S. and Iran on the hostage issue since the failed rescue attempt.

Sunday, August 31, 1980
DAY 303: The Foreign Affairs Commission of the Majlis releases a draft of a plan that could resolve the hostage question. The plan calls for the U.S. to return to Iran the shah's wealth, unfreeze Iranian assets and "acknowledges" past abuses against Iran. The plan has to be presented to the full parliament. At the same time, the commission defends the taking of the hostages as a "natural reaction" on the part of the Iranian people.

Friday
DAY 308: Iranian and Iraqui ground forces clash along their common border with several deaths reported.

Sunday, September 7, 1980
DAY 310: The families of the 52 hostages send a joint letter to the Majlis offering to have family representatives meet with Iranian officials in hopes of ending the stalemate.

Monday
DAY 311: Rajai responds negatively to the Muskie letter. He says the hostages' release could come about "if only we were sure you had repented" and "would not again commit sins against Iran," but that he doubts the U.S. could prove this easily. At the same time, the British close their embassy in Tehran out of fear that its diplomats might be taken hostage in retaliation for the arrest of Iranian protestors in London.

Thurdsay
DAY 314: In his answer to the Muskie letter, Ayatollah Khomeini lists four demands that must be met before the hostages could be released: (1) Return of the shah's wealth; (2) Unfreezing of Iranian assets; (3) Dropping of U.S. claims; and (4) A promise not to interfere in Iranian affairs. Observers see this as a possible breakthrough because no mention was made of trials or a U.S. apology.

Sunday, September 14, 1980
DAY 317: A number of Iranian officials, including Majlis Speaker Hashemi Rafsanjani, tell Western newsmen that merely because Khomeini did not mention certain demands did not mean they would not be required. Rafsanjani specifically said a U.S. apology would be necessary.

Monday
DAY 318: The Majlis, set to open debate on the hostages, instead turns the matter over to the special commission to discuss and report back to the full body. The Foreign Affairs Commission had recommended that the discussion be held by the full body

and 94 members had asked to speak. The decision is seen as a positive development because it removes the hostage issue from internal parliamentary politics.

Tuesday
DAY 319: As border clashes intensify, Iraqi President Saddam Hussein declares his country's 1975 border agreement with Iran to be "null and void."

Friday
DAY 322: Fighting between Iraq and Iran escalates and Iranian President Bani-Sadr orders Iranian reservists called up.

Sunday, September 21, 1980
DAY 324: The fighting between the two countries is now a major war. Iraqui ground forces move across the Iranian border at several points and Iraq's Soviet-built warplanes attack targets all over Iran, including oil facilities, airfields and even Tehran's international airport.

Monday
DAY 325: Speaking to the U.N. General Assembly, Secretary of State Muskie renews his plea for a quick end to the hostage question.

Tuesday
DAY 326: Responding to the Muskie speech, Speaker Rafsanjani declares that the hostages will be released only when "the U.S. has met all our demands." He specifically singles out the return of the shah's wealth, which he says "exceeds 3 billion U.S. dollars."

Saturday
DAY 330: Iraqui President Hussein suggests that a ceasefire might be possible if Iran is willing to hold direct negotiations to settle disputed border claims.

Sunday, September 28, 1980
DAY 331: Prime Minister Rajai says Iran is ready for a protracted war "because we know we are fighting the United States which continues the fight." He also says any Arab state that openly or covertly supports Iraq opens itself to attack by Iran.

Monday

DAY 332: Khomeini rejects any peace offering, saying Iran will fight to the very end. In his speech, the ayatollah rejects any negotiations with Iraq, calling it "corrupt," and insisting that negotiations might be possible only if Iraq "surrenders."

Tuesday

DAY 333: In response to a Saudi request, the U.S. sends four radar command planes and about 300 Air Force personnel to Saudi Arabia to beef up that country's air defense system. The Saudis, who are supporting Iraq, fear an Iranian airstrike against their oil facilities. At the same time, the Pentagon denies a Saudi request for ground-to-air missiles and the crews to man them out of fear that Iran might retaliate against the hostages.

Wednesday

DAY 334: Secretary of State Muskie supports Iraq's call for a ceasefire. Once again, he calls on Iran to end the hostage crisis.

Friday

DAY 336: As the Iran-Iraq war enters its 12th day, fighting continues for control of major cities in Iran's oil region including Abadan, Khurramshahr and Ahwaz. A long war of attrition now seems likely with Iraq unable to deliver a decisive blow because of the effectiveness of the U.S.-supplied Iranian air force.

Sunday, October 5, 1980

DAY 338: Additional air defense early warning equipment and personnel are sent to Saudi Arabia as Iran steps up its threats against Arab countries supporting Iraq.

Tuesday

DAY 340: One positive development has occurred from the war—the emergence of President Bani-Sadr as a major Iranian war hero with the people. Western experts believe Bani-Sadr, given his new power base, now may be able to move to end the hostage situation.

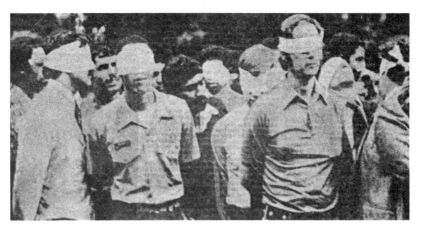

Wednesday

DAY 348: Iran announces that Prime Minister Rajai will go to New York to argue Iran's case against Iraq before the U.N. General Assembly. This marks a major departure in Iranian foreign policy from the time the hostages were taken, which has been to ignore the U.N. Ali Rajai's trip to New York fuels speculation he might be willing to discuss the hostages.

Thursday

DAY 349: President Carter says he would be willing to meet with Rajai while the prime minister is in the U.S., but adds that he remains pessimistic about any real breakthrough in the hostage stalemate.

Friday

DAY 350: Ali Rajai arrives in New York and announces he will have no discussions regarding the hostages while in the United States.

Saturday

DAY 351: Meeting with reporters in New York, Rajai seems to add new demands for release of the hostages, including removal of early warning planes from Saudi Arabia, removal of "U.S. protection from Jordan," "end of U.S. help of Iraq" and a reduction of size of the U.S. fleet in the Indian Ocean. These, Rajai says, are all "obstacles to a solution to the (hostage) problem."

Sunday, October 12, 1980

DAY 345: As the war continues with Iraq on the offensive, Bani-Sadr says Iran might be willing to comply with a U.N. supervised ceasefire if Iraq did so, too. Speaking about the hostages for the first time in weeks, Bani-Sadr says the war is having no effect on the hostage situation and that "the hostage problem will have to be solved on its own merits."

Sunday, October 19, 1980

DAY 352: Secretary of State Muskie again assures Iran that the U.S. remains strictly neutral in the Iran-Iraq conflict. This is echoed later in the day by President Carter at a campaign stop.

DAY 354: As the war with Iraq goes badly, Iranian officials suddenly send new signals to the U.S. that an end to the hostage situation may be at hand. This starts with a news conference by Ali Rajai upon his return from New York in which he says he is sure "the U.S. is now ready to meet Iranian conditions for the hostage's release." Additionally, he says, "The hostages are not a problem for us and we are now in a position to resolve it." Other Iranian officials say a final list of demands for the hostages' release will be made by the Majlis "within a matter of days."

On the **444th day**, ninety days after Bani-Sadr's statement, the 52 U.S. nationals landed first in Athens, then in Algiers, and finally in Frankfurt, West Germany.

For a complete picture of those frantic 90 days, turn to page 5.

The Fall Of The U.S. Embassy: It Shouldn't Have Been A Surprise

To many Western diplomats in Iran, it is confusing why the United States was so surprised that militants stormed and occupied the U.S. embassy compound on November 4. In fact, they still wonder why the United States took no extra precautions to prevent it.

After all, the action that day was the third attempt—and the second success—by the same group to occupy the compound in the nine months that had preceded the event. The only difference this time was that the leftist militants had become a significant political power in the factionalized country and the government was unable or unwilling to do anything about the attack.

The first attack had taken place on the last day of 1978 as hundreds of militants demonstrating against Shah Mohammed Reza Pahlavi and his main protector, the United States, stormed the gates of the embassy compound. They were driven back by tear gas fired by the 19 lightly armed Marine guards on duty. The shah's own troops eventually arrived to disperse the mob.

One Iranian soldier was killed in the riot, which was described as a brief but fierce battle. Dozens of the demonstrators were injured.

The second attempt came in the political vacuum that followed the shah's flight from Iran, but before Ayatollah Ruhollah Khomeini had consolidated his power. On February 14, Valentine's Day in the United States, shortly after 10 A.M., a heavily armed force led by Fedayeen and members of the left-wing Cherikhaye Fedaye Khalq (People's Sacrifice Guerrillas) stormed the embassy.

Despite the warning from the first attempt six weeks earlier, the heavily armed attackers were met by the same 19 lightly armed U.S. Marines. This time, the attackers were carrying machine guns, pistols and automatic rifles, and came in firing volleys of shots into the consular building. The Marines asked permission of Ambassador William Sullivan to defend themselves. Sullivan, however, denied permission and urged surrender instead.

Within a matter of minutes, the heavily armed invaders were in charge of the embassy compound.

One Iranian civilian embassy employee was shot in the chest as he stepped in front of Marine Sgt. Kenneth Kraus to protect him. Kraus himself was hit in the forehead and eyes by shotgun pellets.

In all, the invaders took 18 U.S. nationals hostage (a larger number had managed to escape during the confusion) and, in a scene that was to become all too familiar eventually to U.S. television audience, began parading the hostages around the embassy grounds.

Many of the Marines were kicked and beaten. Said Los Angeles Times correspondent Kenneth Freed, one of those taken, "I thought for sure we all were going to die."

This seizure, however, soon ended, almost as quickly as the attack itself had begun. Forces loyal to Ayatollah Khomeini arrived and took control of the situation. In fact, according to a number of U.S. observers, the pro-Khomeini forces actually began to exchange shots with the attackers.

Finally, with the arrival of Deputy Prime Minister Ibrahim Yazdi, the government forces were able to control the situation and the hostages were led to safety.

The eventual toll was two Iranian civilian employees dead and a half-dozen U.S. diplomats injured, two seriously.

U.S. authorities had the warning repeated late in October following the admission of the shah to the United States for medical treatment. Members of the Revolutionary Council specifically had warned U.S. officials in Iran that the embassy might again be the target if the shah was not expelled immediately from the United States. When the warnings were forwarded to Washington, however, officials at the State Department chose to ignore them. In so doing, they also chose to ignore the growing evidence of a massive anti-U.S. shift of sentiment in Iran, while clinging to the belief that relations between the two countries was improving.

For example, the State Department pointed to what was described as a "cordial" meeting between presidential adviser Zbigniew Brzezinski and then Foreign Minister Yazdi in Algiers, where both had gone for the 25th Anniversary celebration of the start of the Algerian war of independence from France.

What the officials at Foggy Bottom chose to ignore about the meeting was its coverage in Iran on state television, which was controlled by Sadegh Ghotbzadeh. Iranian television used the meeting to point out how the Bazargan government was "sitting at the table with the American wolf." This was followed by a series of speeches by Khomeini in which he condemned the United States in more strident terms.

Specific warnings also were passed on to U.S. embassy officials in Tehran by friends in the Bazargan government. The situation, they told embassy officials, was getting out of Prime Minister Mehdi Bazargan's control.

It is reported that Undersecretary of State David Newsom tried to convince Secretary of State Cyrus Vance to take some action to beef up embassy protection. Instead, Vance simply asked the Bazargan government for assurances that no U.S. nationals would be endangered from reprisals for the shah's admittance to the United States. Such assurances were quickly issued and accepted at the White House, despite the growing evidence of the weakening of Bazargan.

The actual takeover of the embassy began on the early morning of Sunday, November 4, a normal working day in Iran. Some 400 demonstrators gathered outside the main gate of the 27-acre U.S. compound chanting pro-Khomeini slogans. The crowd swelled and turned more anti-U.S. when word arrived from the holy city of Qom that the ayatollah had made still another speech in which he charged that the embassy was a ''nest of spies'' and a ''center of intrigue.''

The ranking diplomat at the embassy, Charge d'Affaires L. Bruce Laingen, and two aides, left for the foreign ministry to demand beefed-up protection. Just after they left, however, at about 11:00 A.M. Tehran time, the situation got out of hand.

Using bolt cutters, the demonstrators cut through a thick chain which had been holding closed the main gates on Taleghani Street. About 100 of the demonstrators then rushed onto the embassy grounds.

As with the attack in February, the U.S. Marine guards were ordered not to oppose the demonstrators, who initially told embassy political officer Victor Tomseth, who was in charge in Laingen's absence, that they simply wanted to hold a sit-in to demonstrate against the shah's admittance to the United States.

The Marines quickly gathered all U.S. nationals who were in the compound in the two-story brick chancellory building, known in the compound as Fort Apache because it was specially reinforced and secured.

On orders from Laingen, embassy personnel began to destroy classified documents and equipment, and finally, at about 3:00 P.M. on orders from Washington relayed through Laingen, the Marines opened the doors of the chancellory and the militants poured in.

In the resulting confusion, a number of U.S. nationals were able to make an escape by simply walking out a back door and down an alley. A hard rain had begun to fall as the order was given to open the doors. As the militants poured in the front, about 14 U.S. and a few Iranian embassy employees pried open a locked rear door and, in groups of three and four, simply walked out.

Once in the alleyway, the groups split up in various directions. Six went to various embassies and friends' houses and eventually were smuggled out of Iran by Canadian embassy officials. A seventh, 27-year-old Kim King of Clatskanie, Ore., simply went to the airport and bought himself a ticket out.

King, a civilian, was in Iran on a tourist visa. A number of other U.S. nationals were not so lucky. They took a wrong turn in an alley and ran into an armed group of militants and were quickly returned to the compound. By then, over 600 ''students'' had gathered and were parading the hostages around the compound in a display which duplicated the one after the fall of the embassy in February.

When the extent of the attack became known, State Department officials called on Foreign Minister Yazdi to send troops to lift the seige. Yazdi and Prime Minister Bazargan phoned Ayatollah Khomeini to get his permission, but were told by his son, Ahmed, to leave the matter alone. Ahmed reportedly said the matter should not be handled by the government and should be left instead to the Revolutionary Council.

Just after the fall of the U.S. Embassy, an unidentified American woman starts a near uproar as she protests to the guards about holding hostages. The guards are calm, however, only instructing her to leave. (WIDE WORLD PHOTOS)

When Bazargan then called Ayatollah Mohammed Behesti, the de-facto head of the council, he was told bluntly that the council supported the actions of the militants. Handcuffed, the Bazargan government resigned.

Clearly, the takeover of the embassy was no spontaneous act. The militants were well-drilled and, if they are to be believed, had prepared for the seizure by studying plans of the embassy which had been made available to them by supporters in the government. Among their leaders were people who spoke in Palestinian dialects and, apparently, were either trained by the Palestine Liberation Organization, or were a part of one of the more militant PLO groups. (Why the PLO would be involved so deeply in the embassy takeover has never been explained. Some observers suggest that, if any PLO terrorists were in the forefront of the attack, it was in the hopes of gaining financial support from the Khomeini regime. No one, however, knows for certain.)

The attackers were so well prepared, in fact, that they even carried identification cards so they could pass through their own sentries and could be told apart from the mob that was expected to gather soon after.

By nightfall, the embassy compound was completely in the hands of the militants who announced they were "Moslem Students of the Imam Khomeini Line." All U.S. nationals, who numbered 63, were taken across the compound to the ambassador's residence, where they were bound, gagged and separated. Iranian employees were taken to a different building and, shortly thereafter, were allowed to leave.

The next day, thousands of Iranians gathered outside the embassy to praise the terrorists and to denounce the United States. The massive demonstration was topped by the appearance of Ahmed Khomeini, the ayatollah's son, who brought word from his father that "this is not an occupation; we have thrown out the occupiers. This is the will of the people."

The hostage crisis had begun.

Two of the Iranian students holding the hostages give an interview to Greek T.V. reporter Liana Kaneli in December 1979. The students insist that the hostages will go on trial if the shah is not returned to Iran. (WIDE WORLD PHOTOS)

Experts Say: U.S. Could Have Blocked Radical Takeover In Iran

Long-time experts on Iran, in both government and the private sector, believe the United States had the ability to prevent the transfer of power in Tehran to a government dominated by the radical clergy and opposed so forcefully to the United States. Had the United States done so, of course, there would have been no takeover of the U.S. embassy and no year-long captivity for 52 U.S. nationals.

That the United States failed to act decisively, the experts say, is mainly the fault of one man, presidential national security adviser Zbigniew Brzezinski, although considerable personal blame also falls on Brzezinski's No. 1 deputy, David Aaron, and on Brzezinski's boss, President Jimmy Carter.

The story is almost a burlesque rendition of international diplomacy. It has its roots in the earliest days of the Carter administration when it became a matter of burning policy to enact some kind of Middle East peace treaty. The president's main advisers believed a major key to any successful Middle East peace was Shah Mohammad Reza Pahlavi.

If some kind of accommodation could be worked out between Egypt and Israel, Carter's advisers believed, it was mandatory to have a complete ally in Iran, one who would guarantee oil to the United States if other Arab nations turned against it and who also would guarantee a stable northern gulf area.

In November 1977, the shah visited Washington and invited President Carter, his family and his closest advisers to be his guest at a lavish New Year's Eve Party in Tehran, Carter accepted and much of the U.S. problems in Iran, and many of the bitter feelings on the part of the militants, is traceable directly to that visit.

The U.S. ambassador to Iran at this time—in fact, all during the period of the exchange of power—was William Sullivan, a man discribed by friend and foe alike as bull-headed, strong-willed, opinionated and very bright.

The bulk of the U.S. information on dissident groups in Iran came from SAVAK, the shah's secret police. So it was generally believed by most in the U.S. government that opposition to the shah came from a small number of semi-fanatics, many with Soviet ties, with the bulk of the Iranian population remaining loyal to the monarch.

However, there were those on the U.S. embassy staff in Tehran and at various consular offices around Iran who were beginning to think differently. One such was Michael Metrinko, a Farsi-speaking consul in Tabriz who was destined to be one of the hostages.

Metrinko, because he could speak the language, had made a very wide circle of contacts within Iranian society and had become convinced that opposition to the shah's authoritarian rule was spreading into all segments of Persian society. Ambassador Sullivan chose to ignore the warnings, preferring to believe the official line coming out of SAVAK that the opposition was a small group of negligible fanatics.

But Sullivan did see enough merit in Metrinko's reports to conclude that it was time for the United States to try to soften the shah's rule or, at least, to begin putting some distance between Washington and Tehran. He strongly recommended to Carter, therefore, that the president's remarks during the nationally televised state dinner on New Year's Eve be "cool but correct." Carter, however, heeded Brzezinski's advice and, instead, lauded the shah at great length and in glowing personal terms as a leader of the Free World who is much beloved by his people and by the United States.

In making such a personal toast, Carter tied himself and the United States to the shah in the minds of the Iranians from that day forward.

Over the next months, oppostion to the shah continued to grow in Iran. But despite the growing evidence to the contrary, and despite the fact that he had counseled the president to tone down his public remarks at the state dinner, Ambassador Sullivan continued to believe that the shah remained in firm control. He continued to cable Washington that the monarch could best be helped through his troubles by the firm and public support of the United States.

This apparently was just what Brzezinski wanted to hear and he consistently advised the president that the shah's troubles were minor, that a strong shah was key to solving the Middle East conflict and that the United States must go all out in its support of the shah.

By the summer of 1978, Sullivan apparently began to have some second thoughts and began cabling Washington about the growing violence being visited upon opposition groups by the shah and SAVAK. He even obtained permission from Undersecretary of State David Newsom to begin establishing secret contacts with some of the opposition groups.

By late summer conviction had grown both in the embassy in Tehran and at the State Department that the shah was in serious trouble. Brzezinski and his deputy Aaron would hear none of it, however, so these fears never reached the oval office.

By late fall, Sullivan had become fully convinced of what some of his staff had argued almost a full year before, that opposition to the shah was widespread, that it involved every segment of Iranian society and that, unless something radical was done by the shah by way of accommodating the opposition, his days on the Peacock Throne were numbered.

The turning point for Sullivan was early November, when he sent a detailed cable to Washington urging a major change in U.S. policy towards the shah. Sullivan correctly saw the emergence of Ayatollah Ruhollah Khomeini, then living in exile in France, as the central opposition to the shah and suggested that immediate and secret feelers be put out to Khomeini. Sullivan saw as imperative the keeping of Iran's military intact and under a pro-U.S. leadership. His idea was to contact Khomeini to determine what it would take to get the ayatollah to agree to accept a pro-Western military if he or his followers ever came to power. Sullivan suggested the way to reach Khomeini was through Mehdi Bazargan, a former engineer, who was highly regarded both by Khomeini and by other factions of the growing opposition to the shah.

The Sullivan cable caused quite a flap in the White House. Reportedly, Carter demanded to know why he had not been told the opposition to the shah had grown so considerably and now cut across a broad segment of Iranian society. Brzezinski reportedly responded that Sullivan was overreacting and that the shah could weather his problems if the United States remained steadfast in its support of him.

Brzezinski also continued to paint the shah's opponents as communists and radicals.

By now a clear division of opinion existed as to what course the United States should follow in Iran. The experts in the State Department were convinced the overthrow of the shah was inevitable, unless radical reforms were forthcoming immediately in the monarchy, reforms they knew the shah was incapable of implementing unless the United States forced him to do so. They recommended, therefore, that either this coercion begin immediately or, if not, then immediate accommodations be sought with the opposition in an effort to get the most pro-U.S. government possible when the shah fell. Either way, the shah had to be cut loose.

Brzezinski still would hear none of this, nor would Aaron. Reportedly, Newsom and other experts at State decided to make one last try and scheduled a briefing of Aaron and other National Security Council staffers on the Iranian situation. The State Department officials went on for hours explaining the depth of opposition to the shah that had grown in Iran. When it was all done, Aaron reportedly dismissed the briefing out of hand and he and Brzezinski continued to tell the president the shah could weather the crisis if only the United States held firm.

Carter reflected this view when he told a December 12 press conference, ''I expect the shah to maintain power in Iran and that the present difficulties will be resolved.'' He then went on to conclude, ''The shah has our support and has our confidence.''

By now, despite what he was telling Carter, Brzezinski had become convinced the only way the shah could maintain control was by using the military. Reportedly, he drafted a letter for the president to send the shah in which Carter would tell the monarch to let the military loose on the opposition.

State Department officials, we are told, went slightly crazy when they saw a draft of the letter. What Brzezinski was suggesting, they concluded, would mean a civil war in which thousands would die if the military agreed to turn on its own people, or a complete disintegration of the military if it did not obey the shah's orders. In either case, they saw the sending of the letter as inviting potential disaster. Secretary of State Cyrus Vance met with Carter to tell him of State's misgivings.

Brzezinski argued the opposite, that the shah must continue to get the full backing of the United States, and Carter agreed. The president said he would accept full responsibility for the letter but did finally agree to Vance's entreaties to tone it down somewhat by making the suggestions for action more ambiguous.

One of the great unanswered mysteries of the whole episode of the fall of the shah is whether that letter was sent. Vance returned to his office from the

White House under the impression the letter was going to be hand-carried to Iran the next day. The White House, however, insists the letter was not sent. It also denies the letter was anything more than one option under discussion. Vance was mistaken if he thought a decision had been made to send the letter.

Meanwhile, back in Iran, things went from bad to worse. Sulivan, the career diplomat, was becoming more and more disgusted with White House policies towards the shah, Brzezinski's insistence that Pahlavi must be supported at all costs, and that no official U.S. contacts could be made with opposition leaders.

This disgust was reflected in Sullivan's cables, which began to be heavily laden with sarcasm. Finally, a particularly impertinent cable came to the president's attention and he ordered Vance to fire Sullivan immediately.

Vance objected saying that firing Sullivan might be interpreted as withdrawal of U.S. support for the shah and could be the act that topples the monarch. Carter reluctantly agreed, and instead ordered Sullivan to be reprimanded. Reportedly, Vance forgot to do so and Sullivan was never aware how unhappy the president was with his Iranian views.

Brzezinski reportedly now hit upon a new argument for continuing to prop up the shah at all costs. If a new regime came to power in Iran that was antagonistic to the United States and to Israel, the flow of oil might be cut back. The United States had guaranteed a constant oil supply to Israel as part of the Camp David negotitions and Brzezinski argued that extra supply would have to come from Iran under the shah.

With both the State Department and the embassy in Tehran now convinced the shah had to go, Brzezinski reportedly made an end run around normal diplomatic channels to deal directly with the shah. The Iranian ambassador to the U.S., Ardeshir Zahedi, became a go-between for the national security adviser. Personally one of the men closest to the shah, the playboy ambassador, one of the social lions of Washington, had a series of meetings with Brzezinski. He then was dispatched to Tehran to bolster the shah's flagging spirits with the news that Jimmy Carter continued to support him completely and that he should hold firm against the rising opposition.

Events began to come to a head in Iran on Christmas Day when, as a taste of what was to occur twice more in the next 12 months, the U.S. embassy was attacked. This act signaled the beginning of the end and was so read by State Department officials. They now stepped up their pleas to Carter that the shah be told that the United States thought he should "take a vacation outside Iran" and that immediate high-level approaches to Khomeini begin. Brzezinski continued to argue against both points and Carter continued to listen to his foreign policy adviser over the careerists at the State Department. He refused to allow any direct contacts with the ayatollah.

By this time it was obvious even to the shah that his situation was desperate and, for the first time, he began holding talks with moderate opposition leaders about including them in the government. The man the shah wanted was Shapur Bakhtiar, a middle-of-the-road opponent of the shah.

The U.S. embassy, however, counseled Washington to oppose naming Bakhtiar because he was unacceptable to most of the opposition. Therefore, his tenure as prime minister would be short-lived and only would postpone the inevitable. Sullivan believed the United States would push the shah to name instead Mehdi Bazargan, a man much more deeply opposed to the shah, one respected by a majority of the shah's foes, a man with whom the embassy experts believed some accommodations might be reached and, most importantly, a man who would accept the military intact and whom the military would accept.

Brzezinski fought against this suggestion. He believed a U.S. intelligence estimate that pictured Bazargan as a wild-eyed fanatic. Carter again agreed and the shah appointed Bakhtiar.

In retrospect, this was the last chance the United States had to influence the future of Iran in a way favorable to U.S. interests. The experts believe that even after all the false starts, even after all the bad decisions, if the shah had turned the government over to Bazargan at that point, there is a chance that much of what was to come could have been, if not avoided, at least toned down.

To the very end, however, Carter continued to listen to Brzezinski, not Vance, and events were set in motion that resulted in the hostage crisis, the Gulf War, the Soviet invasion of Afghanistan, and the total alienation from the United States of the strategically vital Iran.

It even had a deleterious effect on the Mideast peace process, the very thing Brzezinski's adamant stand was meant to protect. When the traditionally pro-U.S. Saudi Arabian monarchy, itself under pressure from Moslem fanatics, saw how poorly the United States helped keep Iran stable, it began adopting a negative line against Washington's efforts at bringing about an Israel-Arab peace. Whereas until then it held silent counsel on the Camp David accords, the Saudi royal house now denounced the treaty and cut off funds for Egypt.

Permitting the shah to fall without securing a friendly government in his place, therefore, had a domino effect as far as the United States is concerned—and a seriously negative one, to be sure.

Dec. 24th. Hostages reading cards at the U.S. Embassy in a picture taken by student captors. At the time, it was believed that at least some of the hostages might be released on the following day, Christmas, 1979 (WIDE WORLD PHOTOS)

Day 443:

Of all the cruelties emanating from Iran, none was so great to the families and loved ones of the 52 U.S. nationals held hostage than that which was perpetrated in the last 24 hours.

For the hostages, it was just a day like any other of the 443 days they had endured until then; they did not know that their freedom was imminent. But for those who knew it should have been their last day, for those who had prayed for that moment when the call would come that required only one word—FREE!—to be understood, it was the longest day in a seemingly never-ending stream of longest days.

And it was the cruelest.

Morning morning, January 19th, had begun with such optimism, such hope. By evening, the opti-

mism and hope had been turned into despair and fear. There had been other "rollercoaster" days, as Rocky Sickmann's father had described them, but none like this one. This day had gone too far on the up side and now it was coming down very hard—and very fast.

First, there was the announcement at 4:58 a.m. EST by President Carter and the telephone calls from the State Department. "They're coming home," the loved ones were told. "The deal has been signed. It's only a matter of hours now."

Then, about 9 a.m., Iranian television began feeding taped footage of some of the hostages being examined by Algerian doctors.

There was Steven Lauterbach having his blood

Christmas tree sent by Seattle-based company is seen being carried inside Embassy by two of the militants. Crates of cards, along with more trees, piled up, all bearing the well-wishes of a saddened nation. (WIDE WORLD PHOTOS)

The Longest Day

pressure and his heart checked. Charles Jones was seen having his heart and lungs examined by a doctor.

There was Phillip Ward and William Keough, John McKeel and Elizabeth Swift, and there was Steven Kirtley. Barry Rosen was there, too, joking with the doctors. Some of the hostages were shown having a hearty meal.

What it all meant was obvious—they were coming home!

And then, the seesaw began. They'll be going to the airport soon, they won't be going to the airport today. The plane can take off even in the dark, the plane cannot take off in the dark.

The hopes began to fade. When Bezhad Nabavi,

the chief Iranian negotiator, appeared before the cameras later that day, the fear began to set in. An "underhanded maneuver" by U.S. banks, he said, threatened the deal. He warned the United States of dire consequences that would result if this latest dirty trick was not immediately withdrawn.

There had been no such "underhanded maneuver," of course, and both the United States and Algeria said so. Were the Iranians trying to get out of the deal?

No, it was just another cruel joke the Iranians were playing. The cruelest joke of all.

Their way of "rubbing the nose of the United States in dirt."

One Man's "Family Honor"; One Woman's Gruesome End

On the morning of March 29, 1980, the body of a young woman was found in a Tehran alley. Cause of death: strangulation.

The young woman was found with a rope around her neck, but the fingermarks on her throat also indicated that she had been first choked by hand.

Within two hours after the body was discovered, a young man presented himself at the central Tehran police station. He confessed to the killing and said he had done it "to save the honor of my family."

The young man has been identified by Iranian authorities only as "Abulnasie A" and his sister only as "A.A." The woman was a 23-year-old student who had attended a Tehran teachers college.

According to the young man's story, he had killed his sister after she had confessed to him that she was pregnant and that the father of the child was "one of the spies in the American embassy." At first, she had said the father was a young Tehran taxi driver, but after the brother had found and beaten the driver, who kept protesting his innocence, the woman "admitted she had been raped by the spy."

The young man in a rage tried to strangle his sister with his bare hands, but succeeded only in causing her to pass out. When she was unconscious, therefore, he decided to hang her and, at the same time, tried to make the death appear a suicide. He then put a rope around her neck and hung her from a post.

The next day, the Iranian public prosecutor identified the U.S. national in question as Marine Staff Sgt. Michael Moeller. In his short statement, the prosecutor said an autopsy had shown the young woman to be "about five months pregnant" and it appeared that, despite what her brother had said about rape, her relationship with Moeller had been "a willing" one. He also announced that "a blood test will establish if the American is the father of the child" and that the killer was being committed to a Tehran mental hospital for treatment.

This is the last word any Iranian authority has spoken about the case. In fact, spokesmen specifically have declined to discuss the case despite being asked by the Swiss embassy to do so. The Swiss are looking after U.S. affairs in Iran these days.

This silence has led to two possible theories of what happened:

1. That Moeller is not the father. The evidence points to the fact that "a willing relationship" almost could not have resulted in the young lady's pregnancy. Moeller was the head of security guards at the embassy. He had been a hostage three days short of five months when the girl's body was found. The young lady was described by Iranian authorities as "about five months pregnant." In the days before it fell, the embassy was the scene of round-the-clock demonstrations. Moeller as chief non-com of the guard also was on about round-the-clock duty. Thus, unless the young woman was one of the student guards at the embassy after the takeover and their relationship occurred then, there is no way he could be the father. If the relationship did begin after the takeover, it would be an embarrassment to both the militants and to the government and thus they have dropped the whole matter.

2. Moeller's wife, who lives at the Quantico, Va., Marine base, has filed a multimillion-dollar class action lawsuit against Iran on behalf of her two children and the other hostage families. Any damages won in the suit would be collectable from Iranian assets currently frozen in the United States—some $8 billion worth. The suit is known to have angered the Iranians and the naming of Moeller may have been a sort of revenge.

U.S. authorities did not believe Moeller was involved. If he was, they say, much more of the incident would have been heard before the hostages were released and it is unlikely Moeller would have been among them in that case.

For the actual wording of the lawsuit as it relates to the Moellers and, by extension, to the lives of all the hostages and their families, please turn to page 50.

The man identified by authorities only as "Abdulnaise A," center, is escorted by police guard after confession to the murder of his sister. The girl was choked, then hanged, because she had allegedly become pregnant by one of the "spies in the Embassy." (WIDE WORLD PHOTOS)

Moeller Vs. Iran

UNITED STATES DISTRICT COURT FOR THE DISTRICT OF COLUMBIA

ANN ELISA MOELLER

    and

AMY CELESTE MOELLER

    and

LINDSEY MARIA MOELLER

    Plaintiffs

    v.

ISLAMIC REPUBLIC OF IRAN,
Tehran, Iran

    Defendant

SERVE: Islamic Republic of Iran
        c/o Embassy of Algeria
        2118 Kalorama Road, N.W.
        Washington, D.C. 20008

        and

        Islamic Republic of Iran
        c/o Embassy of Algeria
        2118 Kalorama Road, N.W.
        Washington, D.C. 20008

COMPLAINT FOR DAMAGES

INTENTIONAL INFLICTION OF EMOTIONAL DISTRESS; INTERFERENCE WITH FAMILY RELATIONSHIPS: FALSE IMPRISONMENT

PARTIES

1. Plaintiff Ann Elisa Moeller is a citizen of the United States, currently residing at Quarters 3704B, MC DEC, Quantico, Virginia. Plaintiffs Amy Celeste Moeller and Lindsey Maria Moeller are minor children residing with their mother, Ann Elisa Moeller, at the same address.

2. Plaintiffs are the wife and children of Michael E. Moeller, who is among several citizens of the United States held hostage and detained against their will in the United States Embassy and compound (the "Embassy") located in Tehran, and in other locations in Iran.

3. Defandant Islamic Republic of Iran ("Iran") is a foreign state under 28 U.S.C. §1603. This action is brought against Iran and all of its agents, officers, employees, servants, designees, officials, agencies and instrumentalities in connection with the facts alleged herein.

JURISDICTION AND VENUE

4. This Court has jurisdiction under 28 U.S.C. §§1130 and 1331. The amount in controversy exceeds the sum of Ten Thousand Dollars ($10,000.00) exclusive of interest and costs.

5. The Embassy is comprised of lands and needful buildings reserved and acquired for the use of the United States and under exclusive or concurrent jurisdiction thereof. The Embassy is within the special maritime and territorial jurisdiction of the United States and is included within the meaning of the "United States" in 28 U.S.C. §1603(c).

6. Defendant's actions causing the personal injuries complained of herein occurred and continue to occur within the continental and territorial jurisdiction of the United States.

7. Venue is properly laid in this judicial district under 28 U.S.C. §1391(f)(4).

THE CONSPIRACY

8. On or about November 4, 1979, a group of Iranians, allegedly "student militants" ("student militants"), took over control of the Embassy by means of force and violence. More than fifty citizens of the United States, including Michael E. Moeller, were among those detained against their will at the Embassy (the "hostages").

9. At all times following the Embassy take-over, Iran, the student militants and various Iranian officials and agents in the United States and in Iran knew that the hostages, including Michael E. Moeller, had spouses and other family located in the United States ("family members").

10. Beginning at or about the time that the student militants took over the Embassy, Iran, together with various Iranian citizens, agents and officials (the "conspirators"), in the United States and in Iran, agreed and conspired to inflict personal injuries upon plaintiffs and relatives of other hostages located in the United States in order to further the purposes and oubjects of the said conspiracy.

11. It was a part of the said conspiracy that Iran,

the student militants and other conspirators would and did make certain demands, including that the United States denounce and extradite to Iran the deposed Shah Mohammed Reza Pahlavi; that the United States return to Iran certain large sums of money allegedly held by the Shah; and that the United States apologize for prior United States support for the Shah.

12. It was further a part of the conspiracy and for the purpose of promoting Iran's political and propaganda objectives, which included securing the demands set forth in paragraph 11, *supra*, that a carefully orchestrated press and media campaign would be conducted through statements of officials of Iran, press releases, and communiques with the United States, and demonstrations in the United States and elsewhere. The focus of the said press and media campaign was the offer of release of the hostages in return for the aggreement by the United States to the said demands of Iran and the conspirators.

13. It was a part of the conspiracy that Iran would and did inflict emotional distress, interfere with marital and other family relationships, and engage in other tortious conduct injuring plaintiffs' and other hostages' family members in the United States for the purpose of pressuring and attempting to induce plaintiffs and others to advocate acceptance of the demands made by Iran and the conspirators.

14. It was further a part of the conspiracy that Iran and the conspirators would continue to detain the hostages, including Michael E. Moeller, against their will, without lawful process and in gross violation of applicable international law. Pursuant to the conspiracy, threats to humiliate, do bodily harm to, or kill the hostages would be and were made by Iran and the conspirators.

COUNT ONE

(INTENTIONAL INFLICTION OF EMOTIONAL DISTRESS)

15. Plaintiffs reallege and incorporate by reference the allegations of paragraphs 1-14.

16. Defendant Iran, together with its agencies and instrumentalities, has engaged in outrageous, wanton, willful, malicious and indecent conduct by which it intentionally inflicted mental and emotional distress and anguish upon plaintiffs.

17. As a result of the emotional and mental distress so inflicted, defendant Iran, together with its agencies and instrumentalities, had caused plaintiffs substantial injury, pain and suffering.

WHEREFORE, plaintiffs pray:

a. For compensatory damages in the amount of Two Million Dollars ($2,000,000.00).

b. For exemplary damages in the amount of Ten Million Dollars ($10,000,000.00).

c. For such other relief as this Court may deem appropriate.

Prior to his resignation, Secretary of State Cyrus Vance, left, and Zbigniew Brzezinski, right, confer with President Carter on the South Lawn of the White House. (WIDE WORLD PHOTOS)

COUNT TWO

(INTERFERENCE WITH FAMILY RELATIONS)

18. Plaintiffs reallege and incorporate by reference the allegations of paragraphs 1-14.

19. Defendant Iran, together with its agencies and instrumentalities, has wrongfrully detained and falsely imprisoned Michael E. Moeller in the Embassy and elsewhere, and intentionally and without justification separated him from his wife and children, the plaintiffs herein.

20. Defendant Iran, together with its agencies and instrumentalities, has willfully interfered with the family relations between plaintiffs and Michael E. Moeller in the United States.

21. As a consequence of the actions of defendant Iran and its agencies and instrumentalities, plaintiffs have been denied the love, society, companionship, services, comfort, conjugal kindness and parental guidance of their familial relationship with Michael E. Moeller.

WHEREFORE, plaintiffs pray:

a. For compensatory damages in the amount of Two Million Dollars ($2,000,000.00).

b. For exemplary damages in the amount of Ten Million Dollars ($10,000,000.00).

c. For such other relief at this Court may deep appropriate.

In the early days of captivity, a U.S. hostage is seen keeping fit with exercises within the embassy compound. (WIDE WORLD PHOTOS)

COUNT THREE

(FALSE IMPRISONMENT)

22. Plaintiffs reallege and incorporate by reference the allegations of paragraphs 1-14.

23. From on or about November 4, 1979, defendant Iran and its agencies and instrumentalities have held Michael E. Moeller against his will and under false arrest and imprisonment at the Embassy and at other locations in Iran.

24. As a direct result of the tortious conduct of defendant Iran and its agencies and instrumentalities plaintiffs have suffered the loss of love, society, companionship, services, comfort, conjugal kindness and parental guidance of their familial relationship with Michael E. Moeller.

WHEREFORE, plaintiff pray:

a. For compensatory damages in the amount of Two Million Dollars ($2,000,000).

b. For exemplary damages in the amount of Ten Million Dollars ($10,000,000).

c. For such other relief as this Court may deem appropriate.

JURY TRIAL DEMAND

Plaintiffs demand a trial by jury of twelve persons insofar as such demand does not defeat the jurisdiction of the Court.

RICHARD BEN-VENISTE
NEIL I. LEVY
Washington, D.C. 20006

Attorney for Plaintiffs
Ann Elisa Moeller
Amy Celeste Moeller
Lindsey Maria Moeller

UNITED STATES DISTRICT COURT FOR THE DISTRICT OF COLUMBIA

ANN ELISA MOELLER, *et al.*,
                Plaintiffs,

    v.

ISLAMIC REPUBLIC OF IRAN,
           Defendant.

Civil Action No. 80-1171

MEMORANDUM OF POINTS AND AUTHORITIES IN SUPPORT OF MOTION OF DEFENDANT THE ISLAMIC REPUBLIC OF IRAN TO DISMISS COMPLAINT

PRELIMARY STATEMENT

Defendant the Islamic Republic of Iran (the "Government of Iran" or "defendant") has moved pursuant to Fed. R. Civ. P. 12 (b) (2), (4), and (5) to dismiss the complaint.[1]

STATEMENT OF FACTS

This is a complaint in three counts brought by plaintiff and her two minor children, in their individual capacity[2] (the "Moellers" or "plaintiffs"), against the Government of Iran. (Compl. ¶2.) The Moellers allege that the Government or Iran is a foreign state under 28 U.S.C. §1603 [28 U.S.C. §1603 (a) (1976)]. (Compl. ¶3.)

The gravamen of the Moellers' complaint [3] is that the Government of Iran caused tortious injuries to the plaintiffs in the United States based on and resulting from the alleged taking as hostage and detaining in the United States Embassy in Tehran, Iran, of the Moellers' husband and father Michael E. Moeller. (Compl. ¶

[1] *By so moving, defendant does not waive any defenses otherwise available to it under the Federal Rules of Civil Procedure, including, but not limited to, lack of subject matter jurisdiction; personal jurisdiction insofar as that defense incorporates subject matter jurisdiction under 28 U.S.C. §1330 (b) (1976); and failure to state a claim upon which relief can be granted. Fed. R. Civ. P. 12 (h) (2), (3).*

[2] *Defendant assumes that the minor children are not infants within the contemplation of Fed. R. Civ. P. 17 (c). Defendant does not, however, thereby waive any defense of lack of capacity.*

[3] *For purpose of this motion only, defendant accepts as well pleaded the allegations of plaintiffs' complaint recited herein. Defendant emphatically denies, for any other purposes, these allegations and all other factual allegations of the complaint. United States based on and resulting from the alleged taking as hostage and detaining in the United States Embassy in Tehran, Iran, of the Moellers' husband and father Michael E. Moeller. (Compl. ¶2.)*

The facts pertinent to service are, as follows: The complaint was filed on May 8, 1980. On that date the Moellers sought and obtained from the Clerk of the Court, pursuant to Fed. R. Civ. P. 4 (c) and Local Rule 1-10 (a), an order appointing Janet Mullaney a special process server to serve process on the Embassy of Algeria in Washington, D.C. on May 29, 1980, Ms. Mullaney filed an affidavit attesting that on May 13, 1980, she served the Islamic Repubic of

Iran c/o the Embassy of Algeria at 2118 Kalorama Road, N.W., Washington, D.C. (The identical affidavit executed four days earlier was filed on May 16, 1980.)

Process filed on May 8, 1980, did not include a notice of suit and a translation into Farsi of the notice of suit; summons and translation thereof; or a translation of the complaint.

I. Because Proper Service of Process Has Not Been Effected, the Complaint Should Be Dismissed.

The Moellers allege that the Government of Iran is a "foreign state.")Compl. ¶3.) As such, defendant must be served in accordance with the provisions of the Foreign Sovereign Immunities Act, 28 U.S.C. §§1330, 1602, *et seq.* (1976) ("FSIA"). However, plaintiffs have not, as of this date, served defendant in any manner authorized by the FSIA.

By the enactment of the FSIA, the United States provided "a statutory procedure for making service upon, and obtaining in personam jurisdiction over, a foreign state." H.R. Rep. No. 94-1487, 94th Cong., 2d Sess. 8. *reprinted in* [1976] U.S. Code Cong. & Ad. News 6606 (hereinafter cited as "House Rep.", "U.S. Code"). (S. Rep. No. 94-310 is identical.) This procedure is the "exclusive" method of service on a foreign state or its political subdivisions, agencies, and instrumentalities." House Rep. at 23, U.S. Code at 6622. No *in personam* jurisdiction over a defendant is acquired unless service of process con-

On Christmas Eve 1980, then President-Elect Ronald Reagan tells reporters, "I don't think you pay ransom for people that have been kidnaped by barbarians." (WIDE WORLD PHOTOS)

At the close of the hostage crisis, Canada's Kenneth Taylor says, "In the opinion of the international community, America's position may have been enhanced. . . Despite the frustration, anger or dismay over what went on, a perception has arisen that you've handled yourself with constraint, responsibility and patience."
(WIDE WORLD PHOTOS)

forms to the literal and explicit requirements of those provisions. *40 D 6262 Realty Corporation* v. *United Arab Emirates Government*, 447 F. Supp. 710 (S.D.N.Y. 1978); *Gray* v. *Permanent Mission of the Peoples Republic of the Congo to the United Nations*, 443 F. Supp. 816 (S.D.N.Y. 1978).

It should be noted that 28 U.S.C. §1330(b) of the FSIA conflates personal and subject matter jurisdiction. Section 1330(b) provides:

(b) Personal jurisdiction over a foreign state shall exist as to every claim for relief over which the district courts have jurisdiction under subsection.

(a) where service has been made under section 1608 of this title.*4/*

Thus, personal jurisdiction with respect to a foreign state depends on the existence of (1) subject matter jurisdiction under Section 1330(a) and (2) effective service under Section 1608 of the FSIA. This motion and memorandum address the latter requirement. Because the defense of personal jurisdiction under the FSIA incorporates the defense of subject matter jurisdiction, defendant addresses by this motion only the issue of effective service under Section 1608. Defendant will have available substantial arguments going to the issue of subject matter jurisdiction under Sections 1330 (a) and (b). By reserving these arguments, defendant does not waive either the defense of lack of subject matter jurisdiction under Section 1330(a) or those aspects of that defense as embraced in the concept of personal jurisdiction under Section

§1330 (b), Fed. R. Civ. P. 12(h) (2), (3).

Section 1330(b) of the FSIA explicitly requires that service be completed before personal jurisdiction exists. Accordingly, in the absence of the strict complaince with the service of process provisions of the FSIA, no personal jurisdiction is acquired over defendant.

Section 1608(a) of the FSIA governing service on a foreign State, provides:

(a) Service in the courts of the United States and of the States shall be made upon a *foreign state or political subdivision of a foreign state*:

(1) by delivery of a copy of the summons and complain in accordance with any special arrangement for service between the plaintiff and the foreign state of political subdivision; or

(2) if no special arrangement exists, by delivery of a copy of the summons and complaints in accordance with an applicable international convention on service of judicial documents; or

(3) if service cannot be made under paragraphs (1) or (2), by sending a copy of the summons and complaint and notice of suit, together with a translation of each into the official language of the foreign state, by any form of mail requiring a signed receipt, to be addressed and dispatched by the clerk of the court to the head of the ministry of foreign affairs of the foreign state concerned, or

(4) if service cannot be made within 30 days under paragraph (3), by sending two copies of the summons and complaint and a notice of suit, together with a translation of each into the official language of the foreign state, by any form of mail requiring a signed receipt, to be addressed and dispatched by the clerk of the court to the Secretary of State in Washington, District of Columbia, to the attention of the Director of Special Consular Services—and the Secretary shall transmit one copy of the papers through diplomatic channels to the foreign state and shall send to the clerk of the court a certified copy of the diplomatic note indicating when the papers were transmitted. [Emphasis added.]

None of the statutory procedures for services was utilized by plaintiffs.*5/* Rather, they sought and obtained authority to serve the Algerian Embassy by special process server. But the FSIA is no carbon copy of the Federal Rules of Civil Procedure. The clerk of the court is authorized to transmit process for service on a foreign state to the Secretary of State pursuant to ¶1608(a) (4). However, the clerk of the court is not authorized to order the mode of service on a foreign state.

If Congress had intended the FSIA to replicate the Federal Rules of Civil Procedure, the language of Rule 4(c) could have been adopted into the later-enacted FSIA. But the Congress went further and carefully prescribed methods for serving process on a foreign sovereign—methods which do not have their counterparts in the Federal Rules. Plaintiffs' resort to Rule 4 procedures was improper and unauthorized, and the Court should reject the attempt to create personal jurisdiction over defendant in this manner. 6/

4/ Section 1330(a) provides:

The district courts shall have original jurisdiction without regard to amount in controversy of any nonjury civil action against a foreign state as defined in section 1603 (a) of this title as to any claim for relief in personam with respect to which the foreign state is not entitled to immunity either under sections 1605-1607 of this title or under any applicable international agreement.

5/ *The record reveals that on June 6, 1980, the Moellers requested pursuant to 28 U.S.C. ¶1608 (a) (3), service by certified mail, return receipt requested, to the Islamic Republic of Iran, Ministry of Foreign Affairs, Tehran, Iran. This method of service conforms to the requirements of Section 1608(a) (3). If proof of service is forthcoming, as required by Section 1608(c) (2), service of process will have been lawfully effected.*

6/ *Defendant points out, for the record, that service via diplomatic channels as provided for by Section 1608(a) (4) quoted supra, is available despite the severing of diplomatic relations with the Government of Iran. Attached as Exhibit A hereto is a copy of a Stipulation and Order entered in another case pending in this Court.* American Bell International, Inc. v. Islamic Republic of Iran, et al., Civ. Act. No. 80-0321 (entered May 19, 1980). *This Stipulation provides that plaintiff in that case will undertake to serve the Government of Iran by diplomatic channels, viz., the Government of Switzerland had agreed to effect service on the Government of Iran by means of diplomatic channels through the Ministry of Foreign Affairs in Tehran, Iran. Apparently, plaintiffs acknowledge the statutory procedure. The record reveals a mailing to the Director of Special Consular Services on June 17, 1980. If service is effected by Section 1608(a) (4), service will be deemed to have been made, pursuant to Section 1608(c) (1), as of the date indicated in the certified copy of the diplomatic note.*

II. Process Is Sufficient.

Personal jurisdiction under the FSIA depends, in part, on the completion of effective service under Section 1608. One element of service—service of process—has been discussed in the immediately preceding section. the second element concerns the process itself. Section 1603(a) (3)-(4) of the FSIA requires that process as to a foreign state include a "notice of suit", which is a notification to the for-

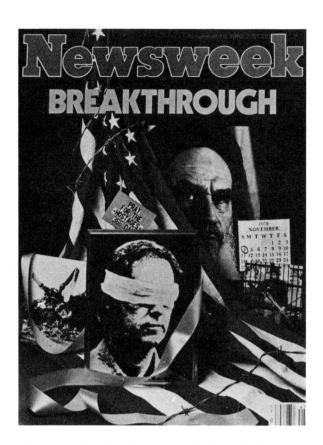

eign sovereign in a form prescribed by the Secretary of State. 22 C.F.R. ¶93 (1980). Moreover, the summons, complaint, and notice of suit must each be accompanied by a translation. 28 U.S.C. ¶1603(a) (3)-(4). The process served on May 13, 1980, did not contain a notice of suit or any translations.

The Moellers conceded the deficiency by filing on June 6, 1980, a document captioned Notice of Suit, as well as translations of the notice of suit and complaint. The absence of the notice of suit and required translations thus renders the May 13, 1980 process insufficient.

Because process is insufficient, the court lacks personal jurisdiction over defendant pursuant to 28 U.S.C. ¶1330(b), and the complaint should, therefore, be dismissed.

CONCLUSION

For the foregoing reasons, this Court shall dismiss the complaint. Alternatively, because the record reveals that plaintiffs have undertaken to serve the Government of Iran in apparent conformance with the FSIA, the Court should enter an order quashing the May 13, 1980 service of process and deeming the process itself ineffective, and allow plaintiffs to proceed with efforts to effect service with lawful process.

Respectfully submitted,

ABOUREZK, SHACK & MENDENHALL, P.C.

Bucking The System

There is an "esprit de corps" in the Foreign Service, much as there is within the military, a set of standards and unwriten rules that all foreign service officers and their families live by.

Uppermost among these unwritten rules is the one which says that foreign service officers and their families publicly must support the official policies of the U.S. government. Privately, one can do as one wishes; but not publicly. When a person no longer can publicly support those policies, that is the time to get out.

So it was not an easy matter for Bonnie Graves and her children the family of John Graves, career Foreign Service officer on a tour of duty in Iran when the embassy was taken, to decide to break publicly with the Carter administration and to come out and say what she has all along thought privately: that the hostages were taken after President Carter wrongly decided to admit the shah into the United States and that, effectively, the hostages' plight was the direct fault of the president.

Bonnie Graves believed that the only way the hostages would be returned is if the U.S. government made some form of conciliatory move. Whether this move took the form of an official apology for admitting the shah and for supporting him in the past, or an official congressional investigation of the shah's activities, she could not say. But, she said, the government had to affirmatively do something to break the impasse then existing.

And so she and her family became advocates of this point of view. They gave interviews, they made speeches, they wrote letters to Congress.

"We are a State Department family and we have broken with tradition and publicly broken ranks," she explained in an interview. "In an official community like ours, that creates shockwaves. But we as a family decided that somebody had to say these things and that we as a hostage family could do it best, especially since we were in fact a career foreign service family."

The decision to go public was one not easily reached by the Graves family. In fact, says Mrs. Graves, "We had some fights that got so loud that the neighbors probably thought we were trying to kill each other." In the end, though, she had the full support of all six of her children, two of whom Adam, 23 and Martin, 20 still live at home.

In fact, the sons probably are more bitter than their mother. Of the lengthy captivity of his father, Martin says, "18 years in government service and look how little his government cares about him."

When President Carter announced new economic sanctions in an effort to put pressure on the Iranian government, Allan was widely quoted as saying, "Jimmy Carter is out of his mind if he really thinks this is going to get the hostages back." For good measure, he added, "It's another half measure that will simply serve to pay off those financial interests that got us into the mess with Iran in the first place."

Of her and the family's actions at the time, Bonnie Graves said she was certain her husband would understand why they acted that way.

"He was always one to work within the system, but he spoke his mind when he thought it was necessary. He will see I am doing what I think I have to do to get them out of there and back home."

President Carter Wants To Know: "Is There A Way To Rescue The Hostages?"

It was a quiet December evening. Several friends were seated around a table in a home near the nation's capital. Anyone watching the scene would have easily pieced together what was going on: These men were playing cards and drinking booze.

Whoever pieced that together, however, would have been wrong. For these friends were former top Central Intelligence Agency officials and they were busily at work trying to honor a request, made "unofficially and off the record," from the White House: Find a way to rescue the hostages being held in Tehran.

Among the men seated around the table were Kermit Roosevelt, who had directed the anti-Mossadegh operation that restored Shah Mohammed Reza Pahlavi to the Peacock Throne in 1953; Col. Stephen Meade, once the CIA's top escape and evasion expert (and a mentor of Col. Charles Beckwith, who was to lead the aborted rescue mission); and Miles Copeland, former CIA political action chief who backed up Roosevelt in the 1953 action.

They were men with such codenames as "Safford," "The Weasel," "Masterson," "The Whistler" and "Major Lincoln," men who, in total, had carried out hundreds of such operations in the past, against far more formidable opposition than a chaotic Iran could muster. (The Whistler, for one, even managed to get into Lubyanka Prison in Moscow to rescue a CIA operative. Circumstances led him to remove the wrong person from Lubyanka; but the point is that he did safely enter and leave the infamous prison despite the heavy security precautions existing there.)

In other words, these were men with vast experience and expertise in the kind of operation that would be required. And they all followed one guiding principle they consider essential for such operations, a principle first enunciated by a member of a Middle-Eastern royal family: "If you kick a king, make sure that you kill him." In other words, either go all the way, or don't go at all.

That principle led the former CIA officials to devise a complex plan to rescue the hostages. Although elements of the plan conform with the one the administration said was implemented, many other elements apparently were not included—and that,

Confessed one Washington official in the heat of crisis, "We have reviewed our assets and our options, and they are precious few."

say the intelligence people, is probably why the eventual rescue mission collapsed in the Iranian desert.

Briefly stated, the plan devised that December night called for turning U.S. allies and potential allies in the Gulf region into the main diplomatic attackers, with the United States offering only a supporting role. It involved using military and paramilitary forces that are indigenous (i.e., Iranians, or people who could pass for Iranians without any difficulty), creating an even more chaotic internal situation than already exists in Iran, sowing the seeds of insurrection and supporting those elements within Iran who could best serve the purpose of the mission, no matter whether those elements were friendly to the United States.

In other words, bring about the downfall of Ayatollah Ruhollah Khomeini and his cohorts by setting the stage for a coup and, in the confusion that would follow, "lift" the hostages out of Tehran.

The task of stirring up major insurrectionary conditions in Iran appeared to be an easy one to the CIA old hands—and for good reason: Mob psychology dictates that rioters will follow their "leaders" even when those "leaders" are making 180-degree turns. In 1953, for example, Kim Roosevelt needed to reverse the growing anti-shah hysteria. "Leaders" of the mobs supporting Prime Minister Mohammed

July 1951, Mohammed Mossadegh, in a gesture of gallantry before Queen Soraya, then wife of Shah Reza Pahlavi of Iran. (WIDE WORLD PHOTOS)

Mossadegh were arrested and new "leaders" put in their place. Soon, the mobs which had been shouting "Death to the shah, long live Mossadegh" began chanting "Death to Mossadegh, long live the shah."

Additionally, there are a number of internal forces already in opposition to the Khomeini regime, including various tribes such as the Qashqais, Bakhtiaris, Lurs and Kurds, and even ordinary Farsis. These forces could be brought into play, the ex-CIA planners reasoned.

The actual raid on the U.S. embassy compound, they decided, had to consist of the following elements:

1. RECONNAISSANCE: By December, U.S. intelligence had detailed maps of the embassy compound, showing where all the various rooms were located, how the buildings were wired, where fuse boxes and light switches could be found, how the plumbing, heating and ventilation systems worked and where key elements of each were situated, and even where the "students" and their hostages were placed throughout the compound. Detailed information also was beginning to come in on booby traps, security, patrols, hour-by-hour manning of watchposts, delivery of food and medical supplies, and even psychological profiles on the individual "students." The information was being supplied by a foreign intelligence service which had managed to infiltrate the "student" ranks.

2. RECRUITMENT OF "STUDENT" MOLES: Under the plan, the friendly foreign agents already inside the compound and U.S. agents outside would offer whatever inducements are necessary to those "students" most likely to be swayed by bribery. (Rarely, until the aborted rescue mission, was the compound manned by more than 40 or 50 students—and, at times, only by around 20—during the evening. The others often were living it up in the city itself, spending time at home with their families, or planning demonstrations for the following day.

In an article released by Independent News Alliance only four days before Charlie's Angels aborted in the desert, Miles Copeland described how this recruitment would be accomplished. "Considering the number of prospective agents—and, to the CIA pro, every one of those 'students' is a potential agent until proven otherwise—the law of averages is on our side," Copeland wrote. "Using recruitment techniques developed over the years, CIA recruiters posing as Iraqi, Libyan or even Iranian 'case officers' could screen the lot of them, pop the question to the most promising few, kill those whose reactions are unsatisfactory, and send the rest back into the target so equipped with psychological booby traps that any attempts to 'double' on us will be immediately detected, and rely on the percentage of holdouts to perform their assigned duties."

Mohammed Mossadegh, as Prime Minister, rides on the shoulders of cheering crowds in Tehran's Majlis Square, outside the Parliament building. (WIDE WORLD PHOTOS)

According to Copeland, the duties of these "moles" would be to keep U.S. intelligence informed of day-to-day changes in target conditions, and to smuggle in and put in place equipment that would be needed before and during the attack (the equipment, by the way, would be rigged to explode when tampered with).

3. COVER: The raid itself would be an undercover operation completely. The raiders themselves, according to the plan, probably would be led to believe they are working for an Arab government or, perhaps, even the PLO. If that cover is blown prior to the raid, a contingency cover would make it appear to the raiders that they are, in fact, working for elements within the Iranian government itself. (Remember, the plan devised that night depended on using indigenous forces for the raid. The planners believed that the raiders, therefore, would feel more comfortable working for an entity indigenous to the area. Also, Moslems working for Moslems presented fewer possibilities for a double-cross.)

Several teams would be employed during the raid. The team entering the compound itself would have to appear to be Iranians who have broken away from demonstrations outside the compound. A second team, which would provide military support, would have to appear as elements of the Iranian military (that they truly might be Iranian troops was a distinct possibility, according to the planners).

Only three U.S. nationals would be used in the operation—Col. Meade himself and two highly trained technicians. Together, they would enter the compound as members of a television news camera crew with passes apparently supplied by the government.

4. PERSONNEL: The main thrust of the raid itself, if Col. Meade had his way, would be carried by Qashqai tribesman, "those tough, dashing, resourceful mountaineers who all look like Anthony Quinn in his heyday and who believe that one government in Tehran is as objectionable as another," as Copeland put it in his INA article.

Of Col. Meade's two U.S. associates, one will be expert in the use of the special equipment planted in the compound by the moles. The other would be a psycho-pharmacist whose job it will be to somehow put out of commission, at least temporarily, people inside and outside the compound (in other words, as Copeland put it, anesthetization), while confusing others into battling amongst themselves through use of behavior-altering agents requiring highly sophisticated techniques of psychological supervision.

5. POSITIONING: A ''staging area'' somewhere within helicopter range of Tehran would be needed, as would at least three ''abort and escape'' points from the time the operation is launched to the time the mission is completed and the hostages rescued. There also would have to be an actual launch point for the attack located within a minute of the compound. Naturally, that point must appear to blend in with the immediate area. It cannot look like a staging area for an imminent attack.

6. THE ATTACK: The planning and execution of the actual attack were considered the easy parts by the planners. The only dangerous moments, if all else goes well, would be the first and the last—and the only danger there is fear of having been double-crossed in the first place.

Meade and his two-man ''TV crew'' would gain access to the compound. Then, following execution of some highly explosive diversionary move which would serve as the kick-off signal, the first team would enter the compound from their assigned entry points, while the ''anesthetization'' process was underway inside.

Next, three helicopters, bearing Iranian Army markings and appearing to be entering the compound to launch a counter-attack, will land at designated points and the hostages loaded onto them.

The second team, meanwhile, disguised as (or actually being) a unit of the regular Iranian army, will seize control of all communications into and out of the compound, as well as all throughout Tehran. The purpose of this is twofold: 1. to prevent calls for help; and, 2. to broadcast martial music, news flashes and ''official'' announcements designed to confuse any potential counterattackers. Elements of what at least would appear to be the Iranian air force would provide safe passage for the helicopters.

7. SAFEHAVEN: A safehaven near Tehran, already chosen, well stocked and well guarded, would be the immediate destination of the rescue helicopters. The local inhabitants in and around the safehaven would be ''friendlies'' who would, among other things, provide guides for a cross-country escape should airborne evacuation be ruled out as impractical.

During the entire operation, U.S. intelligence operatives would be busily implementing a complex set of actions to prevent Iranian police, security and military forces from interfering in time to thwart the rescue attempt.

Also part of this secondary operation would be some form of ''behavior alteration'' designed to turn the mobs against the Khomeini regime.

That, at least, is the plan the former intelligence experts turned over to the White House. To this day, Copeland, Meade and the others insist it would have worked. Whether they are right is only a matter of conjecture, however, because the plan was never implemented.

Or was it? Is there anything in what we already know of the aborted rescue mission that would be inconsistent with this plan?

In truth, there is not. Consider these facts:
● The helicopters used in the aborted attempt were to be disguised as Iranian army helicopters.
● Rescue team members all were to wear Iranian uniforms and all spoke Persian well enough to fool the ''students'' and others long enough, at least, to begin the attack.
● For two weeks prior to the raid itself, various Iranian tribes had begun causing serious trouble for the regime and riots within Tehran were giving the appearance of a city approaching anarchy, thus setting the stage for friendly elements within the government to seize control from Khomeini under the guise of ''restoring order'' in the land.
● The administration claims the operation would have been carried off with minimal to no loss of life, thereby indicating some form of anesthetization.
● Iranian air force fighters destroyed the abandoned helicopters—and whatever evidence of conspiracy they may have contained—before the choppers could be inspected thoroughly by the government.

We never may know what really took place that day. Then again, maybe this time it is better that we do not know. All we can say for certain is that this plan did exist, that it was in the hands of the administration, and that a protege of Col. Meade was assigned to lead the eventual rescue mission.

The rest must be left for historians of another generation to reveal, if they can.

Headline shortly before the rescue attempt. When pushed for specifics, Press Secretary Jody Powell said a White House announcement might be delayed until some decisions could be implemented.

The Secret Negotiations: The Story Now Can Be Told

In early April, a small, highly top secret meeting was held in the oval office. In attendance were President Jimmy Carter, national security adviser Zbigniew Brezinski, Secretary of State Cyrus Vance, Secretary of Defense Harold Brown, Gen. David Jones, chairman of the Joint Chiefs of Staff, and a few top-ranking Carter aides, including Hamilton Jordan and Lloyd Cutler.

The purpose of the meeting was to set in motion a stand-by plan to use military force in an attempt to rescue the 50 hostages being held at the embassy in Tehran and the three diplomats being held at the Iranian foreign ministry.

All those present in the oval office had known that "the military action" was open to them from the start, but many had hoped never to have to make the decision to use it. Now, however, they were only too well aware of the way things stood. The United States, they knew, had come down to the choice of either using force or sit by while the hostages were held indefinitely, a situation which in an election year was politically unacceptable.

On April 24, the military option was taken—and it failed dismally (see page 82). Since that time, the question has been asked over and over: Why did the United States wait until April to attempt a rescue? The military had admitted that agents were in place in Iran since December, that U.S. forces had been specially trained and ready to go since January and that, in fact, weather and other factors had given a January or February raid a far greater chance of success. Why, then, was the raid delayed until late April?

The answer: The United States was secretly negotiating for the hostages' release and did not want to do anything to jeopardize those talks.

For over three months, the White House and top Iranian officials had been involved in secret talks that both sides were certain would result in the freeing of the hostages. Now the story of those negotiations can be told.

To understand the negotiations and why they fell apart in the end, one must understand the very involved internal politics of Iran. And to begin to understand that political situation, one needs to go back in time to mid-1978.

Shah Mohammed Reza Pahlavi's position within Iran was deteriorating rapidly by then. The revolution against his rule, which had spread to every level of the population, was being led by the religious leaders who ruled over the nation's 32 million Shi'ite Moslems. It was these religious leaders who had turned unrest to full-scale revolution and, quite naturally, it was they who assumed that they would inherit the power within Iran once the inevitable occurred and the shah was overthrown.

Meanwhile, some 2,000 miles to the west in a small stucco bungalow in the French community of Neauphle-le-Chateau, outside of Paris, another religious leader of the Shi'ite Moslems, Ayatollah Ruhollah Khomeini, was spending his 15th year in exile. Surrounding Khomeini were various relatives, mujtahids, mullahs and followers.

Among the group, also, were three men whose main concern was how Iran was to be governed after the shah fell. The three were considered the closest to Khomeini and, while united in their hatred for the shah, they were more concerned with keeping Iran a modern state while correcting the abuses and excesses of the shah than turning the nation into a model theocracy, the stated goals of the mullahs back home.

The three were Ibrahim Yazdi, a cancer researcher trained at the University of Texas; Sadegh Ghotbzadeh, educated in the United States and a communications expert; and Abdolhassan Bani-Sadr, an economist trained in French universities.

It is the split between these men and the religious leaders who control the Iranian Religious Party which, in turn, controls the Revolutionary Council that doomed the attempt to negotiate a way out of the hostage situation.

The negotiations actually began a little over a month after the hostages had been taken.

Yazdi, who was the number two man in the government of Prime Minister Mehdi Bazargan, had resigned in the wake of the taking of the hostages and Khomeini's refusal to intervene.

The Revolutionary Council was split. Its conservative religious members sided with the militants for they realized that, as long as they controlled the militants and the militants controlled the hostages, they would keep the upper hand in the internal power struggle within the new regime. The more moderate members of the council, on the other hand, were determined to end the situation.

An event outside gave the moderates their chance and they soon set in motion the process leading to the complex negotiations. That event was the shah's leaving the United States to take up residence in Panama.

The first thing the moderates had to do, however, was find "neutrals" to conduct the negotiations for them.

On Avenue de l'Observatoire, on the Left Bank, are the offices of a three-partner Paris law firm. Each partner had credentials which, when taken together, made them unique to deal with the dual situation of the U.S. hostages in Tehran and the shah in Panama. The firm was selected.

The first partner is Henry Villalon, who for years has been a wheeler and dealer in political and financial circles in Europe and South America and who has some very influential contacts in the United States. The second partner is Francois Cheron, with close ties to Iran. Soon after the hostages had been taken in November, Cheron had been contacted by U.S. officials as a possible go-between. The third partner is Christian Bourguet, who was destined to play a central role in the negotiating process.

Bourguet for a number of years had represented a number of the exiled Iranians in France, including Ghotbzadeh and Bani-Sadr, when the shah sought their expulsion from that country. In addition, the attorney had represented clients who had made spot oil deals for Panama in Iran. So, when Prime Minis-ter Ghotbzadeh heard that the shah had ended up in Panama, he put in a call to his old friend Bourguet in Paris. That call actually set in motion the series of top-level meetings which, in the end, almost succeeded in winning the release of the hostages.

Ghotbzadeh's call on December 15 contained a simple request: Could Bourguet, using the contacts he had made in Panama, contact that government and find out if it would entertain the possible extradition of the shah back to Iran to stand trial.

Thus, what turned out to be a serious attempt by the moderates in Tehran and the United States to work out a deal for the freedom of the hostages in fact began as an attempt by Iran to get the Shah back. Bourguet's original mission was simply to inquire about extradition. The eventual complicated plan to release the hostages evolved over the coming weeks because all sides recognized that it was in everyone's best interest to end the stalemate.

Within a week of getting Ghotbzadeh's call, Bourguet boarded a plane for Panama. There, he held a lengthy meeting with Panama's strongman, Gen. Omar Torrijos Herrera, who told him the situation was controlled by Washington and that, basically, what Panama could do in the situation depended solely on what the White House wanted Panama to do. Torrijos suggested that Bourguet speak to U.S. officials.

Bourguet then returned to Paris, where he reported

Demonstrating against the U.N. Secretary General's presence in Iran, woman holds up news photo of Kurt Waldheim kissing the hand of the Shah's twin sister, Princess Ashraf. (WIDE WORLD PHOTOS)

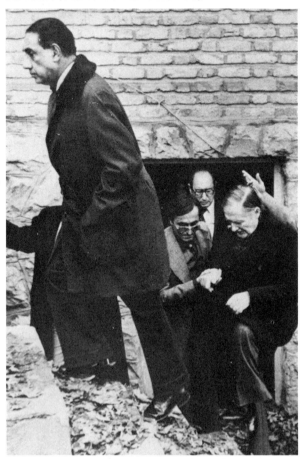

Members of U.N. commission investigate alleged crimes of the Shah. In foreground is Sri Lanka's Hector Jayewardene, followed by Syria's Adib Daoudy and France's Louis Pettiti, leaving what was described as a torture chamber. (WIDE WORLD PHOTOS)

back to Ghotbzadeh and Bani-Sadr. The two, while rivals for power within the moderate faction in Iran, were united in their desire to get the hostages away from the militants in an attempt to begin limiting the power of the conservative clerics.

Shortly after the Christmas holiday season, and with the blessing of Ghotbzadeh and Bani-Sadr, Bourguet secretly flew to Washington, where he met on several occasions with top Carter adviser Hamilton Jordan. The message he received was that, while the United States would not even consider allowing the shah to be extradited, it was willing to discuss almost any other reasonable measure that would end with the hostages' release.

Over the next 30 days, Bourguet went back and forth between the Iranians and the Carter people, and slowly a very fragile and complicated plan began to take shape.

In February, Jordan flew to Paris where, in a series of meetings with Bourguet, the White House chief of staff gave the attorney written power to represent the United States in the hostage matter. On the other side, Bani-Sadr (who was about to be elected the first president under the new Islamic constitution), made it clear that he welcomed the move.

The plan that evolved had three elements. The first was to get U.N. Secretary General Kurt Waldheim to agree to set up a U.N. Commission as part of the plan. The whole idea was to establish a situation in which Iran could claim a "great victory" in the whole matter and then, in a humanitarian gesture, release the hostages. Key to this would be the U.N. commission.

Under the plan, the U.N. commission would hear Iran's grievances against the shah. At the same time, Panama would begin extradition proceedings against the deposed and seriously ailing monarch. It was clearly understood by all the parties that the shah, in fact, never would be returned. However, the legal proceedings in Panama would be allowed to begin so that the Iranian government could point to them and to the commission's work "as signs of good faith." In this way, it could wrest control over the hostages from the militants and then find a way to get them back to the United States.

Most of those involved on both sides of the negotiations thought the plan would work. In fact, it very well may have had it not been for a series of errors on the part of several of the principals involved and a little sabotage on the part of some people who wanted to see the plan fail from the very beginning.

The key error is laid to Secretary General Waldheim. It was absolutely critical that the commission be seen by Iranians as a victory, as pro-Iranian and as the vehicle by which Iran could show the world how bad the shah had been.

Waldheim, however, stumbled badly. The way things turned out was almost the reverse. The secretary general made it seem as though the commission was the United States' idea and one that had been forced on Iran. Almost by definition, if Jimmy Carter was for the commission, Khomeini had to be against it.

(What must not be overlooked in all this is the fact that Khomeini, aside from his deep hatred for the United States in general, has a very genuine hatred for Carter in particular. This is due to the president's New Year's 1978 visit to Tehran when he embraced the shah and sought to prop up the monarch's government at the very time that the pro-religious forces were finally making some headway in bringing the shah down from the Peacock Throne. Khomeini believes the shah was able to hang on for many more months because of the Carter visit.)

Thus, Waldheim's miscalculations doomed the commission to failure even before it arrived in Tehran. It was critical that it appear that the ayatollah supported the work of the commission, but Khomeini refused even to see its members briefly. When it became clear that he would not do so, the effectiveness of the commission was ended.

At the same time, Ghotbzadeh, in an apparent effort to keep the plan on track (or, perhaps, simply because of a gross miscalculation on his part; people who know him have never though of him as being overly bright or subtle), made the grand announcement that he had been told by Gen. Torrijos himself that the shah had been placed under house arrest by the Panamanian government.

The announcement pushed the Panamanians and U.S. officials into a corner. At first, they didn't know how to respond. If they said it was true, it would raise a firestorm among the shah's friends in the United States. If it was flatly denied, it would effectively end the plan. Panamanian President Aristedes Royo attempted to hedge, as did Torrijos, but that did not work, either. It only played right into the hands of the militants.

At this point French communist lawyer Nuri Albala enters the picture. Previously, he had proposed that a major war crimes trial of the shah be held, but was rebuffed. Angered that his plan had been junked in favor of the Bourguet negotiations, he leaked stories to the French press that Ghotbzadeh had traveled to Paris to meet secretly with Jordan at Villalon's home. The story was not true, but it was accepted as fact in Iran and served to further undermine the position of Ghotbzadeh and Bani-Sadr.

In late March, therefore, when Bani-Sadr tried to make his move and take control of the hostages from the militants, as could be expected, they resisted and were backed by Bani-Sadr's rivals on the Revolutionary Council. When the whole matter was dumped into Khomeini's lap, the aged and quite ill ayatollah, confused by all the charges and counter-charges, opted for the status quo. He ordered the hostages to remain in the militants' control.

The plan was thus dead and the shah reacted quickly. All the talk of extradition had made him very nervous and he looked for a safer refuge. He found it with his friend Anwar Sadat in Egypt. Jordan made a trip to Panama to try to convince the shah that no one had any intention of extraditing him back to Iran and that, as he well knew, all the talk was only part of the elaborate charade to win the hostages' release. The shah, however, would not listen and off he went to Egypt, effectively ending the complicated negotiations.

Thus it was early in April that President Carter finally set into motion the rescue attempt. To this day, Bourguet believes that he would have succeeded in winning the freedom of the hostages if a number of people had not fumbled their roles.

Iran's Foreign Minister Sadegh Gotbzadeh, center, smiles with U.N. commissioners following a March 6th meeting. Though planning to leave Iran, they are prompted to stay on after the militants ask the Revolutionary Council to take over responsibility for the captives. From left—Jayewardene, Bedjaoui (Algeria), Daoudy.
(WIDE WORLD PHOTOS)

The one-time Aryamehr (Light of the Aryans) and Shahanshah (King of Kings) succumbed in Egypt at the age of 60 to lymphatic cancer complicated by a hemorrhage of the pancreas, after 18 months in exile. (WIDE WORLD PHOTOS)

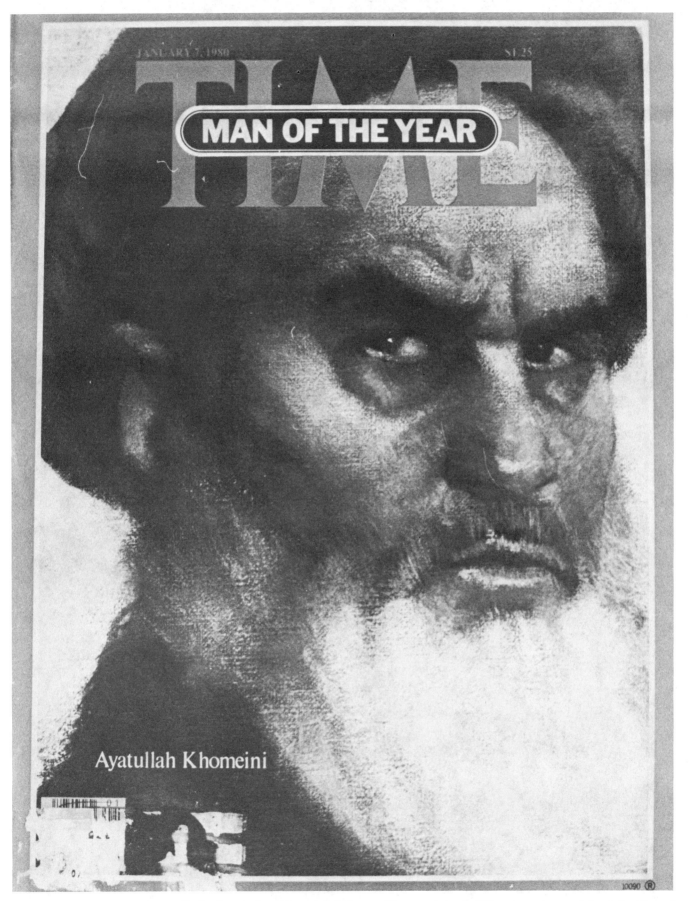

JANUARY 7, 1980

TIME

MAN OF THE YEAR

Ayatullah Khomeini

Defending their controversial choice, Time *explained, "*Time *has always defined the Man of the Year as the person who most affected the news 'for better or worse.' It did so when it named Adolf Hitler in 1938 . . . the Man of the Year has never been restricted to a person* Time *wished to praise."*

Shahpur Bakhtiar, who in December 1979 predicted that Khomeini would ''not last out the winter,'' has waited in Baghdad since the outbreak of the Iran-Iraq war, perhaps to return one day as the leader of a new revolutionary government. (WIDE WORLD PHOTOS)

Foreign Minister Sadegh Ghotbzadeh stated flatly in April 1980 that ''frankly, a resolution of the hostage problem is imperative within two months,'' yet it was another nine months before the hostages were free. (WIDE WORLD PHOTOS)

President Abolhassan Bani-Sadr, whose popularity with his countrymen has waxed and waned, has gone on record saying "For me, the detention of the American hostages is not a trump card for Iran. It even constitutes a weakness." (WIDE WORLD PHOTOS)

Canadian Ambassador Kenneth Taylor becomes an instant hero and all America sings the praise of his government when, thanks to Canada's courage and daring, six hostages escape to freedom. But Sadegh Ghotbzadeh, speaking for Iran, has an ominous reaction: "Sooner or later, somewhere in the world, Canada will pay . . ."

"These troops were going alone into a world of 35 million suspicious and hostile people," wrote Time *magazine. "No other nation had ever tried a military operation so distant and complex. The idea of failure was acknowledged but locked away. It had to be. The belief that success can be achieved in such an exploit may be 60% of the effort."*

In the pre-planning stages, Pentagon computers assessed that of the eight available helicopters, there was a 96.5% probability that 6 would come through to complete the mission. This photo, taken a day after the raid, shows all that remains of a Chinook helicopter and a C-130 transport, both abandoned in the desert of Eastern Iran. (WIDE WORLD PHOTOS)

MAY 5, 1980

$1.25

TIME
Debacle in the Desert

ANDERSON
Breaking Away

BULLETIN: AN ATTEMPT TO RESCUE THE AMERICAN HOSTAGES IN IRAN WAS ABORTED FRIDAY WHEN EIGHT CREW MEMBERS OF A U.S. AIRCRAFT WERE KILLED . . . PRESIDENT CARTER "ACCEPTS FULL RESPONSIBILITY . . ."

Only the first Association Press bulletin read "when eight crew members of a U.S. aircraft were killed." Later bulletins were corrected to read "after" rather than "when," but Time *used the original version to "convey the drama of the situation."*

Becoming Secretary of State after the resignation of Cyrus Vance, Edmund Muskie takes on a heavy burden. His primary mission—the release of the hostages. (WIDE WORLD PHOTOS)

Richard Queen, on coming home after a 250-day captivity, said "I really can't express with words what it's like to be back in America again. I just wish there were 52 more with me." (WIDE WORLD PHOTOS)

Deputy Secretary of State Warren M. Christopher, who once almost quit when passed over for the top State Department position, became chief U.S. negotiator in the hostage issue. In recognition of his invaluable services, President Carter award him the Medal of Honor. (WIDE WORLD PHOTOS)

Minister of State Behzad Neabavi, chief hostage negotiator for Iran, breaks new ground when he announces "If there is a kind of guarantee which is accepted by the Algerian government, we can accept it too." (WIDE WORLD PHOTOS)

"And my heart was filled with the realization of what it means to be free and what it means to be a citizen of the greatest and the strongest and the most decent nation on Earth and I had to fight back the tears."—Jimmy Carter (WIDE WORLD PHOTOS)

DAILY NEWS

Tonight

25¢

New York,
January 20, 1981

**LATEST
STOCKS**

TUESDAY EDITION

Drama at High Noon

Free!

Hostages take off as Reagan is sworn in

14 pages of stories & photos

As he takes the oath of office to become the 40th President of the United States, Ronald Reagan still doesn't know if his administration will begin with a crisis or a celebration. (WIDE WORLD PHOTOS)

Disaster At Desert One The Hostage Raid And Why It Failed

1973 Air Force Academy yearbook photo of Capt. Charles McMillan II. (WIDE WORLD PHOTOS)

Capt. Richard Bakke, USAF, another victim of the ill-fated mission. (WIDE WORLD PHOTOS)

April 24, 1980. The nuclear carrier Nimitz is on station in the Gulf of Oman, some 50 miles off the coast of Iran, where it has been since a mob of revolutionaries joined terrorists in seizing the U.S. embassy in Tehran.

This night is different from all the others, however. For tonight, the men of the Nimitz are not settling down to still another boring night of months-old television programs flown over from the states on video cassettes.

Instead, the carrier is a beehive of activity. Nerves are taut. As the sun goes down, eight large helicopters lift off the carrier's deck.

Their mission: Rescue the 53 U.S. nationals held captive in Iran.

The destination of the eight helicopters is a spot in the Dasht-e-Kavir desert about 600 miles to the north. There they will land to refuel and then fly another 250 miles to Tehran, to land 90 of the best combat troops in the U.S. armed services, troops under the command of Col. Charles Beckwith, considered the best antiterrorist commander in the United States.

"Operation Eagle Claw," commanded directly by the president from the oval office in Washington, is underway.

Within 12 hours, the operation, said to have been in the planning for over six months, or almost from the first day the hostages were taken, will be a disaster. On the salt desert will be the burning remains of two aircraft, four other operational helicopters and the bodies of eight U.S. servicemen killed after a series of mishaps that would leave the entire U.S. military establishment shaken to its very core.

The president and later the generals will announce that the raid failed after an incredible series of mishaps that could not possibly have been foreseen.

But congressional investigators looking into the mess will come to a very different conclusion. They will blame poor planning, poor execution and poor judgment for the failure.

No one knows that, however, as the helicopters leave the Nimitz's deck. There will be no television for the men of the Nimitz this night—and no sleep, either. There is serious work to be done.

To be sure, Operation Eagle Claw was a complex undertaking. After all, the rescuers had to fly, undetected, over 800 miles; they had to infiltrate a heavily guarded garrison, liberate the hostages, and then get themselves and the hostages out of Iran with a very minimal loss of Iranian life, to say nothing of a minimal loss to the hostages and rescuing force.

The plan called for the eight helicopters, carrying most of the 90 commandos, to fly low under and around Iranian radar to the rendezvous in the desert some 250 miles southeast of Tehran.

Earlier, six silent C-130 transports, loaded with additional men, supplies and fuel, had departed from a military airfield near Cairo headed for the "Desert One" location. Once there, the C-130s would be off-loaded and equipment would begin the trip to Tehran by road. The helicopters, meanwhile, would be refueled by the C-130s, loaded with all the commandos, and sent on to a second location in the mountains outside Tehran, codenamed "Figbar." There, they would remain hidden during the coming daylight hours. The C-130s would remain at Desert One until the darkness of the second night began.

At dusk on the second night, trucks and other vehicles would be driven the 55 miles from Tehran to Figbar, where they would be loaded with the commandos. These vehicles would be driven by U.S. agents who had been infiltrated into Iran in the previous week posing as European businessmen and carrying false passports and papers to prove it.

The trucks then would rendezvous at an empty warehouse in the suburbs of Tehran which had been leased by U.S. agents.

In the dead of night, at about 2 AM, using the warren of alleyways around the embassy grounds, the commandos would make their ways into the compound, incapacitate the militants holding them and then proceed with the liberated hostages to several pick-up points within blocks of the embassy. There they would be picked up by the helicopters, which had flown in from Figbar.

The helicopters then would fly on to an abandoned military airfield about 60 miles from Tehran where they would once again rendezvous with the C-130s, which would have flown in from Desert One.

All personnel would be transferred at the point to the Hercules transports, the helicopters would be blown up and the C-130s, with fighter aircraft from the Nimitz flying cover until they were out of Iranian airspace, would fly nonstop to West Germany.

All in all, it was an undertaking that made the Israeli raid at Entebbe look like child's play by comparison.

What happened?

On this ill-fated mission, things began to go wrong almost from the very start. The Nimitz was being shadowed by a Soviet spy ship and it had to steam further away to avoid having the Soviets spot the helicopter takeoffs. When the helicopters finally were able to get into the air, they already were about a half-hour behind schedule.

In order to have enough room to carry the commandos from Desert One to Figbar, and then to carry the commandos and the hostages from the pickup points in Tehran to the waiting Hercules planes, a minimum of 6 helicopters were necessary.

To be on the safe side, mission planners tried to foresee every contingency and sent off eight helicopters from the Nimitz. According to a still secret Pentagon assessment of the raid, its computers told planners that using eight helicopters gave the mission a 96.5 percent probability of having six available to carry out the mission.

No such luck. Things went from bad to worse.

Shortly after takeoff, one of the helicopters had a warning light come on in its cockpit saying it was losing pressure in one of its rotor blades. Following established procedure, the pilot immediately set the helicopter down and another of the helicopters landed with him. Because the time factors in the mission were so critical, because the mission already was running late, and because procedures prohibited the helicopters from breaking radio silence, the pilot of the downed helicopter could not take the time to determine whether he had a real problem in his hydraulic system, whether it was merely a malfunctioning warning light, or how long it might take to rectify whatever problem did exist. So all men and materials were transferred from the downed helicopter to the other one that had landed with it and the helicopter was abandoned.

One down and seven to go.

The mission commanders aboard the Nimitz were not too concerned, however. They had assumed that at least one helicopter would be lost and, while they were bothered that it had happened so early in the

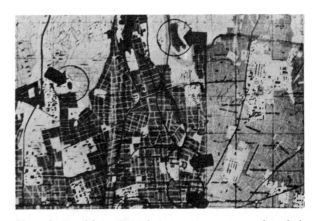

Map obtained from British sources purports to show helicopter landing sites which could have been used in mission. Circles show (top) Embassy and (others) alternate landing sites. (WIDE WORLD PHOTOS)

Iranians race to the American Embassy in Tehran to spread news just heard on Iranian radio—that the U.S. had lost in their commando bid to free the hostages. (WIDE WORLD PHOTOS)

mission, there was no reason yet to be alarmed.

Soon afterward, however, the second major problem of the mission struck. As the remaining seven helicopters were nearing the Iranian town of Bam, they ran head on into what appeared to be a major sandstorm. It struck without warning and, within seconds, the helicopters were flying completely blind. The pilots could not even see a few feet in front of them.

Fear of detection by Iranian radar forced the helicopters to continue flying near ground-level; thus, they did not dare get up over the sandstorm. Because they had no way of telling how widespread the storm was, they had no way of flying around it, either. So they did the only thing they could: they flew on.

Suddenly, one of the helicopters developed a major systems failure. The gyro went first; in quick order, the omni-directional radio system failed and then the tactical navigation system. The pilot, who could not see visually, now also could not see electronically and almost crashed.

He decided to return to the Nimitz, although he did not have enough fuel to reach it. The carrier ended up having to sail at almost flank speed to reach the helicopter before it would have had to ditch for lack of fuel.

Two down and six—the necessary six—to go.

Now the mission planners began to worry. They needed six helicopters to complete the mission and all they had left were six—and there were still several hundred miles of desert to cross before reaching Desert One, the initial rendezvous point. All the planners could do, however, was cross their fingers and hope for the best.

The best was not to be.

By now, the C-130s had landed at the salt flat that was Desert One. A road that was little traveled even in the daytime ran alongside the area and, according to plan, Iranian speaking commandos, wearing Iranian military garb and with vehicles with Iranian markings, set up roadblocks.

Suddenly, a bus appeared on its way to a nearby town. Spy satellite studies of the road over the previous two weeks showed absolutely no traffic on it. In fact, it was little more than a path after midnight; but now, here it was 1 in the morning and there was a bus with 44 Iranian men, women and children (and several goats) on their way from Yazad to Mashhad.

The startled commandos quickly stopped the bus and moved all the Iranians into one of the C-130s and guards were posted.

Finally, the six remaining helicopters landed. One of them, it was discovered, had a faulty hydraulic pump that made it impossible for it to take off again. Ordinarily, that would not have been an impossible problem to solve. A pump was something that could have been fixed in less than an hour. In fact, the planners had thought of the eventuality and a spare pump had been brought along—but it was in the helicopter that was now trying desperately to reach the Nimitz.

Three down and not enough left to go.

The mission had to be scrubbed.

But now disappointment turned into disaster. After conferring with the mission commanders on the Nimitz, the field commander Col. James Kyle relayed the order from the overall mission commander Maj. Gen. James Vaught, who was back in Egypt and in communication with both the Nimitz and with the president: Abort.

The men at Desert One frantically began to refuel the helicopters so that all concerned could get out.

With two of the C-130s already in the air, one of the chopper pilots banked his helicopter in the wrong direction. It was pitch dark and he was flying blind. His wrong move resulted in his rotor blades striking one of the C-130s. Instantly, the helicopter and the Hercules were engulfed in flames.

Absolute panic set in among the aircrews. As the commandos tried to maintain an orderly evacuation, the crews scrambled to get out as quickly as possible. In fact, the evacuation became so hectic that some commandos almost were left on the ground. With the burning aircraft turning the nighttime sky into seeming daylight, all anyone could think about was that the Iranian military had to be on the way. So the decision was made to pack everyone aboard the remaining C-130s, abandon the helicopters, release the bus passengers and make a run for it.

Left behind were four helicopters, piles of classified documents and the bodies of eight servicemen who had died in the fire.

Operation Eagle Claw was now history and one of the blackest marks in U.S. military annals.

Who is to blame for the disaster at Desert One?

In one of the initial assessments of the failure, the Pentagon's chief of naval operations said, "It's hard to imagine a confluence of circumstances that could have been any more unfortunate." In his assessment of the "victory," Ayatollah Ruhollah Khomeini said simply, "God was on the side of the Iranian people."

In fact, the official explanation of the Pentagon was not far removed from the ayatollah's claim: an incredible string of bad luck that no one possibly could have forecast.

Congressional investigators, however, were not so quick to lay the blame at the feet of either Lady Luck or the Deity. From the outset, they believed the blame had to rest with the mission's planners.

To start with, they fault the very basic decision of whom to choose as the planner of the operation.

No one faults the choice of "Chargin' Charlie" Beckwith to lead the commando group. He is the kind of inspirational combat leader whom men will follow through a solid wall and the kind of person of whom novels are written. What's more, he is probably the most experienced anti-terrorist commander in the U.S. military and one who has the open respect and admiration of the anti-terrorist forces of such countries as Israel and Britain. In fact, everyone is in agreement that Beckwith and his "Charlie's Angels" handled themselves in an exemplary manner in the face of tremendous difficulties.

The investigators are not as sure about the choice of Gen. Vaught as overall mission leader and planner. The problem seems to be in Vaught's personality. According to insiders, if there is one man in the active military that could outcharge "Chargin' Charlie," it would be James Vaught. A much-decorated combat veteran, Vaught is described by one investigator as "a super-macho type who believed that he could overcome anything by a simple act of his will."

These investigators believe that, had the mission been planned by more of a strategist and less of a combat commander, various contingencies would have been available and some of the problems might have been overcome.

In his explanation of the mission, President Carter stated that all concerned had trained for months in the deserts of the Southwest and had run the entire mission five times in simulation.

At no time, however, had any of the simulations been run in anything but perfect weather. In fact, whenever a practice run was scheduled and the weather came up bad, the exercise was put off until the weather cleared. So the pilots had no flying experience in bad weather.

Also, no contingency was set up for communication between helicopters, only between the lead helicopter and the mission commander on the Nimitz via special radio. It was never considered that the helicopters would need to communicate with each other except in very simple light code. They did need to communicate.

The helicopter with the bad pump knew at least two hours before landing at the initial staging area that the pump was going bad. Had it been able to communicate this to the lead helicopter, the message could have been relayed to the Nimitz, which knew the spare pump was on its way back aboard the returning helicopter. Some provision then might have been made for another pump to be flown to Desert One and dropped down by parachute.

The most glaring failure in the plan was the abort procedure. Despite the fact that it was always understood that there was a 50-50 chance that the mission

Army Colonel Charles Beckwith, known in Pentagon circles as "the kind of combat leader men will follow through a brick wall, the kind novels are written about." (WIDE WORLD PHOTOS)

Aftermath of the rescue attempt. Human lives, valuable equipment, precious opportunities are lost . . . Vance quits . . . and the hostage question remains.

would have to be scrubbed, not once in all the months of rehearsing did the group practice an abort. Beckwith reportedly told investigators, ''When the abort order came, no one knew quite what to do. We were in a pitch black desert and we were ad-libbing.''

However, the focus on the mission's failure has been directed at the mechanical failures and here a whopping question is open for debate:

Were the wrong kind of helicopters used?

The eight helicopters that took off from the deck of the Nimitz were Navy RH-53D ''Sea Stallions.'' The mission they faced was as tough a one as anyone could ask any helicopter to perform. The whirlybirds had to fly over hot desert (which reduces the amount of lift) to just about their absolute maximum range and each was carrying some 5,000 pounds more weight than is considered their maximum carrying capacity.

The Sea Stallion, however, is a special helicopter designed for the Navy for mine laying and mine sweeping only. The helicopters aboard the Nimitz were not there for a rescue mission, but to lay mines in the event a naval blockade of Iran was ordered.

In fact, the Army has a specially designed helicopter, the CH-47, which is made for just such long-range missions. The Pentagon, however, was afraid that moving a force of these helicopters onto the Nimitz would alert watchers, especially the Soviets, that something was afoot. So instead, the Sea Stal-

lions already aboard were used. This was a grave error.

Planners, however, say it was not an error. The helicopters, they insist, were reliable.

Then did an unexpected accident cause these ''reliable'' helicopters to fail?

The night before the mission, a sailor aboard the Nimitz pushed the wrong button and five of the eight rescue helicopters were throughly doused with a fire-quenching mixture of foam and corrosive sea water. The five immediately were washed down with fresh water and their systems checked.

Given the failures that occurred, was this accident to blame? Pentagon officials say no again, but some suggest the mission should have been delayed to more thoroughly clean the helicopters.

Then there is the question of the storm. It has been described officially by the Pentagon as a sandstorm, known in Arabic as a [fi]khamsin.[FR] (Some biblical scholars have suggested that the Plague of Darkness that descended upon Egypt actually was a [fi]khamsin,[FR] which could be very debilitating.) What actually took place, however, was a [fi]haboob, [FR] a not unusual weather situation in that part of Iran at that time of year. Weather conditions over the desert result in a massive cloud of very fine talcum powder-like dust being raised thousands of feet into the air.

Because these dust storms might have been encountered, the pilots should have been briefed as to the possibility and provisions made for it. Why this did not happen is still an unanswered question.

And, of course, all the above begs the basic question of whether the rescue plan would have worked had there been no mechanical failures. Would the commandos have been able to get into the embassy, would they have been able to overcome the guards without a substantial loss of life and would they have been able to get the hostages out?

In much publicized comments after the raid, Col. Beckwith and others, including both the president and Defense Secretary Harold Brown, were quoted widely as saying that, in effect, as far as planners were concerned, the easiest part of the raid, the one they were most certain would succeed, was the actual rescue.

Investigators are not as certain, however. In fact, they have unearthed one supersecret pre-raid Pentagon study which estimated that as many as 15 of the hostages and as many as 30 of the commandos might have been lost in the raid plus a substantial number of Iranians (which undoubtedly would have brought swift retribution against the over 200 U.S. journalists and other U.S. nationals in Tehran at the time of the raid).

Thus, the raid was ordered even though planners faced the possibility of losing 45 men to rescue 38 and of placing several hundred others in jeopardy of either being killed or of replacing as hostages those rescued at such a high cost.

There are some who would argue that, at such cost, the rescue mission was not worth it.

There are others, however, who say it was worth it at any cost — if only to show the world that the United Staes would not sit by idly while its citizens were held hostage by terrorists and outlaw governments. They point to President Gerald R. Ford's order to rescue the crew of the Mayaguez. A terrible price was paid, they argue, but the message of the mission was heard loud and clear across the globe: The United States was not to be trifled with.

That same message would have been delivered had the Tehran rescue mission succeeded, no mater how many lives were lost.

Instead, however, the disaster at Desert One caused another message—and a dangerously erroneous one—to be sent:

The United States is a paper tiger. Strike at will.

Senior Iranian army officers accompany Ayatollah Sadegh Khalkali to view burned-out U.S. equipment left behind after the failed rescue mission. (WIDE WORLD PHOTOS)

The Aborted Rescue Mission: Have We Been Told The Truth?

Did the Carter Administration tell the truth about the aborted rescue mission?

Maybe it did; and maybe, just maybe, it did not.

That, at least, is the way it seems to some intelligence experts acquainted with Iran and with the kind of planning that goes into such missions as the one which exploded in the sands of the Persian desert.

One such expert is Miles Copeland who, incidentally, joined with other old Central Intelligence Agency hands to plot just such a rescue mission last December at the administration's request.

Copeland, known by the cover name "Major Lincoln," told us of a former CIA counter-intelligence analyst who used to remind his young assistants that they must be slow to make assumptions and quick to discard them as they came upon information which did not add up.

"For example," Copeland said, "if they are shown a script about 80 officers and soldiers wearing U.S. uniforms and flying helicopters clearly marked 'U.S. Air Force,' landing in the middle of one of the most densely populated cities in the world, fighting their way through 100 heavily armed defenders and a maze of booby traps, and lifting 50-odd hostages with little or no loss of life, they must not leap to the conclusion that they are reading a Marx Brother movie.

"Instead, they must postulate a new scenario based on the premise that the officers and the planners behind them know what they are doing, and that the purpose of the mission and of what government spokesmen say about it are other than what they appear."

Asked to elucidate, Copeland urged us to consider the following:

1. The ratio of attackers to defenders. In this case, he says, the ratio was way out of whack.

"It is generally accepted among military planners that the ratio of attackers to defenders, even where environmental factors do not favor one side or the other, should be about 4 to 1," Copeland told us. "No commander in his right mind would send 90 troops to attack 120—unless, of course, there were 'factors bearing on the situation,' as military planners say, that haven't been included in the scenario, such as the presence among the defenders of 'moles' who, upon a given signal, will turn on their associates and assist the attack."

2. The need for surprise. There was nothing in the administration's version of the rescue mission that allowed for any surprise. Yet, says Copeland, without surprise the mission would have failed.

"For an attack to be made in a markedly hostile environment—such as, for example, the environment surrounding the U.S. embassy in Tehran—the maximum element of surprise must be utilized," he says, "preferably by ensuring that, up to the last minute, the attackers blend in with the environment. In the case of an attempt to free those hostages in the embassy, the attackers must either look convincingly like Iranians, or actually be Iranians.

3. The need to control a variety of environmental factors, for example, the water, food, electricity, fuel, communications (both telephone and radio), and even the air going into the embassy compound.

"Also," said Copeland, "there would have to be a certain amount of control over facilities of the city, and even of the country at large—such as, for example, those means by which the police and security forces would receive and act on any alarm signals the attackers might get off.

"Even under minimal, less-than-ideal conditions, auxiliaries of the attackers would not only need the capibility to jam unit-to-unit communications of the government, but actually to feed 'disinformation' into them so as to send them chasing off in a lot of wrong directions."

In short, the intelligence expert told us, in planning from the center outwards, as is necessary in operations where the whole environment is the problem, such a huge degree of indigenous participation is required that the operation has to be indigenous.

If true, of course, then the story the adminstration handed out was far from the whole story. Considering that the version made public indeed does make the United States sound as though Groucho, Chico and Harpo and running things, what motive could the administration have for not telling the whole truth? Said Copeland:

"In times of war, or in conflict situations short of war where there is an 'enemy,' our government may be forgiven for telling the general public something other than the truth. There is no way of being frank and open with our own people without, at the same time, being frank and open with the enemy.

"Anyone whose only experience with conflict has been limited to Saturday night poker games knows that you can't win if you show your hand. So we may assume that the president and the secretary of defense—and, for that matter, a goodly proportion of those lesser officials who've given leaks to outsiders (including myself)—are telling us only what they want the enemy to 'know.'''

But, by simple inference, Copeland says, we can almost know certain things positively.

''We know, for example, that some leaders of the Iranian government have aims which they believe to be constructive and which are not inconsistent with our own once the hostage problem has been resolved to our satisfaction. We also know that some of them, at least indirectly, have been in touch with our government, secretly or not so secretly, and we have good reason to suspect that President Abolhassan Bani-Sadr is among them.

''We also know that there are one or more 'moles' among the non-Iranian elements of the 'students' and that many of the 'students,' including the bona fide Iranians, have motivations which make them eminently susceptible to the kinds of inducements which could be offered them.

''And we know there are tribes, elements in the Iranian army and air force, and in the civilian 'middle Iran' that are prepared to act provided they see sufficient no-strings-attached support from the outside—the act in a purely Iranian operation in which we support them, rather than vice versa.''

It may be years before we know what really did happen in the Iranian desert that fateful and, for eight U.S. servicemen, fatal night. And perhaps, as Copeland said, that is how it should be.

Turned out of office and condemned to death in absentia by Khomeini, Bakhtiar still holds that ''It's not with graffiti and imbecile screamings that you reconstruct a country.'' (WIDE WORLD PHOTOS)

The Ayatollah's Justice

FRIDAY, June 26, 1980—a normal day in Khomeini's Iran:

Iranian news reports listed 22 men and women executed by firing squads today and added that nine people had been executed on Thursday throughout the country. Three women and five men were shot to death in the southern town of Ahvaz on charges of prostitution, white slavery, rebellion against the Islamic republic, exploding bombs and spying for Iraq. One woman was executed in the northeastern city of Mashad for running a "corruption house" and hiding drugs "inside her body," official said. Twelve men were executed at the same time on drug charges. In Tabriz, a man was executed for drug trafficking, homosexual rape and attempted murder.

The government's Society for the Prevention of

In ayatollah Khomeini's Iran, a young boy sells portraits of his idol in Tehran bazaar. (WIDE WORLD PHOTOS)

Sin today banned the playing of music "in all public places, including shops and restaurants." Religious Judge Ayatollah Mohitadi Guilani, who issued the order, said, "The people cannot be permitted to listen to the voice of vulgar male and female singers." Since the Islamic regime seized power, Iranian officials have confiscated records and tape cassettes throughout the country.

The scene: a crowded courtroom in central Tehran.

The trial has been going on for almost five minutes. The five defendants sit silently facing the Judge's bench. Only the bench is empty because the judge in this case also is the prosecutor.

He is circling behind the defendants and he is shouting. "I will exterminate you vermin," he declares.

The defendants are all charged with selling drugs. They are not major drug traffickers, but street-level pushers. They are not allowed to speak in the courtroom or to offer any kind of defense. Suddenly the prosecutor–judge whirls and begins pointing:

"You and you, execution.

"You, life imprisonment.

"You and you, 100 lashes."

As the revolutionary guards take the men out, the prosecutor–judge admonishes them: "Remember every lash must draw blood."

Within two hours, the lashes have been administered and the executions held.

The Justice of Ayatollah Ruhollah Khomeini again has been carried out.

Since the revolution in February 1979, well over 1,000 men and women have faced revolutionary firing squads.

At first, their "crimes" were that they were high-ranking officials of Shah Mohammed Reza Pahlavi's government, or members of his secret police SAVAK. However, after the ayatollah's zealous followers ran out of major officials and secret police, the revolutionary courts turned to those accused of "crimes against Allah,"— offenses ranging from prostitution to drug use to treating a mullah without proper respect.

Then the court turned to those accused of opposition to the government.

In most cases—whether the crime is murder, a crime against Allah, or participation in a demonstration against the ayatollah—the penalty is the same: execution. The firing squads always are at the ready.

The justice system which has prevailed in Iran under the shah, imperfect as it was, was supplanted by the Revolutionary Komiteh (committee), which effectively became both police force and court. Komitehs ranged from local neighborhood units to the Central Revolutionary Komiteh in Tehran presided over by the infamous Ayatollah Sadegh Khalkhali, "the hanging judge" who won worldwide notoriety when he publicly displayed the bodies of the 8 U.S. servicemen who died in the abortive raid to free the hostages.

The regular police force still exists and still handles "normal crimes" such as run-of-the-mill murders, car theft, rapes, etc.

The komitehs investigate crimes against Allah and/or the state (considered the same thing) and trials are held by their own revolutionary courts. The komitehs need no evidence against an accused before they can arrest him; arrests, in fact, often are made after a citizen comes in to say he suspects a friend, neighbor, or enemy of some transgression.

The komitehs run their own jails and can hold the prisoner as long as they like without any kind of formal charge being brought against the person.

Eventually, a trial may take place. More often than not, these trials are secret and often are over in a matter of minutes. In them, the accused has no rights, usually is not even allowed to speak in his or her own defense, let alone be allowed to offer witnesses. Sentence is swiftly pronounced (as noted, it most often is death; at other times, it is severe lashings which usually result in death or disfigurement) and just as swiftly carried out with no benefit of appeal.

Typical of the operation of these star chamber komitehs was a four-day period in late May when over 72 persons were executed on the orders of revolutionary courts. Some of the crimes were serious: drug-dealing and sabotaging of an oil pipeline. Whether the accused were guilty, however, was impossible to determine because they could not speak or offer a defense of any kind. (The sabotaged pipeline is a case in point. It may have been a political act, or it could have been part of a labor dispute; it was never made clear what the motive was, the accused never even had a chance to say they did not do it.) Some of the capital crimes were downright ridiculous: from "publicly insulting the Ayatollah Ruhollah Khomeini" to membership in dissident political groups including the outlawed Moslem People's Republican Party of Azerbaijan (which seeks greater autonomy from Tehran for Iran's Turkish-speaking provinces).

Among the executed were six women. One of the women was executed for "running the largest corruption center" in the country, although this charge was not explained and no details were given; the trial was held in secret.

This week ended with 14 executions. Two military officers, Gen. Mohsen Zadegan and Lt. Abbas Gholis, were put before a firing squad allegedly because they were involved in the plotting of a coup to "reinstate

In February 1980, Khomeini poses with sons, grandsons, and doctors while recuperating from heart ailments. (WIDE WORLD PHOTOS)

the shah." Actually, the evidence showed that if, in fact, there was a plot, more likely it was simply some loose talk about holding a public referendum on what kind of government should be put into place.

Five of those executed were Kurds said to be in the employ of Iraq intelligence. Others executed included seven accused of murder, theft, robbery and drug offenses.

The star chamber proceedings began shortly after the ayatollah returned from France in February 1979. In those days, the Iranian government was headed by Prime Minister Mehdi Bazargan, who almost constantly decried the operation of the revolutionary courts and the komitehs. He said the "komitehs are out of control and have become a law unto themselves." The executions, all of which were still political, he called "irreligious, inhuman and a disgrace."

Bazargan notwithstanding, the political trials and executions continued. Then things began to change. In a secret trial, a man for the first time was executed for violation of Moslem law: a jailer accused of the homosexual rape of a prisoner. This was the start of a new trend and it was followed with a flurry of executions.

This actually worried Khomeini and he stepped in.

The ayatollah ordered a halt to all secret trials and executions, saying that henceforth all trials were to be public and carried out under the direct supervision "of the revolutionary Islamic government."

The prohibition lasted about three weeks.

On the day the order was issued, former Prime Minister Amir Hoveida was on trial on 16 charges ranging from "anti-religious activities," to "turning over assets of the Iranian people to foreigners," to "fostering an Iranian market for foreign consumer goods."

His trial was suspended by the new order, which was issued March 16. The trial resumed on April 6 and Hoveida was executed on April 7. In the next four days, 35 more executions took place.

Despite the ayatollah's order, all the trials and executions were secret. The pattern was established.

By this time, more than 125 executions had taken place and the pace was picking up. As Bazargan was continuing to decry the komitehs' "rule of revenge,"

Another powerful ayatollah, Mohammad Behesti, in favor of putting hostages on trial and intensifying Islamic law. (WIDE WORLD PHOTOS)

more and more former government officials faced firing squads. In the next three weeks, at least 75 more persons were executed.

In early May, the executions took an ominous turn. At first, the trials had been limited to high-ranking officials of the shah's regime. Then there followed the trials of lower-ranking former government officials, all of whom had been charged either with ordering or carrying out killings for the ousted government. Now, however, the revolutionary courts turned their attention to political types from the former government. A speaker of the Parliament was executed, as were a former information minister.

And then came the execution of Habib Elghanian, a wealthy Iranian Jew, executed for "economic imperialism" and "Zionist activity."

This execution caused a worldwide furor, including a threat from Israel to use force to protect the Jewish minority in Iran.

The outcry was so loud that it pushed the ayatollah into action. On May 13, he issued a new order limiting executions to those found guilty of "the killing of others."

By mid-July, the number of executions had risen to almost 400, but the ayatollah's order was being adhered to. All those being executed were accused of killing in the name of the previous government.

But by September, executions again had begun for violations of Moslem law. A favorite charge was "corruption on Earth"; under this charge, the shah's former personal physician, Dr. Jamshid A'Alam, was put to death. His crime: keeping the shah in good health.

In October, with the number of executions topping 600, the ayatollah ordered a complete halt to them. This prohibition continued for five months, but then the problems of the new government began to mount. There was economic and political unrest. The economic unrest, in turn, bred a major crime increase and drug use skyrocketed.

So the solution Khalkhali, by now one of the most powerful figures in Iran, decided upon was to resume the trials and executions. Now the crimes included opposition to the government. By May, over 1,000 had faced the firing squad.

Again the outcry was heard. Stop the executions.

This time, however, Khomeini refused to act. Islamic justice was being meted out, his supporters explained, and the outside world no longer would push their iman into subverting the will of Allah.

Starting in June, the Iranian government under the growing power of Ayatollah Behesti and his mullah-oriented Parliament began a campaign to intensify the application of Islamic law through Iran. With this campaign came a marked increase in the number of executions. One estimate is that in June and July alone almost 250 executions took place.

On July 7, a mass execution was held in public for the first time. On the day, a firing squad—in a busy Tehran intersection—executed seven accused drug dealers. The next day, in another public execution, 10 more drug dealers were shot to death. This brought to more than 200 the estimated number of Iranians executed for drug dealing.

In one two-day period, July 13-14, 55 people were executed. Some were accused drug dealers, others were accused of sexual offenses. In Kerman, a small town in Southern Iran, three men and a woman, accused of sexual offenses, were buried in dirt up to their necks and then stoned to death.

During this period not a week went by without an announcement of another 15 or 20 executions. And these numbers do not include the dozens of military officers who were sent before military firing squads for their alleged involvement in the "plot" to overthrow Khomeini's regime.

Battle of the ayatollahs. January 1980—charred remains of a car and the defaced portraits of Khomeini after clashes between his followers and those of Ayatollah Shariatmadari. (WIDE WORLD PHOTOS)

Ayatollah Ruhollah Khomeini: To Iranians, He's More Than A Man

It was with the blessing of Ayatollah Ruhollah Khomeini that an Iranian mob stormed the U.S. embassy in Tehran on Nov. 4, 1979, and held hostage its 70 occupants, including 62 U.S. nationals, in violation of international law.

It was on Khomeini's orders that the terrorists holding that embassy permitted 15 U.S. nationals —women and blacks—to be released, while keeping the rest and threatening to put them on trial on espionage charges.

And it was on Khomeini's assurance that Allah will protect them that Iranians have dared to thumb their noses at the awesome might of the United States.

Who is Ruhollah Khomeini? Why does he have the kind of power that enables him to enflame Iran's Moslem masses with a mere utterance? And why does he have such a deep-seated hatred for the West in general and the United States in particular?

The first question appears to be an easy one. Khomeini was born in 1901, the simple answer goes, is an aged Moslem religious leader with a long beard, evil-looking black eyebrows and a piercing gaze who eats sparingly and sits cross-legged on the floor. He is a man who walks around haughtily, garbed in a black turban, floor-length robe and flat-bottomed slippers, and rarely laughs at anything but his own witticisms. For 15 years, he was in exile in Iraq and France and, in the latter years, became an embarrassment to his French hosts.

When he was forced to leave Iran, he was just one of a number of ayatollahs (religious leaders). When his followers took command in Iran, however, Khomeini returned to lead his people.

In his 15 years of exile, he had grown from just another ayatollah to the spiritual leader of Iran's Shi'ite Moslems. He was able to accomplish this because, of all of Iran's religious leaders, Khomeini hated Shah Mohammed Reza Pahlavi the most and never relented in his efforts to unseat the monarch from the Peacock Throne.

That is the simple answer only, it also is the superficial one and tells absolutely nothing. The question, it turns out, is not easy at all and, in fact, is so closely tied to the second that only by understanding the answer to the second question can we truly know who Khomeini is.

For Khomeini is more than an ayatollah to the Shi'ites of Iran (there are other ayatollahs, as already

pointed out, but they cannot claim the power of Khomeini); he is their imam.

An imam is the caliph of the Prophet Mohammed and therein lies the secret of Khomeini's powerful grip on a nation hurtling rapidly backwards into the depths of Islam's Dark Ages. Therein, too, lies the reason why the West has been unable to deal effectively with Khomeini. For the West has no conception of what an imam is (just as it has no conception of what Islam is), much less an understanding of why people would follow him.

"Rarely has a man so completely embodied and expressed the will of a people as does Khomeini," says noted anthropologist Dr. Raphael Patai. "True, this will has lain dormant for a long time and the people were made conscious of it only through the exhortations of the ayatollah and the thousands of mullahs who obediently and eagerly do his bidding. In no way, however, does this alter the fact that Khomeini is the manifestation of the people's will to an extent never achieved by a Western leader."

Imam is not a title to be taken lightly, not even by the aged ayatollah to whom it was given by the

Iranian woman in the traditional chador stands vigil outside the Tehran hospital, awaiting word of Khomeini's condition. (WIDE WORLD PHOTOS)

Spotlight over a poster of the Ayatollah Ruhollah Khomeini shines on a nearly deserted street in front of the U.S. Embassy. (WIDE WORLD PHOTOS)

terrorists who took the U.S. embassy. It is all-encompassing and is as close to deification as the Shi'ites dare get without skirting sacrilege. For the imam is appointed by Allah, they say, and thus is divinely inspired and preserved from sin. As the title of imam takes hold of the nation (even President Abolhassan Bani-Sadr and Foreign Minister Sadegh Ghotbzadeh use the title often in public pronouncements), it imbues Khomeini with ever-growing strength among the Shi'ites, who make up the majority of Iran's population.

That Khomeini would accept the title, albeit passively by not repudiating it, indicates the extent of his own ego. That ego has led Khomeini, as imam, to spurn Pope John Paul II, U.S. President Jimmy Carter, Egyptian President Anwar Sadat, U.N. Secretary General Kurt Waldheim and many others, including those who presumably would be on his side, including Palestine Liberation Organization chieftain Yasser Arafat. Khomeini is the imam, appointed by Allah, and there can be no greater than he.

Khomeini never once wavered in his belief that his cause is righteous. And that cause, which brought down the shah, is rooted in a revival of traditional Shi'ite values, values which demand that all controversies—civil and religious—center around the imam. That is, when there is one. There has been no imam in 11 centuries.

This, in itself, explains much about Khomeini and about his power. There has emerged around the doctrine of the imam, the supreme Islamic religious guide, an entire Messianic mythology which is central to Shi'ite philosophy: The twelfth and last imam, who lived in the 9th century, never died, tradition insists; instead, he remains in hiding to this day, waiting for his chance to return and inaugurate a golden age. If the "hidden imam" still lives, there can be no other imam—unless, of course, that imam is the twelfth imam returned from his self-imposed seclusion.

Khomeini, of course, has made no attempt to claim to be the "hidden imam," but he also has made no effort to dissuade his people from believing that he is. If that thought takes serious hold in Iran, there is nothing Khomeini cannot ask of his people; they will follow him even unto certain death. After all, as the Koran declares, "Those who are killed in the path of Allah, He does not let their good deeds go for nothing."

As imam, Khomeini has a ready-made network through which to rule the Iranian masses with the hammerlock grip that comes with divine right and the hierarchical nature of Shi'ite Islam. This network is made up of a class of holy men—ayatollahs, mujtahids and mullahs.

"The Shi'ites believe the imams were and will be again endowed by divine qualities," Dr. Patai recently wrote. "The more extreme Shi'a sects go even further. They say the imams were the incarnations of the deity. While the divine imam is in concealment, his representatives and spokesman, the so-called mujtahids, who are the greatest scholars of the age, wield supreme authority and must be obeyed unquestioningly.

"The mujtahids were and are few (not even every ayatollah can claim to be one), but those of the lower rank of Moslem clergy, the mullahs, are many. Indeed, they are much more numerous in relation to the population than the priests in a Catholic country."

The mullahs are religious teachers, familiar with the Koran, Shi'ite prayers and religious ritual. They are the arbiters of manners and mores, of conduct and conflict. To them people turn for aid in times of need or crisis, receiving prayers, amulets and such to help them.

To the holy men, too, the people turn for guidance and instruction. From cradle to grave, the masses are force-fed the belief that their holy men are the end all and be all, and that Allah demands automatic obedience to the will of these men.

Quite obviously, then, when the holy man involved is the imam, higher even than the mujtahids, the pseudo-reincarntion of the deity, blind obedience becomes as natural as breathing. After all, the caliph of the Prophet Mohammed can do no wrong; it is impossible.

Khomeini's addresses to his people are designed to play on this by using the time-worn religious themes of Shi'ite dogma: Allah's path, the jihad ("holy war"), martyrdom, the assurance that Allah always will help, all old religious tenets applied by Khomeini to new situations.

By reiterating these well-known and well-established doctrines (and, with his near-omniscient authority, thus confirmed what the people from infancy were taught to believe), the imam is able to reassure his Shi'ite followers that they are without question following the true path in anything they do.

Martyrdom, especially, is a favorite Khomeini theme. It is, in fact, an Iranian national ideal. ("This was in response to the fact that the greatest figures in Shi'ite history, beginning with 'Ali, Mohammed's son-in-law and the fountainhead of the Shi'a, were defeated and killed by their enemies and came to be considered holy martyrs," explains Dr. Patai.)

When, in the wake of the aborted U.S. rescue attempt, three revolutionary guards were mistakenly killed by Iranian gunfire, Khomeini congratulated them and said "their deaths raised them to the highest ranks of martyrdom."

Iran, he reminded his followers in one speech, "is a nation of blood and our school is the school of holy war . . . (Iran) has been raised in a school in which martyrdom is considered happiness and an honor, a nation quite willing to sacrifice its life for its reli-

gion." He told his people to "get ready, heeding Almighty God's order and depending on His power, to fight (Islam's) enemies" and "to sacrifice itself for Islam." After all, Khomeini said, Allah "supports the Moslem nation."

Given this cradle-to-grave indoctrination of the Iranian masses in the superiority of their holy men, given the Shi'ite beliefs and traditions ingrained as they are from birth, given the centuries-old wait for the return of "the hidden imam" and, with him, the inauguration of the new Golden Age of Islam, it is easy to see (although to our Western minds, perhaps, still difficult to understand) how anyone widely perceived as the imam would be followed without question, even to ruination and death.

Carrying the holy title, however, also automatically sets Khomeini's course, for to some degree he becomes a prisoner to traditional Shi'ite beliefs. By the very nature of his exalted title, he is set against the infidel West (in this context, the Soviet East is just as West as the rest of the world). It is the infidel, the Koran teaches, who is the enemy and must be subjugated; not the other way around.

(According to the Koran, "there awaits a mighty chastisement" for the unbelieving infidels. To the believers, it says, "Prescribed for you is fighting, though it be hateful to you . . . O believers, take your precautions, then move forward in companies, or move forward all together . . . When you meet the unbelievers, smite their necks and, when you have made wide slaughter among them, tie fast their bonds . . . Thus it is and, if Allah wished, He would crush them Himself, but he tests you against one another.")

This points up an essential difference between the Shi'ites and Islam's overwhelming majority, the Sunnis. The Shi'ites, because of their minority status and constant harassment by the Sunnis in the days of Islam's might, take this Koranic prescription quite literally; the Sunnis, on the other hand, are willing to accept other interpretations on the order smite the necks of the unbelievers.—

As for the United States, it is the worst of the infidels to Khomeini, because it supported his hated blood enemies, Reza Shah and his son, the deposed Shah Mohammed Reza Pahlavi.

Khomeini's feud with the shah began many years ago, long before the monarch's attempts at land and social reforms, which set the rest of the religious community against him. The ayatollah places responsibility for the death of his father on the head of Reza Shah. And Khomeini believes the shah's secret police, SAVAK, was responsible for the mysterious death of one of his two sons in 1977.

Thus, when the shah began land reform and women's emancipation in the early 1960s, Khomeini seized on the issue to begin his efforts to remove his blood enemy from the Peacock Throne. Having accomplished that, Khomeini is now able to take out his anger on the United States for having helped perpetuate the evil shahs in power.

(This is one of the most ironic facts about the recent events in Iran. Khomeini himself lives an ascetic life in the holy city of Qom. He eats sparingly, subsisting mainly on a diet largely made up of fruit and nuts. Iran's holy men, he insists, being merely the stewards of the people, must restrict themselves to a similar life of poverty. Yet it was due to opposite motivations that Khomeini was able to use these same holy men to enflame Iran against the shah.)

(As it turns out, the mullahs and mujtahids as a class may be richer even than the shah's family. Over the centuries, they have built up their tremendous wealth by accumulating vast religious properties. It was because they felt themselves threatened by the shah's "white revolution"—which included revolutionary land reforms which would have broken up vast holdings to be turned over to the people, thus diminishing their wealth and power—that the nation's religious leaders turned on the shah when Khomeini called.)

The biggest unanswered question right now is

Reza Pahlavi's last exile, with Anwar Sadat in Egypt. Upon the Shah's death, Tehran radio proclaims: "The bloodsucker of the century has died at last."

what will happen to Iran if their imam dies. (Awareness of his own mortality indeed may be the only thing preventing Khomeini from declaring himself to be the "hidden imam," who has lived for nearly 1,200 years and, thus, is a man who cannot die.)

In late 1977, Khomeini said he would refuse any political role in Iran because of his advanced age—78 at that time. An Iranian physician who examined him, Dr. Seifeddine Nabavi, nevertheless said the ayatollah had the constitution of a man half his age.

Recent intelligence reports about his health, however, tell a different tale, or at least suggest that things have changed dramatically for the worse. Khomeini suffered a severe heart attack in 1980 which immobilized him for some time. He also suffers from prostate problems and generally has been slowed by old age. The intelligence reports, however, also say Khomeini has become very feeble. His movements are faltering, his voice quivers, his mind apparently wanders. As a result, authority has become badly divided in Iran. Most power now rests with the militant Shiite mullahs, led by Chief Justice Behesti, the so-called "hanging judge of Tehran." These conservative clerics are boldly trying to consolidate their position by gaining complete control of the Iranian political system.

The conservative clergy is being challenged by groups on both right and left—the nationalists in the provinces, the communists in the cities and the educated classes, who opposed the shah but who have also opposed the clergy's confiscation of the wealth they acquired under him. The largest such group is the moderates led by President Bani-Sadr.

So far, widening of the conflict has been prevented only by the personal intervention of Khomeini. However, the intelligence analysts think Khomeini's political power is clearly on the wane. As evidence, they note that many of the ayatollah's longtime aides—clerics and non-clerics who fled with him into exile and returned with him to positions of power—have recently been replaced by mullahs who remained in Iran to fight the shah. The latter owe their allegiance primarily to Beheshti, not Khomeini.

The analysts predict that Khomeini will be able to hold Iran together through his lifetime but that the country will rapidly fall apart thereafter. The Beheshti forces reportedly share this outlook and are moving quickly to consolidate their political power.

They are already uniting behind Ayatollah Hussein Ali Montezari as the future imam. The 58-year-old Ali Montezari, a hard-line conservative cleric allied with Beheshti, may well be strong enough to overcome the active opposition to him among most of the country's anti-clerical forces.

Iran with its imam has become a chaotic, almost anarchic state; wtihout the imam, who knows?

Abolhassan Bani-Sadr: A President In Search of a Power Base

Revolutionary Council meets—Former Prime Minister Mehdi Bazargan is in the extreme foreground, President Abolhassan Bani-Sadr sits at the head of the table, and head of the Islamic Republic Party and the Supreme Court, M. Behesti, sits at the far right. (WIDE WORLD PHOTOS)

Usually, when a man is elected president of a nation with an almost 75 percent vote in a crowded field, one would have to reasonably assume that man has a true power base.

Unfortunately for 46-year-old Marxist-oriented economist Abolhassan Bani-Sadr, the son of the late Ayatollah Sayed Nasrollah Bani-Sadr, of Hamadan, in west Iran, that was nowhere near true in his homeland. Despite Bani-Sadr's landslide victory in Iran's first-ever presidential election, power for many months afterwards continued to rest with the conservative clerics who held control of the Revolutionary Council, and with the militants who held the U.S. nationals hostage.

Bani-Sadr, it turned out, was on the run again, just as he had been, in one way or another, during all the years of his fight against Shah Mohammed Reza Pahlavi.

When the shah fell in January 1979, Bani-Sadr—a "man who is fearlessly independent and has the courage of his own individual convictions inspired by a deep faith in Islam," according to the Tehran Times—returned to his homeland as a leader of the revolution which he had helped lead from the exiled home in France of Ayatollah Rudollah Khomeini.

Nothing has ever come easy for Bani-Sadr, however, and his position in the new Islamic republic created by the ayatollah seemed doomed almost from the start. On November 6, shortly after the new regime took command, he was named acting foreign minister by the ayatollah, while also retaining his post as finance minister. Eighteen days later, he was dismissed from the foreign minister's job because of his moderate views, and particularly those he held regarding the detention of the U.S. nationals by the terrorist students who had taken over the U.S. embassy. The impetus for dumping Bani-Sadr from power was his decision to attend a United Nations meeting on the hostage crisis.

Adversity, however, was nothing new to Bani-Sadr. Long ago, he had predicted that he would emerge as Iran's first president and, although ousted by the all-powerful Khomeini, he refused to take a back seat now. When the ayatollah announced that elections would be held for president, Bani-Sadr announced his candidacy and won by a landslide. Khomeini, whom Bani-Sadr had served as adviser, could not have been too pleased with the election's

result, however. He had ousted Bani-Sadr and, in his place, had appointed Sadegh Ghotbzadeh, another adviser from the French exile days. But when the votes were counted, Khomeini's candidate, Ghotbzadeh, had garnered less than one percent of the vote.

After his election, Bani-Sadr told the press that the hostage crisis could be ended provided the United States agreed not to interfere in Iran's internal affairs. He made no demand for the shah's return to stand trial, or any other demands, for that matter. The holding of the hostages was repugnant to him and he saw the act as not in Iran's best interests. Bani-Sadr also told the world press it was free to report from anywhere in Iran, no matter whether the reports were good or bad for the country. (At the time of his election, most western newsmen had been thrown out of Iran.)

Almost immediately, however, Bani-Sadr's words were proven to be empty ones. The hostages were not going to be released, the militants declared. In this, they were supported by Khomeini. And the western press could not have any such freedom, said Foreign Minister Ghotbzadeh, a communications expert who headed Iranian television until his appointment. In this, Ghotbzadeh also was supported by Khomeini. Bani-Sadr was a leader without a power base.

Only the Iran-Iraq war saved Bani-Sahr, who as president took full command and managed to become a popular figure one more time. But only with the people—not the clergy.

As a youth, Bani-Sadr supported the nationalist movement then headed by Mohammed Mossadegh, destined to become Iran's most controversial prime minister. When Mossadegh's movement collapsed in 1953 as a result of a Central Intelligence Agency-directed coup which allowed the shah to return to Iran, Bani-Sadr went underground with the rest of the Islamic movement.

During the 1960s, Bani-Sadr's anti-shah activities landed him in jail twice, once in 1961 and again in 1964. Eventually, he left Iran and moved to France, where he joined with Khomeini in the ayatollah's blood battle against the shah.

Bani-Sadr has written 30 books on subjects ranging from theology, to sociology and economics. He is married (his wife translated Khomeini's work on the supremacy of religion in politics) and has two daughters and a son.

"These Are The Acts Of Animals!"

In June 1980, Bani-Sadr raises a significant (though generally unheeded) caution: "What happens if the hostages are tried and found not guilty? What then would have been the validity to have held them for seven months?" (WIDE WORLD PHOTOS)

As the Thames Television cameras rolled, Marine Sgt. William Gallegos spoke to an anxious world. It was December 6, 1979, the beginning of the second month of the hostage ordeal, and the world had been waiting for word on the fate of the U.S. nationals being held hostage by terrorists in the U.S. embassy compound in Tehran.

The Thames Television broadcast of an interview with Sgt. Gallegos would give them that word.

After telling his audience that he was being well-treated by his captors, Gallegos said: "I think the shah should be returned and that is not only my feeling, that is the feeling of all the hostages. I think he will get a fair trial, and if he is guilty, he is guilty, and if he is innocent, he is innocent . . .

"Nothing has been done for our release and it has been over a month."

Four days later, Gallegos was interviewed by NBC. Once again, he said he had not been mistreated and spoke well of his captors.

Gallegos' appearances had made him one of the best known of the hostages from the very beginning. "I didn't want to be," he said after his release.

Why, then did Sgt. Gallegos make those two controversial appearances before the world's television cameras?

As he told doctors at the "Freedom Hotel," the U.S. Air Force hospital in Wiesbaden, West Germany, the Iranians induced him to appear on the program by a very simple method: They beat him for two days until he agreed.

That wasn't the only thing his captors had done to the second youngest hostage. He was placed before one of the many mock firing squads; and he spent most of his 444 days in hell in solitary confinement with no human contact allowed.

Gallegos' story is only a small, and not even most horrifying, part of the tales of torture, both physical and mental, that the Iranians put the hostages through during their interminable ordeal; the atrocities were so brutal that it prompted former President Jimmy Carter to call them "unbelievable acts of criminal savagery," adding that "these are the acts of animals."

Following the arrival of the 52 U.S. nationals in Wiesbaden for their brief stay in the Freedom Hotel, they slowly began to unravel their individual tales of horror.

After the first few days of the hostage crisis, the U.S. nationals in the embassy compound were broken up into small groups and never again were they brought together until the final moments before they boarded the Air Algeria plane for freedom. What happened to some did not happen to all; but it really does not matter because all were subjected to torture of one kind or another.

They were, for example, given food that was

infested with insects and maggots, but only after their guards spit in the food; some of the hostages were beaten with rubber hoses; some were manacled to metal chairs for 15 days at a stretch, while others were forced to stand in stationary positions for several days at a time; some of the hostages were forced to stand outside in the severe cold during the night, while others were placed in air-conditioned rooms in the dead of winter with little or no clothes on; one hostage told of having been tied beneath a table for several days with a shotgun pointed at him, another of games of Russian Roulette.

Malcolm Kalp reported to his doctors that he had spent all but 70 of his days as a hostage in solitary confinement and was forbidden to send mail to his loved ones back home. It was his "punishment" for trying to escape. John McKeel was told one day that his mother had died and that he could go home and attend her funeral if only he would cooperate and "tell the truth" to his Iranian captors. McKeel, who lost a tooth when hit in the mouth with a rifle butt by one of his captors, did not know that his mother was alive and well until he called home from West Germany.

Moorhead C. Kennedy, Jr., Richard Queen, and a number of other hostages told of having been placed before mock firing squads. In one of his early letters to his wife, Louisa, Kennedy "said he was willing to accept this with serenity and die if necessary in the cause of his country," his wife told reporters after the ordeal had ended. "But the rest of the letter was just fond last remarks. So I knew from early on," she said. In other words, Mrs. Kennedy was saying, her husband had written, not a letter, but a will.

Marine Sgt. Jimmy Lopez told his Air Force doctors that he was kept in a small, ice-cold cell. On many of his 444 nights, he would awaken to find centipedes crawling all over his face.

· The hostages were kept in a constant state of insecurity and uncertainty, as their guards played good guy-bad guy with them. They were told repeatedly that the United States was making no effort to free them and that their captivity would last for years. Only the occasional letters brought to them in "show visits" gave them any inkling that their captors were lying.

"The evidence now is mounting from the discussions we are having, and it shows much worse and more extensive mistreatment than we previously had evidence of," State Department spokesman Jack Cannon told reporters in Wiesbaden two days after the hostages' release. It will be months before the full story of the physical and mental abuse the hostages were put through can be pieced together. But in a suit filed in the U.S. District Court in Washington, D.C., an earlier hostage, Marine Sgt. Kenneth Kraus, gives some idea of the kind of treatment the 52 U.S.

nationals had to endure.

Sgt. Kraus was not a hostage in the embassy takeover of November 4, 1979; rather, he was a hostage from the earlier takeover on February 14, 1979, Valentine's Day in the United States.

In his suit against the government of Iran, entitled "Complaint—Assault, Abduction, Imprisonment, Torture and Trial," he details the kind of treatment to which he was subjected. A complete text of his suit follows later; however, we will review the major points here. We ask the reader to keep in mind that when Sgt. Kraus was a captive, the situation was not as bad as when the embassy was again seized in November. His treatment, therefore, probably was "better" than those the later hostages were to receive.

As Sgt. Kraus tells his story, at about 10:30 a.m. Tehran time, the U.S. embassy compound was stormed by members of the Islamic Revolutionary Council. Under orders from his superiors, Sgt. Kraus surrendered to the attacking council members. Moments later, all of his personal possessions, including watch and wallet were taken from him and he was placed before a wall, as if to be shot. Shortly thereafter, he was interrogated for approximately 15 minutes, but he refused to give any information to his captors. For this, he "was punched about the face, had a bayonet poked in his ear, and had a rifle put in his face," the court documents say. A second interrogation followed soon after and, when he again "refused to answer their questions," he was hit in the head, stomach and ribs with a rifle, and otherwise assaulted, forcing him to the ground."

While on the ground, Sgt. Kraus had a shotgun placed at his head and he saw the trigger being pulled. The gun, however, had been moved slightly before it was fired; "instead of being struck directly, the shot richocheted off the floor, hitting him in the face, neck, chest and left arm."

He was then carried away, supposedly to a hospital, but his wounds were not treated. The next thing he knew, he was handcuffed, blindfolded and taken from the hospital to a waiting car, "all the while being hit and slapped in the face, his body physically assaulted, and his clothes ripped from his person."

For the next two days and nights, Sgt. Kraus was kept in a military compound. Throughout, he was blindfolded and handcuffed. A blanket was the only article of clothing he was allowed. His meals consisted of one cup of tea a day, one piece of stale bread a day, and very little water.

His next "home," where he would spend five days, was the Islamic Revolutionary Prison, where he was kept in a 15'x10'x12' cell with 25 other prisoners, one of whom was American, and thus did not speak much, if any, English. During the entire time he was in the prison, he was continuously interrogated and urged to sign various anti-U.S., pro-

Iran documents.

Sgt. Kraus never gave in to his captors' requests and was beaten in the head with a rifle for his stubbornness. "On one occasion," the court documents reveal, "a rifle barrel was forced into plaintiff's mouth, the rifle cocked, and the trigger pulled, only at which time he came aware that same was not loaded."

"On another occasion, approximately 20 of his interrogators spat and urinated upon (him).

"On a third occasion, (he) was placed on a table and, while his legs were held in a straightened position, his feet were continuously hit until his legs became numb and the pain in his abdomen and spine became so great that (he) lost consciousness."

According to the court documents, at least some of Sgt. Kraus' interrogators were members of Yasser Arafat's Palestine Liberation Organization, while the others were members of the Islamic Revolutionary Council. Throughout the period of his incarceration, the Marine sergeant was told that he was to be executed following his trial. That trial lasted only ten minutes and was held on February 20, 1979. Kraus was not allowed to defend himself.

Two hours later, Kraus was informed that the court had found him guilty as charged and had sentenced him to death on Washington's Birthday, two days later. Then, on February 21, 1979, Kraus was turned over to U.S. authorities and his long ordeal was over.

As a result of his treatments, or more appropriately *mis*-treatments, after his being shot, Sgt. Kraus suffered severe physical injury to his forehead and parts of his face, chest and left arm. Some of his injuries continue to bother him nearly two years later.

Sgt. Kraus' story, as we said, took place many months before the second hostage crisis. His treatment was mild compared with that of the 52 brave Americans who spent those bitter 444 days in Iranian captivity.

It is clear at this point that the U.S. government and President Carter were aware of the abuses and tortures long before the hostages were released. Kenneth Taylor, the former Canadian ambassador to Tehran, informed his government of them after he helped rescue six U.S. nationals who had escaped from the embassy compound on November 24, 1979.

Many of Carter's critics have been quick to lash out at the former President for having remained silent and "done nothing" after learning of the ordeal the citizens he was sworn to protect were being forced to suffer. Such criticism, however, is unfair; the record clearly shows that Jimmy Carter, no matter whether he was responsible for the embassy takeover in the first place, made every effort during those long 14 months to secure the release of the U.S.

nationals. To have "gone public" with the information of atrocities could only have served to make those atrocities even worse than they were. Instead, he chose to work day and night and to move heaven and earth to secure their freedom. For this he deserves only praise, not condemnation.

As for the hostages, no one is quite certain what the future holds for them. The physical reality of their captivity ended on January 20, 1981. But the psychological reality most likely will continue for some time to come; perhaps even for a lifetime.

In modern history, no other group of hostages has been held by terrorists for longer than 30 days and it is hard, then, to judge the plight of these 52 hostages by the plight of those who came before them. Still, some judgments can be made regarding what the former hostages now must face.

Based on studies of past hostages, the 52 could be subjected to feelings of humiliation, embarrassment, self-deprecation, nightmares, guilt, fear, family problems, and even physical and nervous disorders, according to Brian Michael Jenkins of the Rand Corporation, who has studied 77 incidents of international terrorism in which 348 hostages were released.

"The former hostage feels that he has gone through an experience which no one, save perhaps another former hostage, can understand," told the New York Times in an interview. "The experience is frequently cataclysmic, it may change the hostage's outlook on life itself. Some hostages have undergone profound religious experiences or a deepening of religious faith."

Jenkins, who prepared an unpublished report on hostages for the State Department and the Defense Advance Research Projects Agency, said, "It appears in some cases that the former hostage is treated in much the same way as a rape victim. Both of them are told not to talk about it; the entire episode is to be swept away, kept in the closet. Both kinds of victims also tend to feel that *they* are on trial . . .

"Many former hostages complained that they were treated like social pariahs, as if they were lepers. These are their own words."

Psychiatrist and former Deputy Assistant Secretary of State for Crisis Management Dr. Steve R. Pieczenik told The New York Times that, triggered by subtle cues in the environment, memories of their ordeal might set off physical traumas, extending from mild gastric distress to a serious heart attack.

Obviously, every individual is different and this hostage-taking certainly was different than any other. How each of the 52 U.S. nationals will fare in the years to come depends on each one's physical and psychological make-up. But the scars of their 444 days in hell will take a very long time to heal.

If they heal at all.

The Press Kept Hostage's Secret

For one hostage family, the 14 months the U.S. nationals spent in captivity were doubly frightening because they were living with a secret that, if made public, would undoubtedly have singled their hostage relative out for especially harsh treatment.

During the 14 months, perhaps a dozen or so reporters had learned of the secret and, in each case, were asked by the family to keep it a secret. In every case, the reporter complied, and not a word was printed or broadcast. The secret: hostage John Limbert's wife is an Iranian.

Limbert is a 37-year-old career diplomat who at the time of the seizure was the economics officer in the embassy in Tehran. His father, John Limbert Sr. also was a foreign service officer and the younger Limbert made his first visit to Iran the summer before he entered college to visit his father who was temporarily stationed there. The boy decided that he liked the country so much, he would study Middle-Eastern culture in college.

Four years later, after graduating with honors from Harvard with a major in Russian studies and a minor in Mideast culture, John Limbert Jr. joined the Peace Corps and ended up in Sanandaj, the capital of the Kurdistan portion of Iran. There he met Parvaneh, the daughter of a doctor, and they were married in 1966. Limbert and his new bride remained in Sanandaj for a year and then came to the United States for two years while Limbert worked on his Ph.D. at Harvard in Persian culture.

In 1972, they returned to Iran where they remained for two years. Limbert taught at Pahlavi University and his two children were born during this stay in Iran. The children, Mandanna and Shervin, therefore carry dual citizenship.

In 1974, Limbert and his family returned to Boston so he could finish his doctorate and then Limbert came to Washington to follow in his father's footsteps. He joined the Foreign Service.

After a stint as a desk officer in Washington, he was given successive Middle-Eastern assignments, first to the United Arab Emirates, then Abu Dhabi and finally Saudi Arabia. This was his last posting before he left for Tehran late in the summer of 1979.

Parvaneh Limbert and the children remained in Jeddah because of the declining political situation in Iran. In the months before the fall of the embassy, Limbert would commute to Jeddah to see his family.

Both the family and U.S. officials were terribly afraid of the consequences should word get back to the militants that one of their captives had an Iranian family. They also did not want it published that Limbert was fluent in several Middle Eastern langauges, including Farsi and Arabic. They believed that Limbert would then be given especially harsh treatment and be put to some kind of public relations use by his captors. Or might be considered a spy because of his language abilities.

So Limbert was described only as having a retired Foreign Service officer father and "a wife and two children." The State Department went to extraordinary lengths to protect the fact that the family was Iranian and was living in Saudi Arabia. In Jeddah, the family was kept under tight security both by U.S. embassy officials and the Saudis who shared the family's secret.

The Limbert family not only feared for the safety of John, but also worried about the intense pressure the situation was causing for Parvaneh who, although now a naturalized U.S. citizen, was still Iranian and still loved her country. The ordeal was especially difficult for her because her husband was being held by her countrymen.

But despite the best efforts by the family and the State Department, a small group of reporters, one by one, learned of the secret and most called John Limbert Sr. in Washington to confirm the fact. In each case, Limbert asked that the story be kept secret until John Jr. was free and, in every case, the reporter and their news services complied.

In the aftermath of the freeing of the hostages, Limbert thanked various newspersons for keeping the family secret. As he told one newsman, "This has given me a very high opinion of the press and their professionalism. I will always be grateful."

In Jeddah, Parvaneh also expressed her thanks and then participated in a short and emotional ceremony at the U.S. embassy before flying back to the United States with her children and the coming reunion with her husband.

A footnote: It appears that the militants knew at least of John Limbert's language ability. In some situations, he was used as a translator and several of the returned hostages have remarked that more than one militant had been amazed that Limbert spoke Farsi better than they did. In fact, it is reported that he gave Farsi lessons to at least one of the militants who wanted to improve his language ability.

The 53rd Hostage

Cynthia Dwyer Was the Wrong Person In the Wrong Place at the Wrong Time.

The ordeal finally is over for the 52 U.S. nationals who have been held hostage for over a year. They have been freed and the drama which began with the taking of the U.S. embassy in Tehran in November 1979 is at an end.

For them.

But not for hostage No. 53.

She is still being held and, at times, it seems that she has been forgotten.

Her name is Cynthia Dwyer and to the best of anyone's knowledge she has been held in an Iranian prison for well over six months.

It's a long way from a quiet, tree-lined street in Buffalo, N.Y., to the teeming jail outside Tehran, but the saga of Cynthia Dwyer is a strange one. For she truly was the wrong person in the wrong place at absolutely the wrong time.

Cynthia Brown Dwyer, her husband John, and their three children live in a nice middle-class area of Buffalo. John is an English professor at Buffalo State University and the couple is popular on campus.

Mrs. Dwyer mainly is a housewife, but she often has written for Humanist Magazine. When the Islamic Revolution came to Iran, she is said to have been fascinated by it and often spoke of Ayatollah Ruhollah Khomeini in glowing terms. She very much favored the revolution and had little good to say of the ousted Shah Mohammed Reza Pahlavi.

Mrs. Dwyer was certain the media was missing the real story in Iran by concentrating on the hostages and the revolutionary guard. The real story, she often said, was in the streets with the common people. People who were now much better off and happier under the ayatollah than they had been under the shah.

Using press credentials she had from the Humanist and the Buffalo Police Department, and money from a life insurance policy she cashed in, Cynthia Dwyer applied for a visa, which was granted, and flew to Tehran.

She arrived there last April 15, just two days before President Carter announced his ban on travel

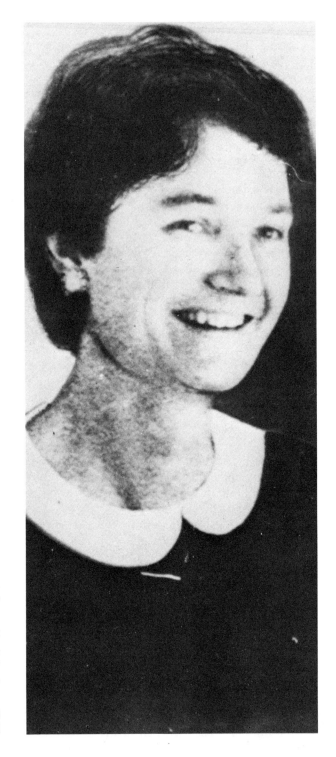

to Iran. She checked into the Tehran Hilton and set forth in search of her story. She was last seen by Westerners five days later on April 20 when she appeared at the gates of the occupied U.S. embassy with some letters for the hostages from their families. The revolutionary guards on duty took the letters and promised they would be delivered.

Five days later, on April 25, the failed rescue attempt was launched and 10 days after that, on May 5, Cynthia Dwyer was taken from her room at the Hilton by revolutionary guards.

"She is accused of being a CIA agent and a spy which is a categorical lie," says husband John from the family home in Buffalo. "She may have said the wrong thing, or simply been in the wrong place at the wrong time, but she was not only not a spy, she favored the revolution."

Since May 5, no one has seen or heard from Cynthia Dwyer. The U.S. government has made inquiries through the Swiss embassy in Tehran, but these inquiries have gone unanswered.

The day after she was taken, the public prosecutor in Tehran said she was in custody as a spy and would be formally charged and tried. Since that one statement, no further word ever has been said about her case nor has any word been received about her. Several subsequent Swiss inquiries have gone unanswered.

This has our State Department worried and somewhat at a loss about what to do. As State Department spokesman John Trattner explained at one point, "She was not seized as the other hostages were, she is not an employee of the U.S. government, we don't even know why she is being held. (Her) situation is so different . . . (from) the other hostages . . ."

As far as her husband and children are concerned, though, Cynthia Dwyer is as much a hostage as were the other 52 and what they are going through is no different than what the other 52 hostage families suffered during their long ordeal.

"The children miss her quite a bit," said John. "I do what I can, but obviously there is so much more she can do for them that I can't. I hope and pray she will come home . . . that this will all be over soon."

No sooner are the rescue planes downed in the desert than Khomeini announces: "Carter is prepared to resort to any crime and inflame the entire world!"

How Much Did Iran Get Back?

1) The United States placed on deposit with the Bank of England in an escrow account for Bank Markazei, the Iranian central bank, under control of the Algerian government, $8 billion of the $12 billion-plus in Iranian assets that had been frozen.

2) Upon certification that the hostages had been placed in U.S. hands in Algeria, the Bank of England transferred to various U.S. and European banks $5.1 billion to pay off in full, **100 cents on the dollar**, all outstanding borrowings by Iran from those banks. The remainder, $2.9 billion, remained in the account that now became the property of Bank Markazei.

3) 1.6 million ounces of gold, which had been on deposit with the Federal Reserve Bank of New York and owned by Bank Markazei, was transferred back to its control and remains on deposit with the Bank of England.

4) The remaining $4 million in Iranian assets will remain in an escrow account in the United States to be used to pay off claims against Iran to be decided by an international arbitration panel. Upon final resolution of those claims, the balance will be transferred back to Iranian control, if a balance exists.

How to pay, what to pay, whether to pay—key considerations in what William F. Buckley Jr. has labeled "a madcap policy of trying to determine how much money we should give Iran for Iran's hospitality to 52 Americans." (WIDE WORLD PHOTOS)

The 52 Who Came Home

Here are the name and brief profiles of the 52 U.S. nationals who were held hostage from Nov. 4, 1979, until Jan. 22, 1981, a span of 444 days.

1. AHERN, THOMAS LEO JR.: 48; McLean, Va., previously of Fond Du Lac, Wis.; wife: Gisela; daughter, 13; 1954 grduate of Notre Dame; has been with the State Department for almost 20 years. Sent to Tehran in June 1979. Job listed as embassy "attache," but really the narcotics control officer. Accused of being a "spy" when the embassy terrorists discovered a Belgian passport with his picture and the phony name "Paul Timmermans."

2. BARNES, CLAIR (CORDY): In his 20s; Of all the hostages, the least is known about him. In fact, his name did not appear on any list until the last several months. Nothing had been officially heard or said about him until a group photograph released by the Iranians after Christmas included him.

3. BELK, WILLIAM E.: 43; West Columbia, S.C.; communications and records officer for the State Department; a 23-year veteran of the Air Force and Marines; wife: Angela; two sons from former marriage.

4. BLUCKER, ROBERT OLOF: 53; North Little Rock, Ark.; a bachelor and 21-year State Department veteran. A specialist in oil, he previously served for seven years in embassy in West Germany. Was assigned to Tehran as economics officer and arrived there only the week before the attack on the embassy.

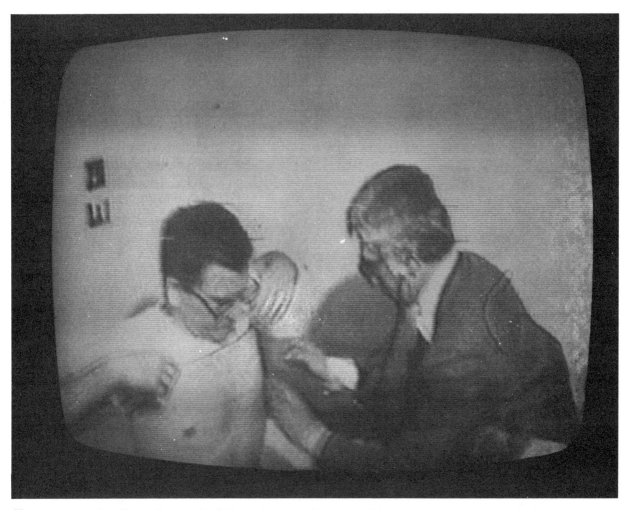

Hostage is examined by an Iranian Red Cross doctor in the occupied U.S. embassy in Tehran. The film was shot by militants and shown on Greek television. (WIDE WORLD PHOTOS)

5. COOKE, DONALD T.: 26; Ellicott, Md.; single. Parents: Ernest and Susan; seven brothers and sisters; serving his first foreign service tour as a State Department employee. Was sent to Iran in winter '78 as vice-consul. Iran was his first choice for a tour of duty.

6. DAUGHERTY, WILLIAM: 34; Tulsa, Okla.: single. Was in Iran as embassy political officer. One of three hostages accused of being CIA agent by militants.

7. ENGELMANN, LT. CMDR. ROBERT: 34; Hurst, Texas. A young career naval officer, had one week to go on his tour of duty in Iran as naval attache when embassy was taken. Shortly before takeover, told his parents he liked Iran and hoped to serve a second tour there.

8. GALLEGOS, WILLIAM (BILLY): 23, Pueblo, Colo.; single. Marine corporal guard; joined Marines in 1977 after high school. First served with 7th Supply Division in Okinawa. Tortured by Iranians for two days until he agreed to be interviewed by NBC News and British television. Parents: Theresa and Richard; sister: Letizia, 19; brothers: Richard, 20, and Ramon, 18.

9. GERMAN, BRUCE: 44; Rockville, Md.; wife: Marge. A 20-year State Department employee, was in Iran as embassy budget officer. In a February letter to Washington Post, complained that hostages had been "forgotten" by U.S. government. In his most recent letter, he complained about his eyesight. Mother: Mrs. Theresa Lodeski, Edwardsville, Pa.

10. GILLETTE, DUANE: 24; Columbia, Pa.; single. Parents: Ivan and Alberta. Joined U.S. Navy after high school. A communications and intelligence specialist transferred to Tehran from Malta in July 1979.

11. GOLACINSKI, ALAN: 31; Silver Spring, MD.; single. A State Department security officer, was sent to Iran in July 1979. Mother, Pearl, went to Paris to talk with French officials to get their aid in hostage release efforts.

12. GRAVES, JOHN: Reston, Va.; Wife: Bonnie; six children. A career foreign service officer in Iran, served since August 1979 as embassy public affairs officer. Previously served in Vietnam, Zaire, Madagascar, Togo and Cameroon. Wife became one of the most outspoken on how U.S. government handled hostage situation.

13. HALL, JOSEPH: 32; Elyria, Ohio (wife now living in the Washington, D.C., area); wife: Cherylnn. Parents: Dorothy and Zane; two sisters. A military attache with rank of warrant officer assigned to Tehran in August; previously assigned to U.S. embassies in Greece and Indonesia; enlisted in Army in 1968 after graduating from high school in Bend, Ore.

14. HERMENING, KEVIN: 21, youngest of the hostages; Oak Creek, Wis.; single. Marine sergeant assigned to Tehran as embassy guard in August 1979. Mother: Barbara Timm; father: Richard; brothers: Kelly, 19, and Christopher, 12; sisters: Laura, 16, and Amy, 15.

15. HOHMAN, DONALD R.: 39; Sacramento, Calif.; married, four children. A Marine Corps medic trained as a nurse, went into the army after high school. Previously served four tours of duty in West Germany. Sent to Iran during summer of 1979.

16. HOLLAND, COL. LELAND: 53, Fairfax, Va.; Wife: Mary, one daughter. Career Army officer, joined service in 1952 after college. Embassy's chief security officer. Wife was with him in Iran until shortly before fall of shah. Previously served in Vietnam, Italy and Germany. Was at Foreign Ministry at time of takeover. Held there. Had been a hostage in Iran once before, in February 1979; was released swiftly. Mother and brother live in Scales Mound, Ill.

17. HOWLAND, MICHAEL H: Bethesda, Md.; married. One of three hostages whom Iranian public prosecutor Hojatolislam Mousari Ardebili asked to have turned over to him.

18. JONES, CHARLES: 40, Detroit. Wife: Hattie; two children. A teletype technician and operator who previously served in Israel. An employee of the International Communications Agency. The only black not released because captors believed him to be a CIA agent.

19. KALP, MALCOLM: 42; Fairfax, Va. Another accused of being CIA agent. Two brothers live in Boston, Mass. area.

20. KENNEDY, MOORHEAD C. JR.: 50; Washington, D.C.; wife: Louisa; sons: Mark, 23, Philip, 21, Andrew, 19, Duncan, 15; 21-plus years with State Department as foreign service officer, given a special temporary three-month assignment in Tehran as economic and commercial officer. Had been there for six weeks at time of takeover. Previously served in Greece, Lebanon and Chile.

21. KEOUGH, WILLIAM F. JR.: 50, Brookline, Mass., formerly of Huntington, N.Y.; divorced, three children: daughters: Katie, 20, and Alyss, 19, of Boston; son: Stephen, in U.S. Navy. Huge man, 6-foot-9, 300-plus pounds. Was in wrong place at wrong time. The superintendent of the American School in Islamabad, Pakistan, was visiting embassy to collect student records. Former superintendent of the American School in Tehran.

22. KIRTLEY, STEVEN WILLIAM: 22; Little Rock, Ark.; single. Parents: Bettie-Jo and Troy; seven brothers and sisters; Marine corporal, a guard at the embassy since June 1979; enlisted in Marines three years ago.

23. KOOB, KATHRYN L.: 42; Farifax, Va., formerly of Jessup, Iowa; single. Parents: Elsie and Harold; five sisters. International Communications Agency and director of the Iran-American Society in Tehran, sent to Tehran in summer 1979. With State Department since 1970. Previously served in Ivory Coast, Upper Volta, Romania and Zambia.

24. KUPKE, FREDERICK LEE: 33; Rensselaer, Ind.; single; part Oklahoma Kiowa Indian. A State Department communications specialist, had only about two weeks to go on his tour when embassy fell. Was in Iran for an eight-week assignment and was due to return to U.S. Nov. 12, 1980. Previously served in Israel and, before that, in Thailand; parents: Arthur and Eleanor.

25. LAINGEN, BRUCE L.: 58; Bethesda, Md., formerly of Minnesota; wife: Penne; sons: Bill, 21, Chip, 19, and James, 14. A 31-year State Department career officer, was formerly deputy assistant secretary of state for European affairs. Sent to Iran in June 1979 as charge d'affaire, our highest-ranking diplomat in the country. Held at Foreign Ministry.

26. LAUTERBACH, STEVEN: 29; North Dayton, Ohio; single. Parents: Margaret and Eugene; brother: Victor; sister: Dale. State Department administrative officer at embassy since April 1979; his first foreign tour of duty. Joined the State Department after five years as a librarian in Fresno, Calif.

27. LEE, GARY EARL: 38; Falls Church, Va., formerly of New York City; wife: Patricia; daughter: Dana, 11. A career administrative officer for the State Department. Masters from Kent State University in 1970, joined State in 1971. Volunteered to serve in Iran six months before takeover because he was bored with Washington desk job. Arrived in May 1979. Previously served in embassies in Bombay, Madras, Damascus and Yemen.

28. LEWIS, PAUL EDWARD: 23; Homer, Ill.; Marine sergeant, single. Parents: Gloria, 43, and Phil, 49; sister: Annette, 19; brothers: William, 13, Patrick, 12. A guard who arrived at the embassy one day before the takeover; was a hometown football star and homecoming king.

29. LIMBERT, JOHN WILLIAM JR.: 37; married to an Iranian woman; son, 9, daughter, 11. A Harvard Ph.D. in Middle Eastern affairs, former Peace Corps volunteer in Iran, and had taught at Pahlavi University. Joined State Department in 1972 as political officer, assigned to embassy in Iran in the summer of 1979. Previously served in Abu Dhabi, the United Arab Emirates and Saudi Arabia. (See ''The Secret The Press Kept '')

30. LOPEZ, JAMES MICHAEL: 28; Globe, Ariz.; single. Parents: Mary, 45, and Jesse, 51; brothers: Richard, 28, Daniel, 19; sisters: Anna, 27, Lori, 17, Marcy, 10. Marine sergeant, a guard at the embassy who arrived in Tehran a month before the takeover. A Marine since April 1977, he helped 6 U.S. nationals escape on Nov. 4, 1975.

31. McKEEL, JOHN D. JR.: 27; Balch Springs, Texas; single. Marine sergeant and embassy guard. Father, John Sr. In a Christmas letter to his father, brought back by U.S. clergymen, said, ''I don't know how much longer we can hold out. We are all coming down sick. I have seen better conditions in a dog pound than we have here. We are not afraid of dying; I just wish it were for a cause. Love, John D.

32. METRINKO, MICHAEL JOHN: 34; Olyphant, Pa.; single. Parents: Harry, 69, and Alice, 65; brothers: Gregory, 37, and Peter, 31. A Georgetown University Foreign Service School graduate, served previous tours in Turkey and Iran. Was a consul in Tabriz. Speaks both Turkish and Farsi. At time of takeover, was embassy political officer.

33. MIELE, JERRY J.: 42; Mount Pleasant, Pa.; single. A 19-year State Department employee, has been in Iran since March 1979.

34. MOELLER, MICHAEL E.: 29; Quantico, Va., formerly of Caruthersville, Mo.; wife: Ann Lisa; two daughters: Amy and Lindsey. Parents: Keith and Doris of Loup City, Neb. Marine staff sergeant in charge of security detail at embassy. Transferred to Tehran from Pakistan in July 1979. Nine years in Marines.

Moeller's wife has filed a multi-million-dollar class-action lawsuit against the Iranian government on behalf of all the hostage families. (See pages 48–55).

In a Christmas 1979 letter to his wife, Moeller complained that his weight had dropped to 145 pounds (he's 6'3"). Iranian captors subsequently improved his diet.

35. MOORE, BERT C.: 45; Mount Vernon, Ohio; wife: Marjorie; three sons, one daughter, ages 16 to 23. Embassy consul for administration; sent to Tehran earlier in 1979 after serving three years at U.S. embassy in Zaire.

36. MOREFIELD, RICHARD H.: 51; San Diego, Calif.; wife: Dorothea; sons: Dan, 21, William, 20, Steven, 16, Kenneth, 14. With State Department for 25 years. Was consul general at embassy since mid-July 1979. Previously assigned to Colombia and, before that, Norway.

37. NEEDHAM, CAPT. PAUL M.: 30; Bellevue, Neb.; divorced; two sons: Paul, 8, and Neal, 5. Parents: Mary, 49, and Paul, 51. An Air Force officer on temporary assignment from Wright-Patterson Air Force Base, Dayton, Ohio. Embassy logistics supply officer.

38. ODE, ROBERT: 64 (eldest of the hostages); Falls Church, Va. With State Department for 35 years. Actually retired in 1975, has served from time to time in special short assignments. Was asked to go to Iran in October for 45 days as senior counsel to head visa section.

39. PERSINGER, GREGORY A.: 24; Seaford, Del.; single. Parents: Jackie and Lawrence; brothers: Lawrence, 27, Greg, 22, Ernest, 15; sister: Donna, 20. A Marine guard assigned to embassy since August 1979.

40. PLOTKIN, JERRY: 46; Sherman Oaks, Calif.; wife: Deborah, no children. A businessman who happened to walk into embassy moments before it was taken. In Tehran since October 1979; had started a personnel company, PSP Technical Services. Was going to try to bring in Korean laborers to work in Iran.

41. RAGAN, REGIS: 39; Johnstown, Pa.; single. Mother: Mrs. Martin J. Ragan. A 19-year Army veteran; master sergeant, in Iran since 1974. Sister: Patricia. Father is deceased. Won Bronze Star in Vietnam.

42. ROEDER, LT. COL. DAVID: 41; Washington, D.C., previously of White Fish Bay, Wis.; wife: Susan; son, 9; daughter, 15. A 20-year veteran of the Air Force, was sent to Tehran 3 days before takeover as air attache. Flew more than 100 combat missions in Vietnam.

43. ROSEN, BARRY: Brooklyn, N.Y.; wife: Barbara. Embassy press attache. A career International Communications Agency employee since 1967. Teacher; director of Iran-American Society; sent to Iran in September 1979.

44. ROYER, WILLIAM BLACKBURN JR.: 49; Houston, Texas; single. Employee of International Communications Agency since 1967. Teacher; director of Iran-American Society; sent to Iran in September 1979. Formerly taught in Morocco and Saudi Arabia.

45. SCHAEFFER, COL. THOMAS E.: 53, Falls Church, Va. Wife: Anita. Embassy military attache.

46. SCOTT, LT. COL. CHARLES W.: 48; Stone Mountain, Ga.; wife: Betty. In Iran for four months as assistant military attache.

47. SHARER, CMDR. DONALD A.: Chesapeake, Va.; wife: Francis. Naval air attache in Iran since April 1979. Was due to transfer to Norfolk, Va., as executive officer in flight squadron.

48. SICKMANN, RODNEY: 23; Krakow, Mo., grew up in Washington, Mo.; single. Parents: Virgil and Tony; sister, Judy Bhlenbeck. A Marine sergeant and embassy guard, arrived in Tehran Oct. 9, 1979, seven days after completing training at embassy school.

49. SUBIC, JOSEPH JR.: 24; Formerly of Bowling Green, Ohio; engaged to a British woman. Parents, Joseph Sr. (a retired Army colonel) and Helen, live in Redford, Mich. A Marine staff sergeant trained as military policeman, he was a guard at embassy.

50. SWIFT, ELIZABETH ANN: 40; political officer; single. Mother: Helen. A ranking foreign service officer in the embassy compound at time of takeover. A 16-year veteran of State Department, previously served in Philippines and Indonesia.

51. TOMSETH, VICTOR L.: 51; Springfield, Ore.; wife: Wallapa (a Thai); children: Christopher, 10, and Aranya, 3. Senior political officer at U.S. embassy in Tehran; sent to Iran in 1976 as consul in Shiraz. Was at foreign ministry at time of takeover. Previously served as cultural affairs officer in Rabat, Morocco, and Jeddah, Saudi Arabia. Also served in Thailand, where he met his wife. Has been in Foreign Service for 15 years. Mother: Lyla.

52. WARD, PHILLIP R.: early 40s; embassy administrative officer. Married, one daughter. Lives in Northern Virginia. Like Cordy Barnes, no further data available.

Documents And Protocols

IN THE UNITED STATES DISTRICT COURT IN AND FOR THE DISTRICT OF COLUMBIA

KENNETH KRAUS
Plaintiff

vs

STATE OF IRAN
Defendant

COMPLAINT—ASSAULT, ABDUCTION, IMPRISONMENT, TORTURE & TRIAL

AND NOW, to wit, comes the plaintiff above-named KENNETH KRAUS, and by his counsel Roger B. Reynolds, Jr., Esquire and George P. Wood, Esquire, files the within cause of action, whereof the following is a statement:

JURISDICTION

1. Jurisdiction of this Court is invoked pursuant to the provisions of Title 28 U.S.C. 1330, 1331, 1332 (a) and 1343.

2. This is a civil action for damages arising under the provisions of Title 28 U.S.C. Sections 1443(1) 1443(2) and 1605(a) (5) and Title 42 U.S.C. Sections 1983, 1985(3), 1986 and 1988 to seek redress for the deprivation by defendant, its officials, agents, instruments, servants and/or employees acting under color of law, of plaintiff's rights, privileges and immunities, secured him by the Constitution of the United States of America, and to seek compensation for personal injuries suffered by him, caused by the intentional and tortious acts and omissions of defendant, its officials, agents, instruments, servants and/or employees, while acting within the scope of their office, duties and/or employment, which personal injury occurred in the United States, as defined in Title 28 U.S.C. Section 1603(c).

3. In addition, plaintiff further invokes pendant and ancillary jurisdiction of this Court for the intentional assault, battery, kidnapping, false imprisonment and malicious prosecution of plaintiff by defendant, its officials, agents, servants and/or employees.

4. In addition, plaintiff further invokes pendant and ancillary jurisdiction of this Court for the deprivation of plaintiff's rights, privileges and immunities as guaranteed him by the Amity, Economic Relations and Consular Rights Treaty of August 15, 1955, (hereinafter referred to as "Consular Rights Treaty of 1955"); the Vienna Convenation on Diplomatic Relations of April 18, 1961; (hereinafter referred to as "Diplomatic Relations Treaty of 1961); the Vienna Convention on Consular Relations and Optional Protocol on Disputes, of April 24, 1963, (hereinafter referred to as "Consular Relations Treaty of 1963"); and, the New York Convention on The Prevention and Punishment of Crimes Against Internationally Protected Persons, Including Diplomatic Agents, of December 14, 1973, (hereinafter referred to as "Internationally Protected Persons Treaty of 1973")

5. The amount in controversy exceeds the sum of Ten Thousand ($10,000.00) Dollars, exclusive of interest and costs.

PARTIES

6. Plaintiff, Kenneth Kraus, is an individual, a citizen of the Commonwealth of Pennsylvania, who resides in Warrington,Bucks County,Pennsylvania.

7. At all times relevant to this Complaint, plaintiff was a citizen of the United States of America, and, a member of the armed services of the United States, to wit, the U.S. Marine Corps, with the rank and grade of Sergeant, E-5.

8. At all times relevant to this Complaint, plaintiff was detached from the U.S. Marine Corps and assigned to duty with the Department of State of the United States Government, who had direct supervision and control over him.

9. At all times relevant to this Complaint, plaintiff was assigned to the United States Embassy at Nicosia, Cyprus, with temporary additional duty at the United States Embassy at Tehran, Iran.

10. At all times relevant to this Complaint, plaintiff resided at, and was a member of the security staff

of the United States Embassy located at Tehran, Iran.

11. At all times relevant to this Complaint, the said United States Embassy was not only a diplomatic mission, but also, provided consular services.

12. At all times relevant to this Complaint, the said United States Embassy and compound in Tehran, Iran, constituted the United States, as defined by Title 28 U.S.C. Section 1603(c).

13. At all times relevant to this Complaint, plaintiff was a member of the staff of the diplomatic mission, located at Tehran, Iran, as defined by Article I, Section (c) of the Diplomatic Relations Treaty of 1961.

14. At all times relevant to this Complaint, plaintiff was a member of the consular post, located at Tehran, Iran, as defined by Article I, Section 1 (6) of the Consular Relations Treaty of 1963.

15. At all times relevant to this Complaint, plaintiff was an internationally protected person, as defined by Article I of the Internationally Protected Persons Treaty of 1973.

16. The United States of America and defendant were signatories to, and subsequently ratified, the Consular Rights Treaty of 1955; the Diplomatic Relations Treaty of 1961; the Consular Relations Treaty of 1963; and, the Internationally Protected Persons Treaty of 1973; and at all times relevant to this Complaint, all of same were in full force and effect.

17. At all times relevant to this Complaint, defendant was a foreign state, as defined by Title 28 U.S.C. Section 1603.

18. At all times relevant to this Complaint, the Ayatollah Ruhollah Khomeini, (hereinafter referred to as ''Khomeini''), was the Chief of State, agent, and instrument of defendant, as defined by Title 28 U.S.C. Section 1603(b).

19. At all times relevant to this Complaint, the Islamic Revolutionary Council, its members, agents, servants and/or employees, (hereinafter referred to as ''Council''), were an agency and/or instrumentality of defendant, as defined by Title 28 U.S.C. Section 1603(b), and were under the direct supervision and control of the Khomeini.

20. At all times relevant to this Complaint, the Komiteh, its members, agents, servants and/or employees, (hereinafter referred to as ''Komiteh''), were an agency and/or instrumentality of defendant, as defined by Title 28 U.S.C. Section 1603(b), and were under the direct supervision and control of the Khomeini.

21. At all times relevant to this Complaint, the Cherikhaye Fedaye Khalag, its members, agents, servants and/or employees, (hereinafter referred to as ''Fedaye''), were an agency and/or instrumentality of defendant, as defined by Title 28 U.S.C. Section 1603(b), and were under the direct supervision and control of the Khomeini.

''The nation voted for the Islamic Republic, and everyone should obey. If you do not obey, you will be annihilated.''—Ayatollah Khomeini (WIDE WORLD PHOTOS)

22. At all times relevant to this Complaint, the Islamic Revolutionary Court, its members, agents, servants and/or employees, (hereinafter referred to as ''Court''), were an agency and/or instrumentality of defendant, as defined by Title 28 U.S.C. Section 1603(b), and were under the direct supervision and control of the Khomeini.

23. At all times relevant to this Complaint, the Council, the Komiteh and the Fedaye acted within the scope of their authority, and pursuant to the specific orders and directions of the Khomeini.

ALLEGATIONS OF FACT

24. On February 14, 1979, at approximately 10:15 o'clock, a.m., plaintiff was situate in the security staff barracks, located at the rear of the United States Embassy compound, Tehran, Iran.

25. At such time, said compound came under fire from machine guns and rifles operated by the Council, the Komiteh, and the Fedaye located outside said compound.

26. At approximately 10:30 o'clock, a.m., the front gates to the said compound were stormed by a mob consisting of the said Council, Komiteh and Fedaye.

27. Plaintiff thereafter took his firearm, a shotgun; left the said security staff barracks; and, led two other Marines to the Embassy commissary, also located at the rear of the aforesaid compound.

28. Already inside said commissary were four-

teen Iranian and six American employees of the said Embassy.

29. Thereafter, said commissary came under attack by the Council, Komiteh and Fedaye, who were firing semi-automatic rifles.

30. In order to ensure the safety of the aforementioned civilians, plaintiff was directed, by radio, by the United States Ambassador William H. Sullivan to surrender.

31. Accordingly, plaintiff and the said two other Marines began to chant "surrender"; but, the firing continued.

32. However, following the killing of one of the said Iranian employees, by the aforesaid attackers, the firing ceased and the attack halted.

33. At such time, plaintiff arranged for the surrender of all personnel, located in the commissary, with the proviso that the remainder of the civilians would be released unharmed.

34. Said individuals then went outside, where plaintiff, and the other Marines, had their weapons, flak vests, helmets, watches and wallets taken by said attackers, each of whom wore an armband signifying that he was a member of the Council.

35. Plaintiff, the other Marines and the American civilian employees were then placed against a wall to be shot, when the attackers were stopped by their commander.

36. All of the Marines were then interrogated by the attackers, for the next ten to fifteen minutes, during which plaintiff was punched about the face, had a bayonet poked in his ear, and had a rifle put in his face.

37. Finally, a group of the attackers took plaintiff back inside the aforesaid commissary, for further interrogation.

38. However, when plaintiff refused to answer their questions, he was hit in the head, stomach and ribs with a rifle, and otherwise assaulted, forcing him to the ground.

39. While plaintiff was on the ground, one of the attackers leveled a shotgun at his head and fired; but, instead of being struck directly, the shot ricocheted off the floor, hitting him in the face, neck, chest and left arm.

40. Subsequently, plaintiff was carried away in a blanket to a hospital, the location of which is unknown, by the Council and Fedaye.

41. Shortly thereafter, his wounds being unattended, plaintiff was handcuffed, blindfolded and escorted from said hospital to a vehicle, by the Council and Komiteh, all the while being hit and slapped in the face, his body physically assaulted, and his clothes ripped from his person.

42. Plaintiff was then transported to a military compound, the location of which is unknown, where he spent the next two nights and days.

43. For his entire stay at said compound, plaintiff was blindfolded and handcuffed; his only clothing was a blanket; he was fed but one cup of tea, one piece of bread and some water per day; and, he was continuously interrogated.

44. Thereafter, plaintiff was transported to the Işlamic Revolutionary Prison, where he was kept for the next five days in a cell fifteen feet long by ten feet wide by twelve feet high, with twenty-five other prisoners, all of whom were Iranian citizens.

45. For the entire of the time he was incarcerated at said prison, plaintiff was guarded and continuously interrogated by the Council.

46. During said incarceration, his interrogators attempted to force plaintiff to sign anti-United States, anti-President Carter, anti-Shah of Iran and pro-Ayatollah Khomeini statements; and, when he refused to sign same, he was beaten and hit in the head with a rifle.

47. On one occasion, a rifle barrel was forced into plaintiff's mouth, the rifle cocked, and the trigger pulled, only at which time he became aware that same was not loaded.

48. On another occasion, approximately twenty of his interrogators spat and urinated upon plaintiff's person.

49. On a third occasion, plaintiff was placed on a table and, while his legs were held in a straightened position, his feet were continuously hit until his legs became numb and the pain in his abdomen and spine

Egypt's Anwar Sadat believes "What Khomeini preaches is not true Islam, for our religion does not speak of vengeance or hatred." (WIDE WORLD PHOTOS)

became so great that plaintiff lost consciousness.

50. On a fourth occasion, plaintiff was interrogated by members of the Palestinian Liberation Organization.

51. During the entire of this period, plaintiff was repeatedly told that he would be executed.

52. Finally, on February 20, 1979, plaintiff was tried before the Court upon the charges of murder, espionage and training savak, said trial lasting no more than ten minutes.

53. Prior to said trial, plaintiff was not presented with a written statement of the charges against him and was denied his right to properly prepare his defense thereto.

54. During said trial, no witnesses testified and plaintiff was denied his rights to counsel, to confront his accusors, to examine and/or cross-examine witness, and, to present a defense.

55. Two hours later, after being returned to his cell, plaintiff was informed that he had been found guilty of all charges and that he would be shot on Thursday, February 22, 1979.

56. The next day, Wednesday, February 21, 1979, plaintiff was transported to another prison, the location of which is unknown; and, later that afternoon, he was taken to the Komiteh Building, where he was released to the custody of the United States diplomatic staff.

57. Plaintiff was then transported to the United States Embassy in Tehran, Iran; and subsequently permitted to depart from Iran.

DAMAGES

58. As a result of his being shot, plaintiff suffered severe physical injury to his forehead, just above the right eye, his right cheek, the right side of his neck, his chest, and his left arm.

59. As a result of the physical beatings of plaintiff, he did suffer injury to his ribs, head, legs, back, abdomen and teeth.

60. Some of the physical injuries suffered by plaintiff, as aforesaid, continue and persist, to wit, the injuries to his right eye, right arm and teeth; and in the future, plaintiff will continue to suffer such injuries.

61. As a result of the shooting, kidnapping, beating, interrogation, torture, threatening, illegal detention and malicious prosecution of plaintiff, he did suffer mental fear, anguish, shock and injury, which mental injuries continue and persist, and in the future, plaintiff will continue to suffer such injuries.

62. As a result of the injuries suffered by him, plaintiff was required to seek, and for the foreseeable future, will be required to seek, medical treatment for same.

63. As a result of that which is averred above in paragraphs 1 through 57, plaintiff has suffered, and will in the future continue to suffer, a loss in wages and earning capacity.

CLAIMS FOR RELIEF

FIRST CAUSE OF ACTION

64. Above paragraphs 1 through 63 are realleged and incorporated herein by reference hereto.

65. Defendant, through its agents and/or instruments, to wit, the Khomeini, Council, Komiteh and Fedaye, intentionally and maliciously, did illegally arrest plaintiff, while in the United States, as defined by Title 28 U.S.C. Section 1603(c).

66. As a direct and proximate result of the conduct alleged above, plaintiff suffered the damages previously set forth.

SECOND CAUSE OF ACTION

67. Above paragraphs 1 through 66 are realleged and incorporated herein by reference hereto.

68. Defendant, through its agents and/or instruments, to wit, the Khomeini, Council, Komiteh and Fedaye, intentionally and maliciously, did assault, batter, torture, threaten and interrogate plaintiff, while in the United States, as defined by Title 28 U.S.C. Section 1603(c.)

69. As a direct and proximate result of the conduct alleged above, plaintiff suffered the damages previously set forth.

THIRD CAUSE OF ACTION

70. Above paragraphs 1 through 69 are realleged and incorporated herein by reference hereto.

71. Defendant, through its agents and/or instruments, to wit, the Khomeini, Council, Komiteh and Fedaye, internationally and maliciously did kidnap and remove plaintiff from the United States, as defined by Title 28 U.S.C. Section 1603(c), and take him to the State of Iran.

72. As a direct and proximate result of the conduct alleged above, plaintiff suffered the damages previously set forth.

FOURTH CAUSE OF ACTION

73. Above paragraphs 1 through 72 are realleged and incorporated herein by reference hereto.

74. Following plaintiff's removal to Iran, defendant, through its agents and/or instruments, to wit, the Khomeini, Council, Komiteh and Fedaye, intentionally and maliciously, did falsely imprison plaintiff.

75. As a direct and proximate result of the conduct alleged hereinabove, plaintiff suffered the damages previously set forth.

FIFTH CAUSE OF ACTION

76. Above paragraphs 1 through 75 are realleged and incorporated herein by reference hereto.

77. Following plaintiff's removal to Iran, defendant, through its agents and/or instruments, to wit, the Khomeini, Council, Komiteh and Fedaye, intentionally and maliciously, did assault, batter, torture, threaten and interrogate plaintiff.

78. As a direct and proximate result of the conduct alleged above, plaintiff suffered the damages previously set forth.

SIXTH CAUSE OF ACTION

79. Above paragraphs 1 through 78 are realleged and incorporated herein by reference hereto.

80. Following plaintiff's removal to Iran, defendant, through its agents and/or instruments, to wit, the Khomeini, Council, Komiteh, Fedays and Court, intentionally and malicously, did prosecute plaintiff, without reasonable or justifiable cause.

81. As a direct and proximate result of the conduct alleged above, plaintiff suffered the damages previously set forth.

SEVENTH CAUSE OF ACTION

82. Above paragraphs 1 through 81 are realleged and incorporated herein by reference hereto.

83. Defendant, through its agents and/or instruments, to wit, the Khomeini, Council, Komiteh and Fedaye, while acting under color of law, did intentionally and maliciously deprive plaintiff, while in the United States, as defined by Title 28 U.S.C. Section 1603(c), of his rights to freedom from cruel and unusual punishment, unlawful arrest, unreasonable search and seizure, and illegal detention and imprisonment, as secured by the Fourth, Fifth and Fourteenth Amendments to the United States Constitution, and by Title 42 U.S.C. Sections 1983, and 1988.

84. As a direct and proximate result of the conduct alleged above, plaintiff suffered the damages previously set forth.

EIGHTH CAUSE OF ACTION

85. Above paragraphs 1 through 84 are realleged and incorporated herein by reference hereto.

86. Defendant, through its agents and/or instruments, to wit, the Khomeini, Council, Komiteh and Fedaye, while acting under color of law, intentionally and maliciously, did conspire with each other, to deprive plaintiff, while in the United States, as defined by Title 28 U.S.C. Section 1603(c), of his rights to freedom from cruel and unusual punishment, unlawful arrest, unreasonable search and seizure, and illegal detention and imprisonment, as secured by the Fourth, Fifth, and Fourteenth Amendments to the United States Constitution, and by Title 42 U.S.C. Sections 1983 and 1988, all in violation of Title 42 U.S.C. Section 1985(3).

87. As a direct and proximate result of the conduct alleged above, plaintiff suffered the damages previously set forth.

NINTH CAUSE OF ACTION

88. Above paragraphs 1 through 87 are realleged and incorporated herein by reference hereto.

89. Defendant, through its agents and/or instruments, to wit, the Khomeini, Council, Komiteh and Fedaye, intentionally and maliciously, did neglect to take appropriate action to prevent that averred above in Paragraph 83, while plaintiff was in the United States, as defined by Title 28 U.S.C. Section 1605(c), all in violation of Title 42 U.S.C. Section 1986.

90. As a direct and proximate result of the conduct alleged above, plaintiff suffered the damages previously set forth.

TENTH CAUSE OF ACTION

91. Above paragraphs 1 through 90 are realleged and incorporated herein by reference hereto.

92. Following plaintiff's removal to Iran, defendant, through its agents and/or instruments, to wit, the Khomeini, Council, Komiteh, Fedaye and Court, while acting under color of law, intentionally and maliciously, did deprive plaintiff of his rights to freedom from cruel and unusual punishment, unlawful arrest, unreasonable search and seizure, illegal detention and imprisonment, and his rights to presentment or indictment of a Grand Jury in a capital case, to a public trial by an impartial jury, to be confronted with witnesses against him, to have compulsory process for obtaining witnesses in his favor and to have assistance of counsel, as secured by the Fourth, Fifth, Sixth and Fourteenth Amendments to the United States Constitution, and by Title 42 U.S.C. Sections 1983 and 1988.

93. As a direct and proximate result of the conduct alleged above, plaintiff suffered the damages previously set forth.

ELEVENTH CAUSE OF ACTION

94. Above paragraphs 1 through 93 are realleged and incorporated herein by reference hereto.

95. Following plaintiff's removal to Iran, defendant, through its agents and/or instruments, to wit, the Khomeini, Council, Komiteh, Fedaye and Court, acting under color of law, intentionally and maliciously, did conspire with each other to deprive plaintiff of his rights to freedom from cruel and unusual punishment, unlawful arrest, unreasonable search and seizure, illegal detention and imprison-

ment, and his rights to presentment or indictment to a grand Jury in a capital case, to a public trial by an impartial jury, to be confronted with witnesses against him, to have compulsory process for obtaining witnesses in his favor and to have assistance of counsel, as secured by the Fourth, Fifth, Sixth and Fourteenth Amendments to the United States Constitution, and by Title 42 U.S.C. Sections 1983 and 1988, all in violation of Title 42 U.S.C. Section 1985(3).

96. As a direct and proximate result of the conduct alleged above, plaintiff suffered the damages previously set forth.

TWELFTH CAUSE OF ACTION

97. Above paragraphs 1 through 96 are realleged and incorporated herein by reference hereto.

98. Following plaintiff's removal to Iran, defendant, through its agents and/or instruments, to wit, the Khomeini, Council, Komiteh, Fedaye and Court, intentionally and maliciously, did neglect to take appropriate action to prevent that averred above in Paragraph 92, in violation of Titale 42 U.S.C. Section 1986.

99. As a direct and proximate result of the conduct alleged above, plaintiff suffered the damages previously set forth.

THIRTEENTH CAUSE OF ACTION

100. Above paragraphs 1 through 99 are realleged and incorporated herein by reference hereto.

101. Defendant, through its agents and/or instruments, to wit, the Khomeini, Council, Komiteh and Fedaye, intentionally and maliciously, did deny plaintiff his rights to be permitted to travel freely and reside at his place of choice in Iran, and to gather and transmit information for dissemination to the public abroad, and otherwise communicate with other persons inside and outside Iran, as secured by Article II, Sections 2(a), 2(b) and 2(d) of the Consular Rights Treaty of 1955.

102. As a direct and proximate result of the conduct alleged above, plaintiff suffered the damages previously set forth.

FOURTEENTH CAUSE OF ACTION

103. Above paragraphs 1 through 102 are realleged and incorporated herein by reference hereto.

104. Defendant, through its agents and/or instruments, to wit, the Khomeini, Council, Komiteh, Fedaye and Court, intentionally and maliciously, did deny plaintiff the most constant protection and security within Iran; did fail and refuse to give plaintiff reasonable and humane treatment while in custody; did fail and refuse to notify plaintiff's diplomatic or consular representative, without unnecessary delay,

of his being in custody; did fail and refuse to promptly inform plaintiff of the accusations against him; did fail and refuse to give plaintiff all facilities reasonably necessary to his defense; and, did fail and refuse to give plaintiff a prompt and impartial disposition of his case, as guaranteed by Article II, Section 4 of the Consular Rights Treaty of 1955.

105. As a direct and proximate result of the conduct alleged above, plaintiff suffered the damages previously set forth.

FIFTEENTH CAUSE OF ACTION

106. Above paragraphs 1 through 105 are realleged and incorporated herein by reference hereto.

107. Defendant, through its agents and/or instruments, to wit, the Khomeini, Council, Komiteh and Fedaye, intentionally and maliciously, did fail and refuse to accord plaintiff fair and equitable treatment; and fail and refuse to refrain from applying unreasonable and discriminatory measures that would impair his legally acquired rights and interests, all in violation of Article IV, Section 1, of the Consular Rights Treaty of 1955.

108. As a direct and proximate result of the conduct alleged above, plaintiff suffered the damages previously set forth.

SIXTEENTH CAUSE OF ACTION

109. Above paragraphs 1 through 108 are realleged

Prime Minister Bazargan, who resigned upon learning of the Embassy takeover, had earlier said, "Khomeini has never been a real politician. He's never had the training needed to face the administrative responsibilities that he now finds on his shoulders." (WIDE WORLD PHOTOS)

On his return to the U.S., Charge d'Affairs Bruce Laingen says of hostage families, "They have demonstrated a nobility of courage which we will never forget," and of the hostages themselves, "We're prepared to go off and become rank-and-file citizens again, and not heroes in the press and panoply of the limelight." (WIDE WORLD PHOTOS)

and incorporated herein by reference hereto.

110. Defendant, through its agents and/or instruments, to wit, the Khomeini, Council, Komiteh and Fedaye, intentionally and maliciously, did violate Article IV, Section 3 of the Consular Rights Treaty of 1955, which provides that plaintiff's residence at the United States Embassy shall not be subject to entry or molestation without just cause, and that official searches of same shall be made only according to law and with careful regard to the convenience of plaintiff.

111. As a direct and proximate result of the conduct alleged above, plaintiff suffered the damages previously set forth.

SEVENTEENTH CAUSE OF ACTION

112. Above paragraphs 1 through 111 are realleged and incorporated herein by reference hereto.

113. Defendant, through its agents and/or instruments, to wit, the Khomeini, Council, Komiteh and Fedaye, intentionally and maliciously, did deny plaintiff the privileges and immunities accorded persons of his rank and status by general international usage; did prevent him from exercising all functions which are in accordance with such usage; and, did treat him in a manner less favorable than similar persons of any Third country, all in violation of Article XIII, Section 1, of the Consular Rights Treaty of 1955.

114. As a direct and proximate result of the con-

duct alleged above, plaintiff suffered the damages previously set forth.

EIGHTEENTH CAUSE OF ACTION

115. Above paragraphs 1 through 114 are realleged and incorporated herein by reference hereto.

116. Defendant, through its agents and/or instruments, to wit, the Khomeini, Council, Komiteh and Fedaye, intentionally and maliciously, did subject plaintiff to local jurisdiction for acts done in his official character and within the scope of his authority, in violation of Article XVIII of the Consular Rights Treaty of 1955, and Article 43 of the Consular Relations Treaty of 1963.

117. As a direct and proximate result of the conduct alleged above, plaintiff suffered the damages previously set forth.

NINETEENTH CAUSE OF ACTION

118. Above paragraphs 1 through 117 are realleged and incorporated herein by reference hereto.

119. Defendant, through its agents and/or instruments, to wit, the Khomeini, Council, Komiteh and Fedaye, intentionally and maliciously, did deny plaintiff his right to communicate with his consular officer, as secured by Article XIX of the Consular Rights Treaty of 1955.

120. As a direct and proximate result of the conduct alleged above, plaintiff suffered the damages previously set forth.

TWENTIETH CAUSE OF ACTION

121. Above paragraphs 1 through 120 are realleged and incorporated herein by reference hereto.

122. Defendant, through its agents and/or instruments, to wit, the Khomeini, Council, Komiteh, Fedaye and Court, intentionally and maliciously, did subject plaintiff to criminal prosecution in violation of Article 9, Section 1 of Diplomatic Relations Treaty of 1961, and Article 23, Section 1, of the Consular Relations Treaty of 1963.

123. As a direct and proximate result of the conduct alleged above, plaintiff suffered the damages previously set forth.

TWENTY-FIRST CAUSE OF ACTION

124. Paragraphs 1 through 123 are realleged and incorporated herein by reference hereto.

125. Defendant, through its agents and/or instruments, to wit, the Khomeini, Council, Komiteh, and Fedaye, intentionally and maliciously, did intrude upon and damage the United States diplomatic mission in Tehran, Iran, including the residence of plaintiff, in violation of Article 22, Section 1 of the

Diplomatic Relations Treaty of 1961.

126. As a direct and proximate result of the conduct alleged above, plaintiff suffered the damages previously set forth.

TWENTY-SECOND CAUSE OF ACTION

127. Above paragraphs 1 through 126 are realleged and incorporated herein by reference hereto.

128. Defendant, through its agents and/or instruments, to wit, the Khomeini, Council, Komiteh and Fedaye, intentionally and maliciously, did fail to fulfill its special duty to take all appropriate steps to protect the premises of the United States mission and consular premises, in Tehran, Iran, including the residence of plaintiff, against any intrusion or damage and to prevent any disturbance of the peace of same or impairment of its dignity, as imposed by Article 22, Section 2, of the Diplomatic Relations Treaty of 1961, and Article 31, Sections 1 and 3 of the Consular Relations Treaty of 1963.

129. As a direct and proximate result of the conduct alleged above, plaintiff suffered the damages previously set forth.

TWENTY-THIRD CAUSE OF ACTION

130. Above paragraphs 1 through 129 are realleged and incorporated herein by reference hereto.

131. Defandant, through its agents and/or instruments, to wit, the Khomeini, Council, Komiteh and Fedaye, intentionally and maliciously, did search and requisition the premises and property of the United States mission in Tehran, Iran, including the residence and property of plaintiff, in violation of Article 22, Section 3, of the Diplomatic Relations Treaty of 1961.

132. As a direct and proximate result of the conduct alleged above, plaintiff suffered the damages previously set forth.

TWENTY-FOURTH CAUSE OF ACTION

133. Above paragraphs 1 through 132 are realleged and incorporated herein by reference hereto.

134. Defendant, through its agents and/or instruments, to wit, the Khomeini, Council, Komiteh and Fedaye, intentionally and maliciously, did deny plaintiff his right to freedom of movement and travel within Iran, as guaranteed by Article 26 of the Diplomatic Relations Treaty of 1961, and Article 34 of the Consular Relations Treaty of 1963.

135. As a direct and proximate result of the conduct alleged above, plaintiff suffered the damages previously set forth.

TWENTY-FIFTH CAUSE OF ACTION

136. Above paragraphs 1 through 135 are realleged and incorporated herein by reference hereto.

137. Defendant, through its agents and/or instruments, to wit, the Khomeini, Council, Komiteh and Fedaye, intentionally and maliciously, did arrest and detain plaintiff, treat him without due respect, and fail and refuse to take all appropriate steps to prevent an attack on his person, freedom and dignity, in violation of Articles 29 and 37, of the Diplomatic Relations Treaty of 1961.

138. As a direct and proximate result of the conduct alleged above, plaintiff suffered the damages previously set forth.

TWENTY-SIXTH CAUSE OF ACTION

139. Above paragraphs 1 through 138 are realleged and incorporated herein by reference hereto.

140. Defendant, through its agents and/or instruments, to wit, the Khomeini, Council, Komiteh, Fedaye and Court, intentionally and maliciously, did criminally prosecute plaintiff, in violation of Article 31, Section 1 and Article 37 of the Diplomatic Relations Treaty of 1961, and Article 43 of the Consular Relations Treaty of 1963.

141. As a direct and proximate result of the conduct alleged above, plaintiff suffered the damages previously set forth.

TWENTY-SEVENTH CAUSE OF ACTION

142. Above paragraphs 1 through 141 are realleged and incorporated herein by reference hereto.

143. Defendant, through its agents and/or instruments, to wit, the Khomeini, Council, Komiteh, Fedaye, intentionally and maliciously, did fail and refuse to provide plaintiff with the facilities to leave Iran at the earliest possible moment, in violation of Article 44 of the Diplomatic Relations Treaty of 1961, and Article 26 of the Consular Relations Treaty of 1963.

144. As a direct and proximate result of the conduct alleged above, plaintiff suffered the damages previously set forth.

TWENTY-EIGHTH CAUSE OF ACTION

145. Above paragraphs 1 through 144 are realleged and incorporated herein by reference hereto.

146. Defendant, through its agents and/or instruments, to wit, the Khomeini, Council, Komiteh and Fedaye, intentionally and maliciously did deny plain-

tiff his right to communicate with his consular office, in violation of Article 36, Section 1(a) of the Consular Relations Treaty of 1963.

147. As a direct and proximate result of the conduct alleged above, plaintiff suffered the damages previously set forth.

TWENTY-NINTH CAUSE OF ACTION

148. Above paragraphs 1 through 147 are realleged and incorporated herein by reference hereto.

149. Defendant, through its agents and/or instruments, to wit, the Khomeini, Council, Komiteh and Fedaye, intentionally and maliciously, did fail to inform plaintiff's consular post, without delay, of his arrest and detention, and did fail and refuse to permit him a visit from his consular officer, in violation of Article 36, Sections 1(b) and 1(c) of the Consular Relations Treaty of 1963.

150. As a direct and proximate result of the conduct alleged above, plaintiff suffered the damages previously set forth.

THIRTIETH CAUSE OF ACTION

151. Above paragraphs 1 through 150 are realleged and incorporated herein by reference hereto.

152. Defendant, through its agents and/or instruments, to wit, the Khomeini, Council, Komiteh and Fedaye, intentionally and maliciously, did fail and refuse to promptly notify the head of the United States consular post, of plaintiff's arrest, detention and pending trial, in violation of Article 42 of the Consular Relations Treaty of 1963.

153. As a direct and proximate result of the conduct alleged above, plaintiff suffered the damages previously set forth.

THIRTY-FIRST CAUSE OF ACTION

154. Above paragraphs 1 through 153 are realleged and incorporated herein by reference hereto.

155. Defendant, through its agents and/or instruments, to wit, the Khomeini, Council, Komiteh, and Fedaye, intentionally and maliciously, did fail and refuse to provide plaintiff with special protection from an attack on his person, freedom and dignity, as required by Article 1 Section 1(b) of the Internationally Protected Persons Treaty of 1973.

156. As a direct and proximate result of the conduct alleged above, plaintiff suffered the damages previously set forth.

THIRTY-SECOND CAUSE OF ACTION

157. Above paragraphs 1 through 156 are re-

alleged and incorporated herein by reference hereto.

158. Defendant, through its agents and/or instruments, to wit, the Khomeini, Council, Komiteh and Fedaye, intentionally and maliciously, did fail and refuse to take all practicable measures to ensure the prevention of (a) those crimes constituting an attack on plaintiff's person and liberty, and the attempt and threat thereof; and (b) a violent attack upon plaintiff's residence, as required by Article 4 of the Internationally Protected Persons Treaty of 1973.

159. As a direct and proximate result of the conduct alleged above, plaintiff suffered the damages previously set forth.

THIRTY-THIRD CAUSE OF ACTION

160. Above paragraphs 1 through 159 are realleged and incorporated herein by reference hereto.

161. Defendant, through its agents and/or instruments, to wit, the Khomeini, Council, Komiteh, Fedaye and Court, by their conduct aforesaid, intentionally and maliciously, did inflict emotional distress upon the plaintiff.

162. As a direct and proximate result of the conduct alleged above, plaintiff suffered the damages previously set forth.

THIRTY-FOURTH CAUSE OF ACTION

163. Above paragraphs 1 through 162 are realleged and incorporated herein by reference hereto.

164. Defendant, through its agents and/or instruments, to wit, the Khomeini, Council, Komiteh and Court, by their conduct as aforesaid, intentionally and maliciously, did act with wilfull, wanton, and reckless negligence in permitting that which occurred to plaintiff, as set forth above.

165. As a direct and proximate result of the conduct alleged above, plaintiff suffered the damages previously set forth.

THIRTY-FIFTH CAUSE OF ACTION

166. Above paragraphs 1 through 165 are realleged and incorporated herein by reference hereto.

167. Defendant, through its agents and/or instruments, to wit, the Khomeini, Council, Komiteh and Court, by their conduct as aforesaid, intentionally and maliciously, did act with wilfull, wanton and reckless negligence in failing to prevent plaintiff from being harmed, as set forth above.

168. As a direct and proximate result of the conduct alleged above, plaintiff suffered the damages previously set forth.

THIRTY-SIXTH CAUSE
OF ACTION

169. Above paragraphs 1 through 159 are re-alleged and incorporated herein by reference hereto.

170. In addition to the causes of action set forth above, causes of action are stated against defendant, under the Fourth, Fifth, Sixth and Fourteenth Amendments to the United States Constitution, independent of other statutory or non-statutory causes of action.

WHEREFORE, in consideration of all of the foregoing, your plaintiff, Kenneth Kraus, respectfully prays your Honorable Court, to enter judgment against defendant State of Iran:

1. For compensatory damages in the amount of Twenty Million ($20,000,000.00) Dollars, exclusive of interests and costs;

2. For punitive damages in the amount of Forty Million ($40,000,000.00) Dollars;

3. For the interest, court costs, expenses and reasonable attorney's fees; and,

4. For such other and further relief as your Honorable Court may deem just, proper and equitable.

Respectfully submitted,

Roger B. Reynolds J., Esq.
George P. Wood, Esq.
N. Marshall Meyers

Attorneys for Plaintiff

JURY

Plaintiff demands trial by jury of twelve as to all claims so triable.

Roger B. Reynolds, Jr., Esq.
George P. Wood, Esq.
N. Marshall Meyers

"Death to Carter" and "Kill the American dogs" chant the Iranian mobs, while Khomeini fuels the fire with "It is a struggle between Islam and the infidels."

Declaration

Following is the English-language text of the Declaration of the Democratic and Popular Republic of Algeria initialed Monday in Algiers by Deputy Secretary of State Warren Christopher. The Algerian declaration was one of three documents signed by Christopher setting down terms for the release of the American hostages in Iran.

The government of the Democratic and Popular Republic of Algeria, having been requested by the governments of the Islamic Republic of Iran and the United States of America to serve as an intermediary in seeking a mutually acceptable resolution of the crisis in their relations arising out the detention of the 52 United States nationals in Iran, has consulted extensively with the two governments as to the commitments which each is willing to make in order to resolve the crisis within the framework of the four points stated in the resolution of Nov. 2, 1980, of the Islamic Consultative Assembly of Iran.

On the basis of formal adherences received from Iran and the United States, the government of Algeria now declares that the following interdependent commitments have been made by the two governments:

General principles

The undertakings reflected in this declaration are based on the following general principles:

A. Within the framework of and pursuant to the provisions of the two Declarations of the Government of the Democratic and Popular Republic of Algeria, the United States will restore the financial position of Iran, in so far as possible, to that which existed prior to Nov. 14, 1979. In this context, the United States commits itself to insure the mobility and free transfer of all Iranian assets within its jurisdiction as set forth in Paragraphs 4 to 9.

B. It is the purpose of both parties, within the framework of and pursuant to the provisions of the two Declarations of the Government of the Democratic and Popular Republic of Algeria, to terminate all litigation as between the government of each party and the nationals of the other, and to bring about the settlement and termination of all such claims through binding arbitration.

Through the procedures provided in the Declaration relating to the Claims Settlement Agreement,

An Executive order from President Carter froze some $8 billion in Iranian assets held by U.S. banks. To unfreeze them thereafter, advised one legal expert, would be ''like putting an omelet back into the egg.'' (WIDE WORLD PHOTOS)

the United States agrees to terminate all legal proceedings in United States courts involving claims of United States persons and institutions against Iran and its state enterprises, to nullify all attachments and judgments obtained therein, to prohibit all further litigation based on such claims, and to bring about the termination of such claims through binding arbitration.

I: Nonintervention in Iranian affairs.

1. The United States pledges that it is and from now on will be the policy of the United States not to intervene, directly or indirectly, politically or militarily, in Iran's internal affairs.

II and III: Return of Iranian assets and settlement of U.S. claims.

2. Iran and the United States (hereinafter ''the parties'') will immediately select a mutually agreeable central bank (hereinafter ''the Central Bank'') to act, under the instructions of the government of Algeria and the Central Bank of Algeria (hereinafter the ''Algerian Central Bank'') as depository of the escrow and security funds hereinafter prescribed and will promptly enter into depository arrangements with the Central Bank in accordance with the terms of this declaration. All funds placed in escrow with the Central Bank pursuant to this declaration shall be held in an account in the name of the Algerian Central Bank. Certain procedures for implementing the obligations set forth in this declaration and in the Declaration of the Democratic and Popular Republic of Algeria concerning the settlement of claims by the government of the United States and the government of the Islamic Republic of Iran (hereinafter ''the Claims Settlement Agreement'') are separately set forth in certain undertakings of the government of the United States of America and the government of the Islamic Republic of Iran with respect to the declaration of the Democratic and Popular Republic of Algeria.

3. The depository arrangements shall provide that, in the event that the government of Algeria certifies to the Algerian Central Bank that the 52 U.S. nationals have safely departed from Iran, the Algerian Central Bank will thereupon instruct the Central Bank to transfer immediately all monies or other assets in escrow with the Central Bank pursuant to this declaration, provided that at any time prior to the making of such certification by the government of Algeria, each of the two parties, Iran and the United States shall have the right of 72 hours notice to terminate its commitments under this declaration.

If such notice is given by the United States and the foregoing certification is made by the government of Algeria within 72-hour period of notice, the Algerian Central Bank will thereupon instruct the Central Bank to transfer such monies and assets. If the 72-hour period of notice by the United States expires without such a certification having been made, or if the notice of termination is delivered by Iran, the Algerian Central Bank will thereupon instruct the Central Bank to return all such monies and assets to the United States, and thereafter the commitments reflected in this declaration shall be of no further force and effect.

Assets in the Federal Reserve Bank

4. Commencing upon completion of the requisite escrow arrangement with the Central Bank, the United States will bring about the transfer to the Central Bank of all gold bullion which is owned by Iran and which is in the custody of the Federal Reserve Bank of New York, together with all other Iranian assets (or the cash equivalent thereof) in the custody of the Federal Reserve Bank of New York, to be held by the Central Bank in escrow until such time as their transfer or return is required by Paragraph 3 above.

Assets in foreign branches of U.S. banks

5. Commencing upon the completion of the requisite escrow arrangements with the Central Bank, the United States will bring about the transfer to the Central Bank, to the account of the Algerian Central Bank, of all Iranian deposits and securities which on or after Nov. 14, 1979 stood upon the books of overseas banking offices of U.S. banks, together with interest thereon through Dec. 31, 1980, to be held by the Central Bank to the account of the Algerian Central Bank, in escrow until such time as their transfer or return is required in accordance with

Paragraph 3 of this Declaration.

Assets in U.S. branches of U.S. banks

6. Commencing with adherence by Iran and the United States to this declaration and the Claims Settlement Agreement attached hereto, and following the conclusion of arrangements with the Central Bank for the establishment of the interest-bearing security account specified in that agreement and Paragraph 7 below, which arrangements will be concluded within 30 days from the date of this declaration, the United States will act to bring about the transfer to the Central Bank within six months from such date of all Iranian deposits and securities in U.S. banking institutions in the United States together with interest thereon, to be held by the Central Bank in escrow until such time as their transfer or return is required by Paragraph 3.

7. As funds received by the Central Bank pursuant to Paragraph 6 above, the Algerian Central Bank shall direct the Central Bank to (1) transfer one-half of each such receipt to Iran and (2) place the other half in a special interest-bearing security account in the Central Bank, until the balance in the security account has reached the level of $1 billion. After the $1 billion balance has been achieved, the Algerian Central Bank shall direct all funds received pursuant to Paragraph 6 to be transferred to Iran. All funds in the security account are to be used for the sole purpose of securing the payment of, and paying, claims against Iran in accordance with the Claims Settlement Agreement. Whenever the Central Bank shall thereafter notify Iran that the balance in the security account has fallen below $500 million, Iran shall promptly make new deposits sufficient to maintain a minimum balance of $500 million in the account. The account shall be so maintained until the President of the Arbitral Tribunal established pursuant to the Claims Settlement Agreement has certified to the Central Bank of Algeria that all arbitral awards against Iran have been satisfied in accordance with the Claims Settlement Agreement, at which point any amount remaining in the security account shall be transferred to Iran.

Other assets in the U.S. and abroad

8. Commencing with the adherence of Iran and the United States to this declaration and the attached Claims Settlement Agreement and the conclusion of arrangements for the establishment of the security account, which arrangements will be concluded within 30 days from the date of this declaration, the United States will act to bring about the transfer to the Central Bank of all Iranian financial assets (meaning funds or securities) which are located in the United States and abroad, apart from those assets referred to in Paragraphs 5 and 6 above, to be held by the Central Bank in escrow until their transfer or return is required by Paragraph 3 above.

9. Commencing with the adherence by Iran and the United States to this declaration and the attached Claims Settlement Agreement and the making by the government of Algeria of the certification described in Paragraph 3 above, the United States will arrange, subject to the provisions of U.S. law applicable prior to Nov. 14, 1979, for the transfer of all Iranian properties which are located in the United States and abroad and which are not within the scope of the preceding paragraphs.

Nullification of sanctions and claims

10. Upon the making by the government of Algeria of the certification described in Paragraph 3 above, the United States will revoke all trade sanctions which were directed against Iran in the period Nov. 4, 1979 to date.

11. Upon the making by the government of Algeria of the certification described in Paragraph 3 above, the United States will promptly withdraw all claims now pending against Iran before the International Court of Justice and will thereafter bar and preclude the prosecution against Iran of any pending or future claims of the United States or United States nationals arising out of events occuring before the date of this declaration related to (A) the seizure o the 52 United States nationals on Nov. 4, 1979, (B) their subsequent detention (C) injury to the United States property or property of the United States nationals within the United States Embassy compound in Tehran after Nov. 3, 1979, and (D) injury to the United

Bani-Sadr, torn between two positions: "The U.S., as a land of free people, can either submit to the humiliation of surrendering a sick man [the Shah] to a regime such as the Islamic Republic of Iran, nor can it take any pleasure in the humiliation of saving the lives of about 50 to 60 of its citizens by turning over this sick man." (WIDE WORLD PHOTOS)

States nationals or their property as a result of popular movements in the course of the Islamic revolution in Iran which were not an act of the government of Iran. The United States will also bar and preclude the prosecution against Iran in the courts of the United States of any pending or future claims asserted by persons other than the United States nationals arising out of the events specified in the preceding sentence.

IV: Return of the assets of the family of the former shah

12. Upon the making by the government of Algeria of the certification describe in Paragraph 3 above, the United States will freeze, and prohibit any transfer of, property and assets in the United States within the control of the estate of the former shah or any close relative of the former shah served as a defendant in U.S. ligitation brought by Iran to recover such property and assets as belonging to Iran. As to any such defendant, including the estate of the former shah, the freeze order will remain in effect until such ligitation is finally terminated. Violation of the freeze order shall be subject to the civil and criminal penalties prescribed by U.S. law.

13. Upon the making by the government of Algeria of the certification described in Paragraph 3 above, the United States will order all persons within U.S. jurisdiction to report to the U.S. Treasury, within 30 days, for transmission to Iran, all information known to them, as of Nov. 3, 1979 and as of the date of the order with respect to the property and assets referred

Major stumbling blocks in any negotiations—the advisability, the feasibility, even the legality of returning the shah's wealth to Iran.

to in Paragraph 12. Violation of the requirement will be subject to civil and criminal penalties described by U.S. law.

14. Upon the making by the government of Algeria of the certification described in Paragraph 3 above, the United States will make known to all appropriate U.S. courts that in any litigation of the kind described in Paragraph 12 above the claims of Iran should not be considered legally barred either by sovereign immunity principles or by the act of state doctrine and that Iranian decrees and judgments relating to such assets should be enforced by such courts in accordance with United States law.

15. As to any judgment of a U.S. court which calls for the transfer of any property of assets to Iran, the United States hereby guarantee the enforcement of the final judgment to the extent that the property or assets exist within the United States.

16. If any dispute arises between the parties as to whether the United States has fulfilled any obligation imposed upon it by Paragraphs 12-15 inclusive, Iran may submit the dispute to binding arbitration by the tribunal established by, and in accordance with the provisions of, the claims settlement agreement. If the tribunal determines that Iran has suffered a loss as a result of a failure by the United States to fulfill such obligation, it shall make an appropriate award in favor of Iran which may be enforced by Iran in the courts of any nation in accordance with its laws.

Settlement of Disputes

17. If any other dispute arises between the parties as to the interpretation or performance of any provision of this declaration, either party may submit the dispute to binding arbitration by the tribunal established by, and in accordance with the provisions of, the claims settlement agreement. Any decision of the tribunal with respect to such dispute, including any award of damages to compensate for a loss resulting from a breach of this declaration or the claims settlement agreement, may be enforced by the prevailing party in the courts of any nation in accordance with its laws.

Claims Agreement

Following is the English-language text of the agreement signed by Deputy Secretary of State Warren Christopher to set up a method to settle claims filed by the United States or its citizens against Iran and claims filed by Iran or its citizens agains the United States:

The Government of the Democratic and Popular Republic of Algeria, on the basis of formal notice of adherence received from the Government of the Islamic Republic of Iran and the Government of the United States of America, now declares that Iran and the United States have agreed as follows:

"Thank you, America, and God bless all of you."—
Bruce Laingen (WIDE WORLD PHOTOS)

Article I

Iran and the United States will promote the settlement of the claims described in Article II by the parties directly concerned. Any such claims not settled within six months from the date of entry into force of this agreement shall be submitted to binding third-party arbitration in accordance with the terms of the agreement. The aforementioned six months' period may be extended once by three months at the request of either party.

Article II

1. An International Arbitral Tribunal (the Iran-United States Claims Tribunal) is hereby established for the purpose of deciding claims of nationals of the United States against Iran and claims of nationals of Iran against the United States and any counterclaim which arises out of the same contract, transaction or occurrence that constitutes the subject matter of that national's claim, if such claims and counterclaims are outstanding on the date of this agreement, whether or not filed with any court, and arise out of debts, contracts (including transactions which are the subject of letters of credit or bank guarantees), expropriations or other measures affecting property rights, excluding claims described in Paragraph 11 of the Declaration of the Government of Algeria of Jan. 19, 1981, and claims arising out of the actions of the United States in response to the conduct described in such paragraph, and excluding claims arising under a binding contract between the parties specifically providing that any disputes thereunder shall be within the sole jurisdiction of the competent Iranian courts in response to the Majlis position.

2. The Tribunal shall also have jurisdiction over official claims of the United States and Iran against each other arising out of contractual arrangements between them for the purchase and sale of goods and services.

3. The Tribunal shall have jurisdiction, as specified in Paragraphs 16-17 of the Declaration of the Government of Algeria of Jan. 19, 1981, over any dispute as to the interpretation or performance of any provision of that declaration.

Article III

1. The Tribunal shall consist of nine members or such larger multiple of three as Iran and the United States may agree are necessary to conduct its business expeditiously. Within 90 days after the entry

into force of this agreement, each government shall appoint one-third of the members. Within 30 days after their appointment, the members so appointed shall by mutual agreement select the remaining third of the Tribunal. Claims may be decided by the full Tribunal or by a panel of three members of the Tribunal as the President shall determine. Each such panel shall be composed by the President and shall consist of one member appointed by each of the three methods set forth above.

2. Members of the Tribunal shall be appointed and the Tribunal shall conduct its business in accordance with the arbitration rules of the United Nations Commission on International Trade Law (UN-CITRAL) expect to the extent modified by the parties or by the Tribunal to ensure that this agreement can be carried out. The UNCITRAL rules for appointing members of three-member Tribunals shall apply *mutatis mutandis* to the appointment of the Tribunal.

3. Claims of nationals of the United States and Iran that are within the scope of this agreement shall be presented to the Tribunal either by claimants themselves, or, in the case of claims of less than $250,000, by the Government of such national.

4. No claim may be filed with the Tribunal more than one year after the entry into force of this agreement or six months after the date the President is appointed, whichever is later. These deadlines do no apply to the procedures contemplated by Paragraphs 16 and 17 of the Declaration of the Government of Algeria of Jan. 19, 1981.

Article IV

1. All decisions and awards of the Tribunal shall be final and binding.

2. The President of the Tribunal shall certify, as prescribed in Paragraph 7 of the Declaration of the Government of Algeria of Jan. 19, 1981, when all arbitral awards under this agreement have been satisfied.

3. Any award which the Tribunal may render against either government shall be enforceable against such government in the courts of any nation in accordance with its laws.

Article V

The Tribunal shall decide all cases on the basis of respect for law, applying such choice of law rules and principles of commercial and international law as the Tribunal determines to be applicable, taking into account relevant usages of the trade, contract provisions and changed circumstances.

Article VI

1. The seat of the Tribunal shall be The Hague, The Netherlands, or any other place agreed by Iran and the United States.

2. Each government shall designate an agent at

the seat of the Tribunal to represent it to the Tribunal and to receive notices or other communications directed to it or to its nationals, agencies, instrumentalities, or entities in connection with proceedings before the Tribunal.

3. The expenses of the Tribunal shall be borne equally by the two governments.

4. Any question concerning the interpretation or application of this agreement shall be decided by the Tribunal upon the request of either Iran or the United States.

Article VII

For the purposes of this agreement:

1. A "national" of Iran or of the United States, as the case may be, means (a) a natural person who is a citizen of Iran or the United States; and (b) a corporation or other legal entity which is organized under the laws of Iran or the United States or any of its states or territories, the District of Columbia or the Commonwealth of Puerto Rico, if collectively, natural persons who are citizens of such country hold, directly or indirectly, an interest in such corporation or entity equivalent to 50 percent or more of its capital stock.

2. "Claims of nationals" of Iran or the United States, as the case may be, means claims owned continuously, from the date on which the claim arose to the date on which this agreement enters into force, by nationals of that state, including claims that are owned indirectly by such nationals through ownership of capital stock or other proprietary interests in juridical persons, provided that the ownership interests of such nationals, collectively, were sufficient at the time the claim arose to control the corporation or other entity, and provided, further, that the corporation or other entity is not itself entitled to bring a claim under the terms of this agreement. Claims referred to the Arbitral Tribunal shall, as of the date of filing of such claims with the Tribunal, be considered excluded from the jurisdiction of the courts of Iran, or of the United States, or of any other court.

3. "Iran" means the Government of Iran, any political subdivision of Iran, and any agency, instrumentality, or entity controlled by the Government of Iran or any political subdivision thereof.

4. The "United States" means the Government of the United States, any political subdivision of the United States, any agency, instrumentality or entity controlled by the Government of the United States or any political subdivision thereof.

Article VIII

This agreement shall enter into force when the Government of Algeria has received from both Iran and the United States a notification of adherence to the agreement.

"Let us renew our determination, our courage and our strength. Let us renew our faith and our hope. We have every right to dream heroic dreams."—Ronald Reagan (WIDE WORLD PHOTOS)